FRACTURE

KEN LOZITO

ACOUSTICAL BOOKS LLC

Published by Acoustical Books, LLC

KenLozito.com

Cover design by Jeff Brown

IF YOU WOULD LIKE TO BE NOTIFIED WHEN MY NEXT BOOK IS RELEASED VISIT

WWW.KENLOZITO.COM

ISBN: 978-1-945223-31-0

1

WINTER WAS OFFICIALLY OVER, but Connor could still feel it on the gust of wind that brushed past his face. He was farther north, well away from any colonial settlements. After hiking to the top of a hill, he turned to where the fragmented remnants of an ancient Ovarrow city disappeared into the glistening undergrowth. He wondered if any of the Ovarrow who'd been brought out of stasis remembered what the city had been like before the ice age. Probably not, and he supposed that could be a blessing, but he doubted it.

He didn't have to be there. Several teams of CDF soldiers were scouting locations for Ovarrow settlements beyond what had already been discovered, but Connor enjoyed getting away. His years on New Earth had awakened a burgeoning desire to explore every inch of it. Humanity's first interstellar colony world was a wondrous mix of mammalian life, some of which appeared familiar, while others were so strange that in light of recent events, scientists had begun to theorize whether those life-forms had evolved on this planet at all. Discovering alien technology that allowed for travel between universes tended to turn some of the mysteries of New Earth on their heads. Regardless, New Earth was humanity's only home and was as dangerous as it was awe-inspiring.

Connor activated his combat-enabled multipurpose protection suit. The MPS series twelve had recently been approved for military use as an alternative to the heavy Nexstar-powered armor. The nanosuit had several modes of operation and could double as a heavy layer of clothing. Once the nanosuit was in combat mode, the onboard AI integrated with Connor's neural implants and could operate in a variety of modes to protect him.

The helmet extended from the ring around Connor's neck, covering his head and seamlessly attaching to the front. The highly advanced suit of armor was capable of protecting him from everything but the heaviest ordnance—a long way from the prototype he'd used nearly two years earlier.

The helmet's internal heads-up display showed the location of the recon drones the survey team was using to map out the area. They were particularly interested in whether there were any hidden bunkers that might contain Ovarrow in stasis pods, but Connor already knew there was very little chance of that. He and Lenora had scouted this area over a year ago. There'd been no stasis pods then, and there probably weren't any now. However, it didn't hurt to take one last look before offering the area up as a potential Ovarrow settlement site so they could rebuild their civilization.

Connor activated the stealth field and took off at a run. Doubtless, the CDF soldier monitoring him was currently alerting his superior that General Connor Gates had suddenly disappeared from their scanners. Eventually—probably seconds from now—they'd alert Samson, who'd lead his team to track Connor down.

Connor couldn't do anything about the impact his footprints had on the low-lying shrubs he ran through. The MPS wasn't able to fly. What it *could* do was enable Connor to run as fast as a rover could cover ground at top speed. Nanorobotic actuators were specifically aligned to his body type, which allowed him to move almost effortlessly. He was required to exert minimal effort to initiate movement, but then the suit took over. The new series twelve MPSs were in short supply and were restricted to select Spec Ops platoons, but Connor planned to expand their usage.

He bolted toward a nearby grove of trees and launched himself into the air. Using his momentum to swing around near the top of the tree, he changed directions. Samson's team would have a *little* bit of difficulty tracking him, but he couldn't make it too easy for them. He kept this up until he'd left the grove behind.

An alert flashed on his internal heads-up display, and then a live video feed appeared from one of the reconnaissance drones that had been scouting the outlying areas northwest of his position. Several warning indicators appeared on the HUD, and a solitary screech pierced the air, carrying a deadly promise to anyone within earshot.

Ryklars.

Answering ryklar calls sounded from farther away. There was always more than one of them. The recon drone was just under five hundred meters away, but the ryklars were much closer.

Ryklars were New Earth predators that had been genetically enhanced by the Ovarrow. Controlled with high-frequency sound waves, they'd been used as weapons of war. They were pack hunters, and a pack could reach sizes of a hundred or more.

Connor had seen them coordinate their hunting efforts before and had even been on the receiving end. Ryklars had highly acute senses, but that wasn't what made them exemplary hunters. They were capable of running at speeds that rivaled old Earth's cheetahs, but they could sustain it for much longer. They had spotted fur on their backs and arms, which made them difficult to spot in grassland and forested areas. They also had the ability to conceal their body heat. Colonial scientists had determined that ryklars had been genetically enhanced to give them this ability. In addition, their claws were capable of tearing through battle steel. Over the years since the colonists had lived on New Earth, they'd increased the armor capability of all their vehicles with ryklars in mind.

Connor knew the MPS specs inside out. In theory, it could resist a ryklar attack, but he didn't want to test that; however, he *was* curious to see just how close he could get to the pack while avoiding detection.

He slowed his pace so he could move as quietly as possible, careful to check the area in front of him, and only the spongy crunching of dead leaves and twigs marked his passing. The closer he'd gotten to the ryklars, the louder their screeches had become. This was a big pack. He was certain he could outrun them if it came down to it, and he began to wonder what all the fuss was about. Ryklars were fairly predictable when not under Ovarrow influence, and they'd even displayed complex social structures that hinted at a species on the verge of an evolutionary leap.

Connor checked the recon drone's scan data. There were no Ovarrow signals that would activate any of the ryklars' latent protocols, some of which included the clean-sweep protocol that forced the ryklars to kill all living creatures found in Ovarrow cities. This meant that whatever was happening with the ryklars now was a natural occurrence from within the pack.

He slowed down even more and crept his way forward, using the blooming shrubbery as cover and automatically checking the holster for his weapon. The heavy-gauge pistol carried lethal darts capable of bringing down a ryklar at close range, and he also carried a combat knife. He wasn't equipped to fight hundreds of ryklars, but it was enough of a deterrence should the need arise.

With the MPS stealth mode enabled, Connor blended in with his surroundings. The MPS computer used images of the surrounding area and projected them in a holographic field around him. This technology wasn't new, but it had never been used on a weapon system that had such a small footprint. The MPS was essentially wearable armor that could double as clothing.

Connor angled his approach so he could keep the high ground, giving him the best vantage point from which to observe the ryklars. He eased his way through the shrubs, resisting the urge to crawl on the ground in order to remain hidden. He didn't have to do that, but "old habits die hard," as the saying went. Connor crouched and watched as the spotted predators gathered around a smaller group of ryklars where most of the noise was coming from.

At the center was a ryklar whose spotted golden hide showed streaks of gray and old battle scars acquired throughout its long life. It had its two front arms in front of it, and its secondary, longer, thickly muscled arms were off to the sides, but its overall countenance was as impassive as a ryklar could look. The tips of the stubby tentacles on its lower face were blood red, indicating that despite outward appearances, the ryklar was becoming agitated. Five younger ryklars were darting in toward the older one in a feigned attack and then quickly changing course at the last minute. Several others also tried to dart in.

Connor focused on the veteran, and the MPS filtered out the others. A deep growl rumbled from its chest. The gray veteran ryklar was the pack leader, and it was being challenged.

Connor spotted a large shape out of the corners of his eyes, and he went still. The breath caught in his throat, but he didn't want to risk turning his head toward it. Instead, he used the MPS cameras to show him a video feed of the area next to him and caught the faint outline of something brushing against the shrubs.

"I didn't want to startle you, General," Samson said quietly, his voice coming through the speakers in Connor's helmet.

"I have to say, you found me a lot faster than I thought you would."

"It would've taken longer if it were someone else," Samson replied without offering any further explanation.

Samson was a former Ghost, an elite special forces platoon from the old NA Alliance Military. They'd known each other for a long time and were friends, despite the falling out they'd had since they were both shanghaied to join the colony.

"Keep the rest of the team back. I want to watch this," Connor said.

Samson went quiet for a moment, and Connor knew he'd muted the comlink so he could send a broadcast to the other soldiers.

"You know what this is, right?" Samson asked.

"Looks like the pack leader is being challenged."

"So, what are you watching for? Either those younglings will work themselves up and give that veteran a real challenge, or they'll scamper out of here."

"That's not always how it happens. It's not a simple one-against-one type of fight. I would've thought you'd have seen that, given how remote you used to live."

Samson was quiet for a few moments, considering. "I didn't spend my time studying ryklars. They left me alone, and I left them alone. It was a good arrangement."

Connor watched as the five younglings, large enough and deadly enough to be considered adults, stalked closer to the pack leader. The other ryklars rocked from side to side, showing a bit of anxiousness at the display. Despite the viciousness of a ryklar attack, they were actually quite disciplined. They preferred a rigid hierarchy, and it was in times like these that the hierarchy was challenged. It wasn't simply a fight to determine who became leader, but a fight to determine the future of the pack down to its youngest member.

Two ryklars darted in toward the veteran but didn't stop this time. They collided in a furious battle—a raging inferno of vicious snarls and claws. The aged veteran hadn't attained his position and held it for so long without being among the deadliest of the pack's fighters.

Connor watched the ryklars engage. It wasn't simple, mindless fury but a delicate dance between seasoned combatants. It had taken him years to notice the subtleties of ryklar combat. There was posturing, but a veteran wouldn't seek to kill its challengers, at least not initially. The veteran would seek to disable them. When challenges for pack supremacy ended in death, it could be disastrous for the entire pack.

The two ryklars that attacked had been seriously wounded and now had dark, blood-soaked slashes in their hides. The remaining three challengers moved in closer, circling the veteran. When other ryklars started to come closer, the veteran hissed at them and they stopped. They were its loyal lieutenants, but the veteran wouldn't allow them to interfere. This was its fight, despite the five-to-one odds.

The wounded ryklars joined the others, and the five of them attacked the veteran all at once, overwhelming whatever defense it could muster. They pulled him off balance, and he went down. Screeches and snarls sounded. The grizzled veteran scrambled, throwing off some of his attackers, and Connor saw that its bearded tentacles had become even redder as it gave in to its fury. One of the ryklars went down, clutching its middle in a futile attempt to keep its life from bleeding out. Another ryklar darted in. The veteran scrambled around it, using it as a shield to block the follow-up attack by the other three. Unable to stop themselves, they collided with their ally's claws, rending through flesh. The ryklar screeched in pain as it went through its death throes.

This is it. There's no stopping it now, Connor thought grimly.

The three ryklars backed away, and the veteran pursued them.

They'd crossed the line, and now the pack would pay the price. The veteran had already proven to be their better. The challengers would die.

When the battle was over, the veteran ryklar had a few new battle scars, and five attackers lay dead or dying in a quivering mess on the ground.

Connor glanced at the rest of the pack. The forest was suddenly awash in red, showing the ryklars' agitation. Scuffles broke out among them, and the pack leader roared. The nearest ryklars immediately snapped to attention, but there were others farther away that scattered, leaving the pack.

"What's the matter with them?" Samson asked.

"The pack is dead, or at least weakened," Connor said and began backing away through the shrubs.

Samson followed him, waiting a few moments for them to be well away from the area. "I don't understand. Why did the pack break apart because of a simple challenge to the pack leader?"

"The ryklars are predators, but they're more than that. They're good at killing, but when it comes to pack hierarchy, they don't handle transition of power very well. They do fight among themselves, but despite their ferociousness toward other species, a challenge to the pack leader rarely ends in death because of the risk of the pack splintering. Given the overwhelming odds, the pack leader could have abdicated his position."

"Do they do that? Stop being the pack leader so the pack stays together?"

Connor's eyebrows raised and he shrugged. "Sometimes. Depends on the leader, I guess."

Samson glanced behind them. They could still hear the ryklars screeching, though they were farther away. The once powerful pack had fragmented. "I'll never understand this planet. There are some things that remind me of Earth, but sometimes it's just so alien."

They walked in silence until they met up with several other CDF soldiers under Samson's command.

"I still don't understand why the pack split apart. If anything, wouldn't the fact that the pack leader won have solidified his hold over the pack, given that he'd been challenged and it failed?"

"You're still thinking of the ryklars as simple animals. Remember, they're genetically enhanced, which includes their brains. Look at it this way. Even though the pack leader was challenged, he allowed himself to be put in a position where he killed members of the pack. A large portion of the ryklars will likely remain, but a sizable chunk will choose to leave, having lost faith in him. This will make the pack weaker overall."

Samson eyed Connor for a minute. "You know an awful lot about these things."

"Studying them had been a hobby of mine for a while—at least until I rejoined the CDF. I've even seen the smaller factions join other packs and then exact revenge upon their old packs. Who does that remind you of?" Connor asked.

Samson thought about it for a minute. He was a soldier through and through, and one of the things he was good at was measuring the capacity of an enemy's willingness to fight. "So, we have something in common with the ryklars. Would you rather they sit down around a conference table and come to a peaceful resolution for their differences?" He paused for a moment. "Sometimes you have to be ruthless. I know you know that. Do you think the Krake will be civilized when they come here?"

"I'll be sure to share your philosophy of shooting first and asking questions later with the defense committee," Connor said.

"It does simplify things. Seriously, the committee can't really be considering how they could work with the Krake if they found a way to communicate with them. Given what they've done to the Ovarrow and the data you retrieved, I seriously doubt they're open to peace."

Connor didn't need to be reminded. He'd gone over that data many times. "It's not that simple," he said, snorting in disbelief. "Okay, from *your* perspective it's simple. I give you a weapon, I tell you to achieve an objective, and it's done. But dealing with civilians can be complicated."

Samson arched a thick eyebrow and smiled a little, but it didn't make his face look friendly. "Complicated," he repeated. "Is that what we're calling it now?"

Since Connor had invited Samson back into the CDF, he'd gotten used to some of his old friend's moods. Sometimes Samson had a simplified way of reading into a situation that was useful. This wasn't one of those times.

"I don't mean to be a hard-ass about this," Samson continued. "And I know I'm not telling you anything new."

Connor looked at him for a moment and then nodded. "I thought after the Vemus War we could leave all that behind us. I want there to be a better way, but . . ." He let the thought go unfinished.

There were a few times in a soldier's life when events would shape the kind of soldier they'd become. For Connor, the first time was when he killed an enemy combatant. He'd never forget his first kill. He'd felt numb in the beginning, and then he tried to rationalize it when he could think clearly again. He'd thought he was supposed to feel conflicted about it, but he didn't. He never did. It was then that he had to accept that fighting was something he was exceptionally good at, and possibly the *only* thing he was really good at. It didn't make him a monster, although there were some people who probably thought of him that way. He was a protector, and he would protect this colony until his dying breath.

2

THE CDF HELLCAT set down at an impromptu landing zone out in the middle of nowhere. Connor had picked this site because it was hundreds of kilometers away from any colonial outpost and because they could control the environment.

"General Gates," Lieutenant Solari said, "General Hayes is inbound and will be here in a few minutes. The other attendees will arrive shortly."

"Thank you, Lieutenant," Connor replied and left the cockpit.

He went to the back of the Hellcat where the CDF infantry unit waited. Captain Kathy Morris came over to him.

"Have your platoon secure the area. The others will be arriving shortly."

"Yes, General," Morris replied and began issuing orders to her platoon.

Connor walked down the exit ramp and stepped onto solid ground, hearing Samson's heavy footfalls behind him. Samson was a few inches taller than Connor and outweighed him by more than sixty pounds of solid muscle.

There were vast areas of the supercontinent that were home to wide-open plains. One of the reasons Connor had selected this area was that there was very little chance anyone could spy on them.

Several reconnaissance drones flew overhead, and Connor glanced at Samson, wondering if he'd ask any of the questions that were obviously forming in his mind. Samson had only rejoined the colony in the past three months and was still prone to long bouts of silence.

"I'm glad you asked," Connor said. "The reason we're out here in the middle of nowhere is because we can secure the area and prevent anyone else from listening in."

Samson eyed him for a few moments. "I didn't ask. I'm just following orders."

"You were wondering. I could tell."

"If Wil and Kasey could see us now."

Connor sighed heavily, remembering his friends. All of them had been former members of the Ghost Platoon, but Wil and Kasey had died protecting the colony. "At least you're here."

Samson snorted, which sounded more like a bull clearing its throat. "You'll get more use out of me when the Krake actually arrive, or when we take the fight to them. I hate all the strategy stuff beforehand."

"You're only as good as the weapons you use," Connor replied.

Samson eyed him for a moment. "Unless you think some of the people coming to this meeting aren't friends."

High above, a Hellcat flew across the pale gray sky, lining up with the LZ, engines shrieking in a dopplered wail as it came in low and fast. Connor glanced at it before turning back to Samson. "If we only surround ourselves with people we trust, not much would get done."

"So, you trust me now," Samson said, which was more of a statement than a question.

"Now that you're weapons qualified again, I trust you won't shoot me in the back."

Samson's mouth split into a broad grin. "I was just keeping you on your toes."

The Hellcat landed, next in a line of several others en route to the LZ. Some of the Hellcats were smaller than the troop-carrier-sized transport, and they had different insignias for the branch of service they operated under. Two of the ships were tan and green for Field Ops, while the Hellcats from the CDF were battle-steel gray with a blue and gold stripe across the middle. They were designed for both atmospheric flight and lower orbit, but they didn't have the range of a combat shuttle.

Nathan Hayes walked down the exit ramp of the nearest CDF Hellcat and gave Connor a wave before heading in his direction.

As Nathan walked over, he looked over at the other ships landing close by. "This is something new," he said, looking around at the open grasslands surrounding them.

"It's time for it."

"I'm pretty certain we can secure our communications at any of the CDF bases," Nathan replied.

Connor nodded. "Probably, but there are other ways to listen in. It'll be a good idea for us to lay our cards out on the table before meeting with the Colonial Defense Committee."

More people disembarked from their ships, and Connor saw Damon Mills, Director of Field Ops, walking over to him. A woman in a Field Ops uniform walked at his side, and her name appeared on Connor's internal heads-up display.

Captain Leslie Tyler.

Age 51.

Senior Field Ops agent in charge of Search and Rescue at Sierra.

Captain Tyler looked barely into her twenties due to the prolonging treatments all colonists were privy to. Connor looked at her record with appreciation, glad that Search and Rescue was in such capable hands.

Damon Mills had had a career in law enforcement back on old Earth. His skin was weatherworn, and he sported an outdoorsman's deep tan. He looked to have an almost permanent scowl on his face, and he could be somewhat abrasive at times. Connor remembered getting off to a rocky start with Damon when he'd first gotten to the colony, but over the years, they'd come to a mutual respect for one another. They might never be what Connor would consider close friends, but he trusted Damon, which was why he'd invited him.

"Thanks for making time to come here," Connor said to Damon.

Damon rubbed his eyes for a moment and nodded. "Of course."

"Were you up all night?"

Damon nodded by way of tilting his head to the side once and smiling a little. "There's never a dull moment, is there? Believe me, we're all busy, and I'm happy for a little bit of a change for a few hours, at least. Lots of fresh air around here," he said while glancing around.

A text message appeared on Connor's internal heads-up display.

C. Weber: *Suppressor net ready to engage. One invitee overdue.*

C. Gates: *Acknowledged. Come on out and join us now.*

More people arrived, mostly from Field Ops, with Franklin Mallory arriving last. An older man, Franklin was taller than Connor, and the short beard he wore emphasized the long lines of his face from his high cheekbones to the straight slash of his mouth. Fresh worry lines adorned his friend's face, and Connor's stomach knotted into a ball of acidic regret.

"Franklin, thanks for coming," Connor said.

Franklin Mallory looked as if he'd rather be somewhere else, impatient to get back to work, and Connor understood why. His son was a prominent figure associated with a rogue terrorist organization, and it tended to make for many sleepless nights.

"Connor," Franklin replied in acknowledgment.

Major Natalia Vassar joined them and gave Connor a meaningful nod. She was a short woman, and her reputation among the officers was that she was tiny but fierce.

"Gentlemen and ladies," Connor said, "this is Major Natalia Vassar, and she's with CDF Intelligence. She's activated a suppressor net, so don't be alarmed if you find yourselves suddenly cut off from all communications with the rest of the colony. There's nothing wrong with your equipment. It's just a precaution to prevent other people from listening in on this meeting."

Several people frowned, but it was Damon who voiced the unspoken objection. "Don't you think this is over the top? What if there's an emergency?"

Connor looked at Damon and smiled. "We'll be fine. We all have well-trained people in our respective organizations, and they have protocols to follow in an emergency. I promise not to keep any of you longer than absolutely necessary."

Franklin Mallory cleared his throat. "What's this about, Connor?"

"I wanted to have an open and honest conversation with all of you. You were asked to bring at least one person that you absolutely trust," Connor said and looked around at all of them. More than a few glanced at Samson, whose form towered off to Connor's right. Gesturing toward Samson, Connor continued. "This is Captain Samson. For those of you who haven't met him yet, he's a former member of the Ghost Platoon of the NA Alliance Military. He's recently rejoined the CDF and is part of Spec Ops in charge of Ranger 7th company."

Hearing that Samson was a former member of Connor's old

Ghost Platoon drew a few curious looks in his direction. People like Franklin and Damon, who'd been there at the beginning of the colony, knew firsthand that not all the Ghosts had acclimated to colonial living. Samson was one of those who hadn't. He'd spent the last eight years living alone, getting as far away from colonial population centers as possible.

Samson returned their curious gazes with what he probably considered a nonthreatening look.

"I'm going to cut to the chase," Connor said. "The Krake represent a threat that's like nothing we've ever faced. All our preparation for the Vemus was designed to meet a threat coming from deep space. And though the Krake could attack us from space, they could also attack us on the ground and could already be here without our knowledge." Connor paused for a few moments to glance at the Field Ops people, who looked as if they weren't sure how to react to this news. "The purpose of the Colonial Defense Force is to protect the colony from outside threats. Given what we know about the Krake, this responsibility is going to be shared directly with Field Ops. There's a very real possibility that our conflict with them will happen on the planet, and the CDF and Field Ops need to be able to coordinate together."

Damon jutted his chin up once, indicating that he wanted to speak, and Connor nodded. "We still have the civilian readiness plans we put together in the event that the Vemus invaded us. Wouldn't that be enough?"

"That's the thing, Damon. I don't know if they are. We can plug the security holes as best we can, but the situation is different. The Krake could already be here. How would we know? How would they attack us? *Would* they attack us?"

"If you didn't believe the Krake would attack us at some point, we wouldn't be here," Franklin said.

Connor nodded. "You're right. I believe it's not a matter of *if* but *when*. The other thing that concerns me is that our best source of information is also the source of a major division between colony members. I'm talking about the Ovarrow," he said, using the NEIIS name for themselves.

"Given what the Ovarrow have done to their planet," Nathan began, "trusting them to be our allies has given me a lot of sleepless nights. I'm willing to confess to that. You and I have discussed this before, but for the rest of you, here's what I think. I do agree that the Ovarrow represent a source of the intel we need, but they're alien. They fought a war—many wars—among themselves and possibly against the Krake, and look where it left them."

Franklin Mallory crossed his arms in front of his chest and exhaled. "We still don't understand why the Krake would even come here."

"Actually," Connor said, "we've uncovered evidence from their military base that indicates they allocate a lot of resources for exploring different universes and interacting with intelligent species. I say 'interact' because the evidence we have indicates that the Krake don't simply launch an all-out campaign to conquer a target. We can talk about this for hours and days, and we already have within our various circles. What I'm looking for from all of you are ideas for how to prepare for the Krake. And I recognize that some of our ideas may not be popular with certain groups of civilians or even with each other, for that matter."

They were silent for a few moments before Franklin Mallory spoke.

"When Tobias Quinn was drafting the Colonial Charter, he had to account for the possibility that there might be factions of the colony that broke off from the main group. There are ways for them to legally do this. It's their right."

"I understand that it's their right," Connor said, "but we barely survived a war with the Vemus, and it took the effort of the entire colony to do it. The Vemus sent a fighting force across interstellar space to get us. What we're facing here has the potential to be a fighting force that doesn't have to travel so far. It's already here but in a different universe. I know it's difficult to accept, but if we make this a numbers game, then the odds are overwhelmingly in their favor."

"Excuse me," Leslie Tyler said. "How can you be so sure? We haven't even found the . . ." she paused for a moment, searching for the right words, ". . . home universe of the Krake. So, this is all speculation as to what their capabilities are."

"You're right; we haven't found it. But they're a spacefaring race, which means they must have certain technological and manufacturing capabilities that can only come from a heavily populated planet. They might even have colonies. We don't know. They could be drawing from resources that come from multiple worlds. Regardless, it will be our job to come up with a way to stop them from wiping us out."

Connor watched the others as his words were mulled over.

"So why all the secrecy?" Damon said, gesturing around them.

Connor looked at Damon, and then his gaze went to Franklin Mallory. "It's because of Lars and the rogue group he's part of."

Franklin's gaze hardened, and he glanced away.

"I know this hasn't been easy for you," Connor said, "but Lars and his group are driving a wedge into the colony."

Franklin looked at Connor. "I don't condone my son's actions, but Lars isn't forcing his ideas on anyone. They just happen to be in conflict with what your ideas for protecting the colony are."

Connor was quiet for a few moments, considering, and as each moment passed, he saw the others shift uncomfortably. Franklin was worried about his son and angry with him at the same time. Connor could tell Franklin wanted to defend his son's actions, and Connor also wanted to help protect Lars and get him to stop doing what he was doing. "All right, you have a point, but the fact of the matter is that we're putting forth a motion to have the actions of Lars and the rogue group declared illegal. Like it or not, if Lars keeps on his current path, his actions will be declared criminal."

Franklin Mallory's broad shoulders drew up tight, and a groan escaped his lips. As he lifted his eyes, the pain in his expression stabbed at Connor's chest. But Franklin quickly replaced that pain with a scowl and clenched his fists.

"I think we need a few minutes here," Nathan said, gesturing for some of the others to walk away.

Damon came to Franklin's side, trying to get him to walk away, and Franklin took a few steps. He was shaking his head, and his face had become several shades of red as he glared at Connor. "My son is not a criminal, and I don't care what motion you get passed. He is not a criminal! He's doing what *you* taught him to do. He's doing what *I* taught him to do. He's trying to protect this colony."

Connor met Franklin's gaze. He knew what it was like to grieve for a son—that gut-wrenching pain that kept stabbing until it drove you to your knees. It was a pain that Connor carried within himself, too, and it would never leave. At least Franklin's son was alive, and there was still a chance to save him from himself, but Connor wouldn't give him false hope. "Lars is treading a very thin line that he's come dangerously close to crossing. Did you forget what happened to Noah? Or the fact that he led a group that almost opened fire on a CDF squad that was protecting Dash? Lars is pulling Ovarrow from their stasis pods, questioning them, and then murdering them. In that respect, he's already crossed the line. How long do you think it will be before he does the same thing to a colonist who's standing in his way? Do you want to stand in front of another father or mother and tell *them* that Lars's actions aren't criminal? What about the Ovarrow? Don't they have a right to live just like you or me? I don't like this either. He's a good kid. They all were, but they're making grave mistakes— mistakes that are going to put them on the wrong side—"

"Stop!" Damon shouted. "Just stop."

Angry tears had gathered in Franklin's eyes. It was a gaze full of pain that touched on bitterness, and perhaps even hatred. Franklin shook his head, and his shoulders slumped. "Where did I go wrong? How could I have let this happen?"

Connor stepped closer to him. "It's not just you," he said, his voice thick with emotion.

Franklin squeezed his eyes shut for a moment, exhaling a heavy breath. "I don't know how to protect him," he said and looked at Connor. "How can I protect him? I feel like I should've been able to stop . . . like I should've known what he was going to do."

Connor swallowed hard. "It's not your fault." Even as he spoke, he knew Franklin would never listen or accept it.

"Like hell it isn't! I raised him. I should've known."

"You didn't make Lars do what he did. Sometimes, kids start out on a path and then can't find a way out of it," Connor said as he reached out to put his hand on Franklin's shoulder. "And Lars didn't start doing this on his own. Someone else put him on this path, and that's who we need to find."

Franklin wiped away his tears and nodded, his breath coming in gasps as he struggled to control himself. Then he nodded again and allowed Damon to lead him away.

Connor watched them go. Anger like a coiled viper yearned to strike out from him. He hated this—hated whoever was corrupting young men and women to do horrible things. Yet, if he'd been desperate enough, wouldn't he have taken similarly terrible actions to protect the colony? Connor would have liked to deny such a thought. He knew he'd push himself beyond the brink to fight the Krake while keeping his integrity intact, but a more ruthless side of himself whispered that he'd sacrifice even that to save the colony. What *wouldn't* he do to ensure the colony's survival—the survival of the entire human race? These thoughts were like fire in his mind, and they burned as he realized it was those same ideas that had probably been used to corrupt Lars. Connor whispered a curse and shook his head. He'd thought he was alone, but then he saw that Samson was standing close by.

"This won't end well," Samson said and walked away.

Connor stood there for a few moments, denying what Samson had said. There had to be a way to stop Lars and the rest of the people involved, rooting out the entire terrorist organization. He had to believe there was some hope they could reach Lars and get him to stop what he was doing.

Connor couldn't imagine what Franklin was going through. He hadn't been around to raise his own son; he'd only gotten to mourn his loss. And now, his daughter was barely old enough to walk.

His thoughts traveled back to that first shuttle ride from the *Ark* down to New Earth. Lenora had been there, but so had Sean, Noah, and Lars—three young men bursting with youthful vigor and massive potential. The three of them had somehow wriggled their way into becoming family to him, and Connor wanted to protect them all, but he knew this was something he couldn't do. Noah was still was in a coma and, despite their best efforts, showed no signs of waking from it. Sean was lost, trapped in another universe, and Lars was here on New Earth but beyond Connor's reach. Sometimes he felt helpless, but he had to do what he could. What good was protecting the colony when it almost seemed like everything was working against him? As deplorable as Lars's actions toward the Ovarrow had been, the fact of the matter was that in different circumstances, Connor might've been tempted to do the same if it meant saving the lives of his family. He needed to get in front of Lars so he could try to convince him that what he was doing was wrong and that there was a better way to protect the colony. He just hoped he'd get that chance before it was too late.

3

PHOENIX STATION MAINTAINED its orbit approximately a hundred sixty million kilometers from New Earth. This put one of New Earth's main lines of defense well past Sagan's orbit but not near Gigantor's orbit. Over four thousand people resided there, and Colonel Savanah Cross was in charge of overseeing the station's activities. First and foremost, Phoenix Station was a military installation, but more than half its residents were civilians. Since there were so many civilians working there, it seemed appropriate that Savanah's counterpart was a civilian. Julius Sheppard was a good man who had a way of dealing with people.

Colonial defensive initiatives beyond Phoenix Station were comprised of missile-defense platforms stationed throughout the star system. With the advent of subspace communication, there were plans to make better use of those automated defense platforms, given the threat the Krake represented. One of the problems they'd identified from encountering the Vemus and the destruction of Titan Station was their limited communication capabilities back to New Earth.

Savannah frowned. Perhaps that assessment was a bit unfair.

They were aware of the communication limitations that came with maintaining defense outposts so far from New Earth, and they'd had to account for the lag in comms as part of their strategy. It had been necessary, given the threat coming from old Earth. They also had a relay of listening outposts further out in the system that would send an alert should any latent Vemus attack force make its way to New Earth. The chances of that happening were extremely low, but vigilance was the key to survival.

Savanah's current command, while military in nature, also had a similar job description to that of a governor on New Earth. She was responsible for the station in its entirety, including the civilians. Phoenix Station was essentially a city in its own rights—a city with heavy weaponry and a burgeoning shipbuilding capability. One day, they'd rival the shipyards at the lunar base. Savannah smiled at the thought. Her husband, Nathan, was largely responsible for everything Lunar Base had become, and perhaps there was a bit of a competitive streak in her where her husband was concerned. However, she was extremely proud of the work she'd accomplished during her tenure at Phoenix Station. It could be trying at times, given that she hadn't gotten to see Nathan very often for the past year. They essentially split their son Oliver's time between the two of them, but she knew this arrangement could only work on a temporary basis, particularly since she and Nathan wanted more children—many more children. Savannah wasn't about to let her career in the CDF stand in the way of that, but it wasn't time to go home just yet. She had important work to do. She wouldn't allow herself the luxury of returning to New Earth until they'd found Trident Battle Group.

Sean Quinn had been overdue for almost three months now. Neither Connor nor Nathan believed that Trident Battle Group had been lost to the Krake, and she shared their opinion. Despite this, their current reconnaissance efforts into the alternate universe had been severely lacking, in her opinion. The latest report was on a holoscreen in front of her, and she glared at it.

The door to her office chimed and Major Vance Peterson stuck his head through the doorway. "We have a one o'clock."

Savannah nodded and waved him inside. Peterson entered and glanced at the data on her holoscreen, seeing it through the now-translucent screen. "It doesn't inspire a lot of confidence, does it?"

"No, it does not. At this rate, it'll take us a year to recon the star system, and we don't have a year."

Peterson frowned. "I want to find them just as much as you do, but did something else happened that I'm not aware of?"

Savanah powered off her holoscreen and leaned back in her chair. "It's taking too long. The restriction of using only limited reconnaissance probes isn't going to get the job done. We thought it was the safest thing to do, but I'm not so sure anymore."

Peterson pursed his lips in thought. "Are you looking for ideas?"

Savannah shook her head and then, after a moment, shrugged. "Of course, but I already have an idea. I just need to get approval to use it."

Peterson was about to reply when the comlink she'd been waiting for chimed on the nearby wallscreen. A large image of Connor Gates' face appeared.

"General Gates," Savanah greeted.

"Colonel Cross. Major Peterson. How are things on Phoenix Station today?"

Savanah proceeded to give Connor a brief status report on current projects at Phoenix Station. "Have you had a chance to review the latest reconnaissance report from the alternate universe?" Savannah asked.

Connor shook his head. "No, I haven't, but judging by the look on your face, it isn't good."

"Sir, we've reached the limitations of what our reconnaissance drones are capable of. They're simply not up to the task. We've equipped them with high-powered telescopes and limited sensor arrays, but it's not enough. We need to send a team through."

Connor was silent while he considered.

"I'm sending you a new file, sir. The Raven class scout ship, SR-01, is ready for service."

Connor's eyebrows raised slightly. "Ready for service," he repeated. "I thought that ship was still several months from completion in favor of completing space gate components."

"Sir, we already have four completed space gates deployed in the star system. Instead of prioritizing another space gate, I allocated some resources to complete the scout ship."

"I see."

"Sir, I believe this is our best chance to find out what happened to Trident Battle Group. Sending more recon drones isn't going to give us any new data soon enough."

"Is there any supporting evidence that warrants sending another team to the alternate universe? I'm asking because that's what Governor Wolf and the rest of the defense committee will ask me."

Savannah felt the tightening in shoulders spread down her arms and into her abdomen. She shook her head. "There's been no new evidence to support that Trident Battle Group is still there. However, I have a plan that involves the use of the scout ship in coordination with the space gates we've deployed."

"Savannah, I'm not trying to be a hard-ass about this. I want to know what happened to them as much as you do. Send your plan over. Also, what team did you have in mind for the mission?"

Savannah felt the beginnings of a smile. "I think you'll approve. Actually, I think you know him."

4

CONNOR'S HELLCAT set down in the landing zone at the colonial government campus in Sierra. When Sierra had been rebuilt after the Vemus War, they'd taken the opportunity to change the design of the city. It had been rebuilt during a time of great uncertainty after they'd learned that something horrible had happened back on Earth.

The Vemus was a rare form of symbiotic viral and bacterial life form that attacked mammalian life on Earth. Earth scientists had tried to modify it to make humans immune—and Connor suspected they were trying to make all mammals immune—but there were others who saw an opportunity to acquire power. Billions of lives had been lost, and the calamity of Earth had reached out across interstellar space to invade the colony. It'd been almost three years since the end of the Vemus War, but Connor could still see the scars that impacted colonial society. Peaceful cities didn't have rail guns on their roofs or hidden missile-defense platforms buried under the ground in parks throughout the city. Peaceful cities didn't have military bases nearby with an alert force ready to defend the city should an invader appear. Perhaps one day there would be cities on New Earth that didn't require those types of defenses, but Connor suspected he'd be an old man by then.

There were multiple landing zones throughout Sierra. When the city had been redesigned, they'd taken evacuation plans into account should the residents need to flee quickly. Both New Haven and Delphi also had these accommodations in place. Sanctuary was a much smaller city in comparison. Due to its remote location and the fact there was already an underground bunker capable of withstanding an orbital bombardment, it was one of the safest cities in the event they were invaded.

Connor had to attend a Colonial Defense Force committee meeting later in the day, but he'd arrived early to meet with Governor Dana Wolf. Nathan had advised Connor to meet with various colonial leaders outside of committee meetings in order to facilitate working relationships with them. Despite his initial reluctance due to time constraints, Connor had to admit that his friend had been right. Meeting with colonial leaders *had* helped make getting things done a little bit easier. Above all, Connor wanted to avoid a situation like the one he'd faced during Stanton Parish's administration. Connor didn't thing about Parish much, but since Connor had been instrumental in removing Stanton Parish from power with the help of Tobias Quinn, certain political leaders mistrusted him, even though Connor's actions had been necessary and legal under the Colonial Charter.

After the war, Connor had distanced himself from the Colonial Defense Force, but now that he was back in the military, he'd made an effort to "play nice," as his wife preferred to call it. Lenora had the uncanny ability to see right to the heart of matters, and Connor had come to rely on her insights, especially when dealing with civilians.

He shook his head as he walked across the campus. They were all people, but he'd always thought of himself as a soldier—a military man—even when he'd retired. Perhaps that was part of the problem. Civilians were a breed apart from soldiers. There'd been divisions among the different branches of the old NA Alliance Military, and the CDF was no different. It came from being competitive. They all had their traditions and their own ways of saber-rattling.

Connor walked into the main entrance of the administration building where the governor's office resided. He glanced up at the murals depicting scenes from Earth's history, then the *Ark*, the colonists first coming to New Earth, and the building of the cities. Across the main hall were more murals of colonists exploring New Earth, but there were two that Connor liked to take a few moments to observe. These were the murals for the Colonial Defense Force and Field Ops. They showed figures of CDF soldiers in blue and gold dress uniforms standing before a setting sun and then shifted to a scene beyond the planet showing various types of warships. The entire space-scape had been done in an outline form, depicting the heads and shoulders of the men and women who comprised the CDF.

Tobias Quinn had been an advocate of remembering where they'd come from. Without those things to remind them of who they were, they may have lost sight of their heritage. There were times when Connor and Tobias hadn't seen eye to eye on some important issues, but there'd always been mutual respect. During the time Tobias's widow, Ashley Quinn, had been acting governor, Connor had no longer been in the CDF, but they respected each other and were friends—more than friends. They were family. She was like a sister to him, but it was getting increasingly difficult to see her. The fact that her son Sean was still missing worried her beyond words, despite his assurances.

Connor acknowledged a few friendly greetings of people he passed on his way to Governor Wolf's office. When he walked in, the young secretary told him to go on inside, as the governor was expecting him.

Connor walked into the office and saw Governor Wolf standing amid a trio of holoscreens. She was reviewing various reports, and Connor noted the ever-growing list of tasks she'd noted. The amber holoscreens became translucent, giving him a clear view of her face, and she waved him over.

Connor noticed that her office had been reconfigured, looking much like his own. He didn't spend hours sitting at a desk, reviewing reports on a holoscreen. He alternated, but mostly he stood up and worked as he saw Dana Wolf working right then.

She smiled at him. "I took a page out of your book. I got tired of sitting around on my ass."

"Imitation is the sincerest form of flattery, but your secret is safe with me."

Dana grinned. "And where did *you* learn it from?"

"I didn't always have a desk at the places I was stationed, but the work still had to get done."

She nodded. She was an older woman, but Connor couldn't guess her age. She looked older than him, but with prolonging that could mean anything. The human lifespan was currently well over two hundred years.

"Did you see the new banners on your way in?"

Connor frowned and thought for a few seconds. He'd been so focused on his own thoughts that he must have missed them. "I didn't."

"It's a major milestone. The colony has doubled in size in the past twelve years. In another year, our population will be over seven hundred thousand."

She walked over to the side table and poured two glasses of dark brown liquid, added a few cubes of ice, and handed one to Connor. "Nathan Hayes gave me this, and I have to admit this latest cask of bourbon has made me a customer."

Connor took the glass and had a sip. Nathan had given him a case of it as well. "I thought you preferred wine."

She nodded. "I do, and my husband does as well, but sometimes it's nice to have something a little bit different. Don't tell my husband. He's got ideas for growing grapes and starting his own winery."

Connor took another taste, and the bourbon warmed his chest.

"Before we get started," Wolf said, "I wanted to ask how John Rollins' recovery is going."

Connor liked that she asked, although he had no doubt she'd read about Rollins' current medical status and feedback from his psychological evaluation. But there was always information that couldn't be conveyed in a report. "Physically he's doing much better. The doctors are happy that he's put on some weight, but he's still very thin."

Rollins had been held captive by the Krake, and when he'd been rescued, they'd found him starved almost to death.

"I'm sure you read that he has severe PTSD," Connor continued. "It's going to take time for him to come around, but he'll never be the same. He wasn't able to communicate with the other prisoners, and the isolation was untenable. There's some memory suppression going on, which is to be expected. What he *has* shared with us is more of a confirmation of what we already knew or suspected based on the information we'd gotten from the base and from the Ovarrow."

"I know everything that can be done is being done by the doctors, but if there's anything I can do, please don't hesitate to ask."

Connor nodded and finished his bourbon.

"Going back to the population of the colony, I've done a little bit of research. Did you know that almost ten percent of the population is serving in the CDF?"

"I wouldn't be much of a general if I didn't know the number of people in the CDF, but I don't expect that having ten percent of the population serving in the military will be something that's maintained as the colony grows."

Wolf finished her bourbon and set the glass down on the table. "I've been looking at the history of the NA Alliance, as well as the Asia Pac Alliance and the member nations that comprised them. Historically, the percentage of the population serving in the military was only that high during times of war. What we have here is something that has become ongoing. If you add Field Ops into it, the numbers reach twenty percent of the population that's devoted in some way to colonial defense. When I examined the original charters that preceded the *Ark* program, there was a much different picture being painted."

"They never expected to need a military. They believed a police force would be enough to keep the colony safe, and they might have been right in other circumstances. You seem to be preoccupied with the numbers. What are you worried about?" Connor asked.

"What do you imagine your daughter will do when she becomes an adult? I know she's just a baby, but these years will go by quickly."

At the mention of his daughter, Connor felt the edges of his lips curve upward. Diaz had called it that dopey fatherly smile that descended when a man became a father. "Whatever she wants to do," he answered.

"Fair enough, but would you want her to choose a dangerous occupation like yours? Hopefully, by the time she's an adult, colonial life will be much more settled than it is right now."

"I hope so, too. Otherwise . . . I don't want my daughter to have to do some of the things I've done, but if I'm understanding you correctly, I think you're implying that at some point you'd like to reduce the number of active military personnel."

"Eventually," she said and tilted her head to the side by way of a single nod. "We were meant to be explorers and pioneers. I understand the need for what we've done and will continue to do, but what I don't want is our legacy to be a military state that falls under a dictatorship."

There it was, Connor thought, *an acknowledgment of the fear that's been mostly unspoken.* "Let's hope we'll be smarter than that. It's not what *I* want."

Wolf smiled. It was friendly and reached her eyes. "Oh, I believe you, Connor. I have no issues trusting you, but things change. Eventually you and I won't be here, and what the people who *are* here will have is the groundwork we've laid for them. It's a concern of mine."

Connor didn't know how to respond to that. What could he say? How was he supposed to know what the next generation was going to do with the legacy they built for them?

"It's just something to think about. Anyway, it's time for us to go," Dana said. They started walking toward the door, and she stopped. "I'm glad you make an effort for us to speak outside of those meetings."

"Thank you for being open to it. I hope that whoever serves as governor in the future will have the same policy you do."

Governor Wolf still had another year left before she could be reelected, and that would be the last term she'd serve as governor. In the Colonial Charter, there was a strict two-term limit on any political office. There would be no career politicians on the colony.

This Colonial Defense Committee meeting wasn't a run-of-the-mill affair. There'd been outside agencies invited, given some of the things they were discussing. This included representatives from the legislative and judicial branches of the colonial government, along with Meredith Cain, who was the head of the Colonial Intelligence Bureau. Bob Mullins and Kurt Johnson,

Dana's advisors, were also in attendance, as well as Franklin Mallory and Damon Mills. On the CDF side were Connor, Nathan, and Colonel Celeste Belonét. Celeste would be returning to her post at the lunar base, but Connor wanted representation from various CDF senior officers. If circumstances required that they interact with civilian leadership, it wouldn't be as foreign to them as it had been to Connor when he first created the CDF.

"The next order of business," Kurt Johnson said, "has to do with our state of defense readiness in the event of a threat to any of the colonial cities."

Connor noticed that Johnson hadn't mentioned the Krake and was inclined to believe Johnson would've liked to include the Ovarrow as a potential threat to the colony. He glanced at Nathan and gave him a nod.

Nathan cleared his throat. "We've established designated patrol areas in the vicinity of colonial cities that are outside those areas designated for Field Ops. We've established criteria for Field Ops to communicate with CDF alert forces that are on standby to investigate anomalies the Field Ops agents determine necessary."

"How long do you think these patrols will be necessary?" Johnson asked.

Until the Krake were no longer a threat, was the answer Connor wanted to give.

"We'll continue to reevaluate their effectiveness in the coming months and bring it up for this committee's review in six months," Nathan answered.

Johnson nodded and then looked at Governor Wolf. "There have been some concerns raised in each of our major cities about the fact that we have heavily armed ships flying overhead. People are worried there could be an accident waiting to happen."

Connor leaned forward. "Now what would give them that impression?"

Johnson looked at Connor. "I don't understand your question, General Gates."

"There's always been a CDF base at colonial population centers. This is nothing new. Heavily armed ships coming to and from those bases aren't new, is my point. So, I'm left wondering why there's a sudden concern, unless somebody put those ideas into their heads."

"I don't know anything about a campaign to influence the hearts and minds of the colonists. But the patrols by the CDF have increased, and it's a valid concern."

"I haven't heard of any of these concerns at Sanctuary, and to the best of my knowledge, the base commanders haven't received any word of such concerns from the local colonists. There have never been any accidents involving weapons misfire. So, where did these reports come from? Why the sudden concern? These are the same ships that are there for their protection," Connor said.

There was an edge to his voice, and he knew it. The meeting had gone on pretty long, and that stretched his patience sometimes.

Johnson tapped his fingers on the table. "I'm merely voicing the concerns that have been brought to the governor's office, General Gates. I didn't make them up."

"Fair enough. I think the concerns might be a symptom of the attitude that's been growing lately regarding the Ovarrow settlement," Connor said.

Camp Alpha had been a staging area for bringing NEIIS, now known as the Ovarrow, out of stasis. In order for an alliance to work, they'd agreed to help the Ovarrow reestablish themselves in one of their abandoned cities, which was over three hundred kilometers from the nearest colonial city.

"Our office has received those concerns as well. There's a general mistrust of the Ovarrow," Johnson replied.

Connor looked at Governor Wolf. "I don't mean to circle back to what we've already covered, but I think it applies here. This is going back to the activity of the rogue group. It's the responsibility of colonial leadership to condemn their actions. The longer this doesn't happen, the more anxious people will become, and they'll start to believe we approve of such actions. I don't think anyone in this room would advocate murdering helpless victims of any race, including the Ovarrow. At least now it's been declared a war crime."

The rest of the defense committee waited for Governor Wolf to reply to Connor. "You're right, General Gates. We need to be clear on our stance regarding the Ovarrow; however, regardless of this administration's stance, people still won't trust them. Right or wrong, they have the right not to trust them."

"I understand," Connor replied. "And I'm not saying we should welcome them into our homes, but if we want an alliance with them, we need to have the right attitude about it at home. If you take my meaning."

"What do you suggest we do?" Johnson asked. "Given the current circumstances, what would you say to the average person about the Ovarrow?"

Connor took a few seconds to consider his answer. "We need an effort to demystify them. Right now, they're one of the colony's greatest mysteries—a civilization that once thrived on this planet—and now we find out they're still here. It's enough to make anyone anxious. I know one of the reasons I'm more comfortable with it is because my wife's an archaeologist. I worked with her, going to the sites to uncover their history."

Johnson nodded and tapped his chin with his fingers. "It's their history that most people find alarming."

"If someone read our history and hadn't interacted with us, they might be just as concerned about *our* intentions. Their history isn't perfect, and neither is ours. I thought one of the pillars the colony was founded on was second chances. It says it right on this building as you walk inside. This is our fresh start. A chance for new beginnings."

"I think I understand," Johnson said, and Connor doubted it. "How should the average person react if they encounter an Ovarrow? Will they be attacked? Should they attempt to communicate?" Johnson asked and then turned toward the other committee members. "Is it even possible to equip every person who leaves the city with a NEIIS . . ." he paused and frowned, then looked at Connor. "I'm sorry, old habits. An Ovarrow translator? Most people want to be reassured that it's safe to encounter them."

"This isn't just about what I want," Connor said. "This is a collective decision, and we have to live with the consequences. If you're worried about how to deal with the Ovarrow, then you need to have other experts in the room to help facilitate those questions. This committee is for the defense of the colony."

Johnson was about to reply, but Governor Wolf spoke first. "You're absolutely right, General Gates. Perhaps this is a takeaway from this meeting that we need to address outside of this committee. I can think of a few people whose opinion I would highly value on the subject."

Johnson held up his hands, letting the matter drop, and Connor nodded. "Going back to our state of readiness. We can secure our cities and keep a fairly close watch on the surrounding areas, but what we can't do is monitor activity on the entire planet. Also, there are various research efforts and exploration initiatives throughout the continent and in some of the oceans. I think we need to encourage people to report suspicious activity. And not just abroad but inside our cities as well."

Johnson's eyebrows lifted, and he looked at Governor Wolf. "Inside our own cities? Why would we do that?"

Dana gestured for Connor to continue.

"Because despite our efforts, mainly by Field Ops and Security, we haven't been able to arrest any of the rogue group. I don't want to create a society of suspicion, but we do need help. I've had quite a number of conversations with Damon Mills about this," Connor said.

Damon, who was sitting across from him, nodded. "It's true. Connor and I have spoken about this at length. I think the new laws will help. As many of you know, I come from a background in law enforcement, and we do need informers if we're going to find this rogue group."

"Also," Connor began, "we've been analyzing the data taken from the Krake military base. The Ovarrow testimonies regarding the Krake indicate that they don't simply invade a world. They study it first and then they try to influence the events that occur. I don't think the Krake's standard operating procedure really applies to us because we're different species. Presumably, we're something they've never encountered before. Regardless, we need to be informed if something doesn't look right to the average person. Then we can investigate."

"This is a good suggestion," Damon said. "I'll have my office coordinate with the other mayors, and we'll put something out for the general population."

"Excuse me, Governor Wolf," a woman said. The voice was clipped and precise. Connor turned toward it and saw that Meredith Cain had spoken. "Regarding the Krake data, my office hasn't received anything to analyze. We've sent multiple requests to the CDF for this."

Wolf looked at Connor.

"We've been holding back on it because we think the data we've retrieved might not be safe. Meaning that the data is filled with misinformation."

"That's just it, General Gates. The Colonial Intelligence Bureau is supposed to be able to disseminate the information and maybe make some connections. I'm not asking the CDF to hand over the data for our exclusive use. I just want my people to have access to it, and perhaps they might offer a fresh perspective."

That wasn't all she was asking for, and Connor knew it. Meredith Cain might have been a bit on the quiet side, but when she did speak, it wasn't without purpose. He'd had his eye on her for a long time, but he couldn't connect her to the rogue group Lars Mallory was involved with.

"I think we can arrange for the data to be accessed by vetted personnel from the Intelligence Bureau," Connor said.

Meredith smiled. "That would be very much appreciated."

The meeting ended shortly after that, and Connor was walking with Nathan to the landing zone.

"I don't know about you, but I expected it," Nathan said and then added, "the request from the CIB."

"I know. Officially, there's no reason not to share the data with them."

"The older the colony gets, the more complex it is. I guess we can't expect to hold all the cards forever," Nathan replied.

"You're right, I know. It's just that the rogue group and Lars Mallory . . . They're not operating in a vacuum. They have support, and I suspect there were people in that meeting who agree with some of their efforts. There's no evidence, of course, but how else would they have evaded Field Ops for so long?"

"I know better than to question those instincts."

"What do you think, Nathan?"

"I think you're right, but I'm not sure what we can do about it without evidence. Sure, we can have our intelligence analysts watching the Colonial Intelligence Bureau, and they're likely watching us. Isn't that the name of the game? And wasn't that how things were done back on Earth?"

Connor drew in a deep breath and sighed. "Probably . . . no, not probably. More people, more complexity."

"Well, at least now we can legally pursue the rogue group, as long as they're not in any colonial city. That's a step in the right direction and will make things more difficult for them," Nathan said.

"The mandate is to capture them. They've been smart up to this point, avoiding a confrontation with the CDF and Field Ops. The closest they came to an actual conflict was with the squad we had escorting Dash to a remote Ovarrow site. I know we made progress in that meeting, but sometimes it feels like it takes so long to get anything done."

Nathan smiled. "Beats the alternative, meaning that the Krake could already be here and we'd be fighting them. I count that as a blessing."

Connor nodded. He could always count on Nathan to look at the brighter side of things. There was just so much to do and so little time. The fact was that Connor couldn't guess what the Krake would do if they ever did arrive on New Earth. He'd spent a career envisioning worst-case scenarios, but when he thought about what the Krake were capable of, he felt that his imagination might come up short. If that was the case, a lot of people would pay the price.

5

LARS MALLORY STOOD outside the exam room door. They'd been using this base of operations for almost a month. With colonial efforts focused on bringing the Ovarrow out of stasis and transporting them to their makeshift city, there were fewer resources hunting for him and the people under his command. It was almost time to move again, but Lars had decided to wait, which was a risk because the location was known and occasionally monitored by the Office of NEIIS Investigation. Lars supposed they'd have to change ONI to a more appropriate name now that the latest trend was to refer to the NEIIS as the Ovarrow. OOI didn't quite roll off the tongue like the ONI did, but Lars didn't really care what they called themselves.

The exam room door opened, and Tonya Wagner looked at him. "We're ready to begin anytime," she said and looked around. "Evans and Clark running late again?"

"They'll be here. It's not like whoever's inside is going anywhere. Did you confirm the faction before we took this pod?" Lars asked.

Tonya nodded her pretty head. She had dark brown eyes and

pale skin, and her hair had a natural curl to it despite how short she kept it. She was tall and lithe, and she could run with the best of them on any survival trek.

"Of course. The three-triangle symbol, just like the other ones we've been focused on," she replied.

They'd been focused on the same Ovarrow symbol as the one on the stasis pod Connor had accidentally revived. For as long as they'd been searching, they hadn't found another Ovarrow that was anything like Siloc. That was irritating at first—that is until Lars had figured out that Siloc was way more than he appeared to be. On more than one occasion, Lars had thought about sending that information to Connor. It would have to be untraceable, of course, but Connor hadn't been wrong in killing that Ovarrow.

A message appeared on Lars's internal heads-up display. "Evans said they're about five minutes out. They're bringing some new recruits."

Tonya smiled broadly. Seeing the reaction of the new recruits to an Ovarrow was always interesting. The colonial news net did an admirable job of circulating press pieces about the Ovarrow, but it was all contrived, of course. Lars enjoyed circulating his own set of propaganda to influence the masses, a source of frustration for some.

He heard people coming down the passageway that led outside, and the muffled conversation became louder as the group got closer. He heard Evans ordering them to be quiet, and the group of recruits quieted down.

Evans came around the corner first and jutted his chin up toward Lars. "We need to talk."

"All right," Lars said and looked at the man standing behind Evans. "Justin, why don't you take the others inside? We'll be there in a minute."

"Will do, sir," Justin Clark replied.

The group quietly walked by, with some of the new recruits

sneaking a glance at him. Lars was making a name for himself, at least among the people who knew better than to think they could share their planet with a species like the Ovarrow.

"We're outlaws now. Have you heard the latest?"

Lars shook his head. "No, what happened?"

"The governor's office released a statement condemning any activity that harms the Ovarrow. It does go into some specifics, and basically everything we've been doing is now illegal," Evans said and tapped a few commands on his wrist computer.

"They were bound to catch up with it sooner or later. It's a legal loophole at best, and there was a limited window of opportunity."

"Yeah, but they didn't vote on this. They just made it a law. This goes against everything else they've been telling us."

Evans was a hothead, and this was the latest thing to get his goat. It also confirmed that Evans didn't understand how laws were passed in the colony. Lars shrugged. "You can't let this get you all riled up."

"The hell I can't. Why aren't you angry? They're condemning our actions."

"They can pass all the laws they want. We have actual support outside the colonial government, and the message is getting out there. There's a growing segment of the population questioning the proposed alliance with the Ovarrow."

Evans curled his lips. "Not fast enough. We need to do more. People are still too complacent," he said and shook his head, glaring at nothing.

"Colton, you've got to calm down," Lars said and moved so he could get in front of his friend's line of sight. "You hear me? You're no good to anyone like this."

Evans shook his head and clenched his teeth. His hands were balled into fists.

"Look, why don't you take a walk? I've got this. Get some fresh air. Then we could talk more about these laws and how it affects what we need to do."

Evans regarded him for a few moments, at first looking as if he were going to protest. His left hand was in his pocket, and he seemed to be caressing something inside. Lars had a pretty good idea of what it was. And he didn't like it.

Evans bobbed his head up and down. "Okay. I'm going to go check the perimeter."

Lars watched him go. He even walked as if he had excessive energy. Too many stimulants. Lars shook his head and sighed. He needed to keep a closer eye on his friend. Evans was dedicated to what they were doing, but Lars had to redirect Evans' frantic energy at times. He had to be careful not to let it become a distraction or allow Evans to be put in a position to do something drastic.

The door to the exam room opened, and Tonya stood inside the doorway. "We're ready for you, sir."

Lars saw that the stasis pod was now open. The Ovarrow that had been inside was restrained, still looking disoriented and confused. Lars drew in a deep breath and stepped toward the door. His footsteps were heavy and carried a sense of finality with them. "All right, let's get started."

6

SANCTUARY HAD BEGUN as a forward operating research base that Lenora had gotten off the ground. For years it had been home to a small group of archaeologists, engineers, and other research scientists. As such, Field Ops had always had a presence there, and it had been a small, tightknit community. Then, when the Vemus War had finally reached them, Sanctuary had become one of the designated bunker sites to safely hold colonists.

Lenora walked through the ruins of an Ovarrow city. To her left were the geothermal power taps that had been used to provide electricity to the vault below. The Ovarrow vault was a treasure trove of recorded history. They'd made more progress translating it in the past year than they had in all the previous years combined.

Sanctuary had grown to become a city-size settlement after the Vemus War when colonial refugees had elected to stay rather than return to the other cities to rebuild. Connor's presence there had drawn no small amount of former CDF soldiers, and he'd been instrumental in getting Sanctuary the support it needed to become an actual colonial city.

She glanced wistfully up at the clear blue skies and smiled, missing him as Mayor Gates. After all those years of preparing for a war, it seemed that Connor had finally found some peace. She knew rejoining the CDF hadn't been an easy decision for him to make, but it was different this time. *He* was different. She still worried about him; that would never change. But Connor wasn't quite so consumed with preparing for the worst like he'd been after that first clash with the Vemus. The Krake certainly worried him, and if she was being honest with herself, they worried her, too.

She'd been studying archaeological records since they'd first landed on this planet, and she'd been piecing together everything she could about the Ovarrow civilization that used to live there. But she never would've expected to find stasis pods with those beings inside. Who would?

Lenora reached the interior of the abandoned city and went inside the archives, heading for the computing core. She could access all the information from her lab at the Colonial Research Institute; however, sometimes she just felt that she had a different perspective when accessing the data from its original location. Some of her students understood this. Dash certainly understood it as he trekked off to every possible Ovarrow ruin he could find.

The archives were quiet. Coming down there was a reminder that a few hundred years ago, New Earth had been a much different place. Sometimes she brought Lauren with her. She tried to bring her daughter with her everywhere she went. When she did, she didn't get as much done as she would have, but she didn't mind so much. Becoming a mother had changed her perspective on work and life. But both she and Connor had demanding jobs, and given the current state of affairs, they needed to continue to work hard. Connor was focused on coming up with a way to protect them from the Krake, and Lenora believed that the answers and the insight they needed to come up with a strategy lay within the Ovarrow archives. This was how she could best contribute.

There were monitoring systems at the archives, and she'd sent her credentials through so she could just walk right in. She descended to the level where the computing core was and got to work. There were some key systems she wanted to access using the updated translator Dash had created. The new translator made some of the more obscure data repositories she'd found more accessible.

Lenora had been lost in her work for a few hours when she heard somebody walking down the corridor towards the computing core. She turned as they entered the room.

Dash smiled and waved at her. "Still prefer to work in the archives?"

Lenora stood up, stretched her arms in front of her, and rolled her shoulders. She'd been sitting a long time. "It does carry a certain amount of authenticity."

Dash nodded. "That it does."

"I was actually just giving the new translator a try on the archives."

Dash perked up. "Revision number seven, right? How'd it do?"

"It does open some doors, but it also raises more questions. At least now we can categorize more of what we *can* access. I can even task the AI at the research institute with trying to find any connections within the data that we might've missed. Some of the history makes more sense now."

"That's what I found at the capital city, but the archives there weren't as well protected as this one. Anyway, I don't get to spend much time there," Dash said.

"What brings you down here?" Lenora asked.

"I was visiting an old friend at Field Ops, and after seeing him, I thought I'd check in with you. Do you need any help with anything?"

"We still need to validate what the Ovarrow told us. The fact of the matter is that they can come out of stasis and tell us anything they want, and we wouldn't know whether it was the truth," Lenora said.

"So far, everything has checked out. I wonder how they'd react if they knew about this place."

A comlink chimed from Lenora's tablet computer, and she glanced at it for a moment before accepting the call. A small holoscreen appeared above it that showed Governor Wolf's face.

"Dr. Bishop, thank you for taking my call."

"Of course, Governor Wolf. What can I do for you?"

Dash came to her side within view of the camera. Wolf looked at him. "Mr. DeWitt, I'm glad you're there, too." She looked back at Lenora. "Dr. Bishop, I have a request. There's been a lot of debate on the proposed alliance with the Ovarrow. As someone who's studied the archaeological record, I believe you can provide a fresh perspective on the Ovarrow and possibly help improve our relations with them."

Lenora leaned toward the holoscreen. "I'm happy to give you my opinion, but I'm not a diplomat."

Governor Wolf smiled. "That's good because I don't need another diplomat. And I would value your opinion. However, it's a lot to discuss, and I was hoping you'd be open to making a short trip to Sierra."

Lenora frowned for a moment as her thoughts immediately turned to Lauren.

"We can arrange help with childcare while you're here, if that helps," Governor Wolf said and looked at Dash. "Mr. DeWitt, Darius Cohen has requested that you come as well."

Lenora glanced at Dash.

"Darius is the lead diplomatic representative for the Ovarrow," he said.

"Can I count on you to join us?" Governor Wolf asked.

Lenora considered the request for a few more moments. "I'll come. When is this meeting?"

"We're kind of in the middle of it now, but we'll also be reconvening in a few hours."

They wanted her there *now*. "I'll be there as soon as I can. I'll let your office know when I arrive."

"A C-cat is already is en route to Sanctuary and will be there soon. It'll collect you and bring you straight to us."

The comlink closed and Lenora saw Dash grinning a little. "What?" she asked.

Dash shook his head and smiled. "It's not important."

Lenora narrowed her gaze. "If you were going to remark about my piloting skills, I'll have you know I've been flying ships almost as long as you've been alive."

Lenora was an excellent pilot. She just happened to make a few other pilots nervous when she flew.

"I know. I've flown with you, remember?"

She rolled her eyes. "Come on, I have some things I need to take care of."

"Yes, Dr. Bishop," Dash replied.

Lenora gave him a playful swat on the arm. "I'll give you 'Dr. Bishop.'"

7

SAVANNAH WALKED on the elevated pathway above the secondary hangar bay on Phoenix Station. This bay was used for ships in need of repair or for ships whose flight status hadn't yet been confirmed.

She'd risen through the ranks with the goal of commanding a warship, which she'd done for a while. Her first real ship command had been aboard the destroyer *Banshee*, which had been taken by the Vemus. Most of the crew had died, and she'd led the survivors through the enemy ship in hopes of commandeering a vessel to escape. Having survived that ordeal, she'd been put in command of Phoenix Station. At first, the station had been built from a patchwork of the battleship cruiser they'd been attempting to build. The current iteration was version two-point-zero and was designed from the beginning to be a space station capable of being among their first line of defense from an invading fleet.

It was quiet as far as hangar bays went, with the more active areas of the station being currently used. That wasn't a coincidence. Major Vance Peterson walked toward her from the opposite end of the elevated pathway. He'd just been speaking with his assistant, who had hastened in the opposite direction.

Peterson glanced down at the area below them. Several rows of Talon-V space fighters were being readied for active duty. It was impractical to bring all types of CDF ships into the hangar bay. They were simply too big, which was why most hangar bays housed the shuttles and other smaller spacecraft, while larger vessels docked with the space station itself.

She walked over to Peterson and they kept walking down a long corridor that extended out away from the station.

"I have a list of alternates in case this doesn't work out, Colonel," Peterson said.

"It's nice to have, but it won't be necessary."

Peterson pursed his lips thoughtfully. "If you say so."

"You don't know him like I do."

"I read his record. It's exemplary. He's received awards for distinguished service. Instrumental in bringing about the end of the Vemus War," Peterson said.

"Did you read down to the part where it was actually his brother he was attempting to rescue? That's when the Vemus Alpha entered the star system."

Peterson frowned as he read more of the report and then nodded. "I see."

A warning alarm sounded from the airlock on the far side of the corridor, indicating that there was a brief exposure to vacuum. A shuttle docked and then the locks switched to green. Several CDF personnel entered the station. Among them was a tall, athletic man with dark hair. He saw her and immediately headed in her direction.

He came to a stop and snapped a crisp salute. "Captain Jon Walker reporting for duty, Colonel."

Savannah returned the salute. "At ease, Captain."

Walker glanced at Peterson for a moment and then looked

back at Savannah. "I didn't expect the commanding officer of Phoenix Station to meet me at the airlock."

"I wanted to show you something before your briefing, Captain," Savannah said, and without waiting for a reply, she walked to the other side of the corridor. There was a window of polarized glass that prevented anyone from seeing through it. Savannah set the window to clear, revealing the ship on the other side. Her gaze slid over the sleek lines of the vessel. It had twin engine pods near the rear, with secondary engines on top of the cigar-shaped ship.

Walker came over to her side. "It looks like a small frigate, Colonel," he said.

"It's much more than that, Captain," Savannah replied. "That's your new ship if you accept the mission we have for you."

"I wasn't under the impression that missions were optional, Colonel."

"This is a different kind of mission."

Savannah watched as Walker peered at the ship. "I know that's not a frigate. It has more sensor arrays. The hull looks different than the battle steel we use on standard CDF vessels. I'd say it's some kind of scout ship. A quick one, judging by the engines."

Savannah nodded in approval. "Very good, Captain Walker. That is the Raven class scout ship SR–01, the first of its kind. The hull is comprised of a new flexible alloy designed to thwart active scans."

Walker's thick eyebrows came together for a moment. Then he leaned toward the window, his eyes shining with desire. Savannah knew Walker's type. He was a pilot to his bones. She missed commanding a warship, but she wouldn't give up her current command to return to the gleaming decks of one. She could tell Walker wasn't done with them though.

He looked back at her and waited.

"Captain Walker, I'm sure you're aware of the disappearance of the Trident Battle Group. I want you to use this ship to find them."

Walker licked his lips for a moment and frowned.

"We've been putting together a plan to scout the alternate universe the Trident Battle Group went to, and there's a high probability of enemy forces operating in the area. We have a list of candidates selected for this mission, and you're at the top of the list. You have the most experience flying undetected among enemy forces. I believe that experience will be crucial for the success of the mission."

Walker scratched the side of his face and drew in a deep breath. Then he shook his head. "Now I understand why I would need to volunteer. This is a suicide mission. I thought the reconnaissance drones were making progress finding Trident Battle Group."

"Not quickly enough. It's been almost three months since we lost contact. We need to find out what happened to them. We already have a crew for the Raven, and all it needs is a captain. The mission is yours if you want it."

Major Peterson looked as if he was going to say something, and Savannah silenced him with a look.

Walker turned away from her for a moment, considering. "I'm sorry, Colonel. But you have the wrong man for this job."

He walked away, and Savannah could feel the proverbial door being shut in her face. She didn't like it one bit, and she didn't have time for self-absorbed antics. "Are you really content with making supply runs? Is that the extent of your legacy? You think that if you continue to make supply runs you can somehow fool yourself that you're still a pilot? That you're still capable of commanding a ship? Your record might indicate that you're a hero of the Vemus War, but your more recent record indicates a man who's barely keeping it together. I remember who you were. General Hayes and General Gates also remember, and it's with their approval that I'm extending this mission to you. Your choice is to either accept the mission to get out there and find Trident Battle Group, helping your fellow CDF soldiers in the process, or you can walk away. Scurry off this space station and crawl back to New Earth, but I guarantee you'll never fly for the CDF again. Those are your choices, Captain."

Savannah turned and walked away with Major Peterson at her side. She counted the seconds as she put more distance between herself and Jon Walker. She'd been on the receiving end of a kick in the ass once by Connor and hadn't liked it. She also didn't like having to be the one to do the kicking, but it was necessary.

"I'll call in the alternates, Colonel," Peterson said quietly.

Savannah nodded. She'd been sure that once she'd shown Walker that ship, it would spur some of that decisive gumption required by those officers who commanded ships. She might've been wrong.

"Colonel Cross," Walker called out as he hastened toward her. Savannah didn't turn around nor did she slow down. Walker repeated himself and circled in front of her. "What kind of reconnaissance do you need?"

Savannah gave him her stone-cold glare. "Time is a luxury, Captain. And I won't waste any if you're not one hundred percent committed to this."

"Understood, Colonel Cross," Walker replied. "Colonel Sean Quinn is the reason my family is still alive. I owe him, and I'll do everything I can to find him and the rest of the battle group. I promise."

Savannah regarded him for a moment. She'd already made up her mind, but she didn't want to appear to give in too quickly. She wanted Walker to believe she might not let him go. "All right then. The plan is as follows: We send the Raven through the space gate. You scout the area and come back through it at predefined times and coordinates."

Walker pressed his lips together and was silent for a few seconds. "You want to send the scout ship through the space gate here and come back through this space gate?" he said, gesturing away from him. "If we really want to scout the entire system, why not position a space gate at a predetermined set of coordinates? That way, our entry point isn't the same as our egress point. Since we have more than two gates, we could have multiple egress points should the need arise. I think it would be important to keep our options open, given the fact that there's a high probability of enemy ships in the area."

Savannah felt Peterson's gaze slip toward her and then back at Walker. She looked at her XO. "See, I told you. He's the right man for the job." She looked at Walker. "Welcome to Operation Sherlock, Captain Walker."

Walker's eyes widened for a moment. "Thank you, Colonel. I have a request."

Savannah felt her eyebrows raise. "What is it?"

"You mentioned earlier that you had a crew for the Raven. I'd like some additional crew members to be added to the roster. People I've worked with who I know are reliable."

Savannah resumed walking, and Walker and Peterson kept pace at her side. "We can discuss it, and we'll go over the specifics of the plan."

"Yes, Colonel," Walker said. "When do I leave?"

"Sooner than you'd like, but not soon enough."

Walker nodded. "Understood, Colonel."

8

THE CDF BASE at Sanctuary had grown considerably in the past eighteen months. All colonial cities had their own dedicated defensive force, but what made the base at Sanctuary different had to do with the city itself. The Colonial Research Institute drew in some of the finest minds in the colony, and this made the city a hotbed of ingenuity and technological advancement. In addition, the CDF base also had a significant section of its capacity devoted to weapons development and defense. What had begun as a stockpiling effort, with Connor doing his own weapons development, had expanded. Noah had really helped bring it along. Connor missed Noah, but he could still see his friend's contributions all around him. Civilian experts also worked at designated areas on the base.

Connor walked down the hallway, heading for an observation room with live feeds of the Ovarrow settlement. Samson caught up to him and settled into a pace matching Connor's.

"I thought you were on a training exercise," Connor said.

"This is just as important. I gave the teams their assigned tasks," Samson said. Connor raised his eyebrows and Samson continued. "This is as close as I can get to observing the enemy. I'm well aware that the Ovarrow aren't considered the enemy, but the Krake certainly are. This is as close as I can get to them until we can start using the Arch again."

"We'll get a chance, just not right now."

"I know. I know. We have a limited amount of resources and a whole lot more words to simply say we can't do it right now, but we *should* be doing it, Connor."

They reached the end of the hallway and turned down another one.

"You know how this works, Samson. We need buy-in and approval. Plus, we're still analyzing the data from the Krake base. The intelligence analysts are building profiles of the different universes. Then we have to review them to see which ones we want to recon. It's going to happen sooner than we think though."

They reached the observation room and walked inside. Carl Flint and Dr. Eric Young were already inside.

"Hello, Connor. I'm glad you're here," Eric said. "I've been meaning to talk to you, but your schedule has been pretty booked up."

Connor had first met Eric when he'd encountered Siloc, the Ovarrow they'd accidentally brought out of stasis. Dr. Eric Young was a psychologist who specialized in crisis management and coping strategies for traumatized situations. Eric had been surprisingly helpful during that time, and Connor had extended an invitation for him to advise the CDF as they learned to deal with the Ovarrow. Since the Office of NEIIS Intelligence was being absorbed into the Colonial Intelligence Bureau, Connor wanted his own intelligence assets within the CDF so they'd have reliable subject matter experts on hand. In essence, he'd done what he'd normally do in this situation and gone recruiting. Nathan often accused him of poaching the best talent, and it helped that Sanctuary held a certain amount of allure for colonists.

"It can't be helped," Connor replied.

"I understand, and I've been working with the other officers here on base, just as you asked. We're learning more about the Ovarrow each passing day. Certain behavioral patterns that were difficult to observe in a smaller group are now much easier to see as their population has grown," Eric said.

He was right about that. They'd put considerable effort into helping the Ovarrow become more independent, and that also necessitated bringing more of their people out of stasis. The Ovarrow population was over ten thousand refugees.

Connor had been part of the effort to offload over three hundred thousand colonists when they'd first arrived at New Earth. Accidentally awakened in one of the earlier groups, he'd learned that there was a balance between bringing people out of stasis and ensuring that they had adequate shelter, food, and relevant work detail. What was different with the Ovarrow was that they didn't know who was in stasis. Not exactly. Having the Ovarrow involved with bringing their own species out of stasis sped up the process considerably. It made explaining things to them much easier than when it had been a purely human-based operation.

The Ovarrow city was a hundred kilometers from Camp Alpha, which was more of a forward operating base but with significant military and civilian presence.

"There are teams of scientists observing the Ovarrow and their interactions; however, I'm beginning to suspect they're aware they're being watched as closely as they were when there were only a few hundred of them at Camp Alpha," Eric said.

"Do you think it's a problem?" Connor asked.

They had stealth recon drones regularly patrolling the areas, which should have been undetected by the Ovarrow, but maybe they were wrong about that. Or the Ovarrow could simply assume they were being watched and work under that assumption.

Eric's head swayed from side to side. "It's difficult to say. Usually when people know they're being observed, they put on a performance. Given the situation the Ovarrow find themselves in, they're more anxious than they might otherwise be. It's hard to say because we still don't know when their stasis pod systems were supposed to bring them out. According to their experts, it was when the danger of the Krake had passed. How their systems were going to decide that is a bit of a mystery."

"I'm aware of this," Connor replied. "It's also important to remember that their system was flawed and breaking. Stasis pods were going offline because of a lack of resources. Their fail-safe was to eliminate the occupant rather than have them wake up earlier than intended. I believe that sheds a lot of light on how seriously they took this effort."

Samson whistled softly and shook his head. "I've witnessed the result of ruthless policies before, but this is extreme."

"The Ovarrow who got to go into a stasis pod were the lucky ones. Think about that for a little while," Connor said.

Eric nodded. "It does explain some of the violent outbursts that were observed at Camp Alpha. Having a cure for the rapid-aging illness was a big help."

That was something else that had taken them all by surprise, including the Ovarrow. They'd gone into stasis with only some of them knowing that when they woke up, they could be dead within a month. Faulty stasis tech resulted in rapid cellular degeneration, or extreme, rapid aging. They either hadn't yet perfected using stasis tech, or they just didn't understand the tech they'd stolen from the Krake.

"What else?" Connor said.

"In some respects, they're . . ." Eric said and paused for a moment, frowning in thought. "That's not right. The way they handle conflict is tied to establishing dominance. In some respects, it's like we're dealing with a primitive or immature species."

"They fought wars," Connor replied. "A lot of them. There hasn't been enough time for them to get away from that mentality. Constant war is a cycle, and it will take time for it to loosen its hold on how they deal with things."

"Except that's not what we're doing," Samson said.

"What do you mean?" Eric asked.

"We're pulling them out of stasis and telling them their worst enemy is still around and we'd like their help to fight them. How would you react?" Samson said.

"We can't keep them ignorant of the Krake. They just need some time to adapt," Connor said.

"I understand that. I've even noted it in my own observations. What's interesting is that the establishment of dominance isn't divided by males and females. They have similar stature in their society, but you're right, they've been conditioned to react to conflict in what we might consider the most brutal way possible," Eric said.

Samson cleared his throat. "Are you saying the Ovarrow are simply misguided?"

Eric nodded. "That's one way of putting it. Might be a bit oversimplistic, but it does get the point across."

Connor considered this for a few seconds. "They've been brutalized and manipulated, but on the other hand they've embraced the things they've been a victim of. I've seen that kind of behavior before."

"Where?" Eric asked.

"Back on Earth," Connor said. "My job, along with Samson's, was counterintelligence and insurgents. It was my job to deal with groups that manipulated other groups of people. There are lots of different ways to do this. Mostly it's preying on biases and prejudices. I think you see a lot of that with the Ovarrow."

"How are we supposed to deal with this?" Flint asked. He'd been listening and hadn't spoken until then.

Connor glanced at Eric and waited for him to answer. "If we interfere and force them to be civilized to each other, they'll resent it. What we need to deal with is the group mentality. Maybe focus on keeping the violence from escalating out of control."

Flint frowned and pressed his lips together. "How?"

"The Ovarrow need to feel that they can control their own destiny. Otherwise, they won't be able to help us or themselves," Connor replied.

"Just so I understand—we need to let them do their thing unless they're about to get out of control, at which point we step in and course correct for them?" Flint asked.

"It's a start, but again we're simplifying what's happening," Eric replied.

Samson shook his head. "This might make more sense if we were dealing with people, but they're an alien species. We can watch them all we want, but on a fundamental level, we might never understand them."

Connor looked over at the holoscreens that showed live video feeds of the Ovarrow city. The Ovarrow spent much of their time trying to provide for themselves, restoring systems in their abandoned cities. The colony provided ryklar deterrent systems so they could establish themselves without the threat of being attacked. They still had limited access to transportation beyond the city.

"I have a question for you, Connor. What do you think the Krake would do if they found this place based on what you know now? Given that this is a former world they used to control," Eric said.

"They'd probably observe us for a while. This place is one of their experiments that went wrong, and they'd likely want to understand why—how the outcome didn't match with their predictions. It also depends on how they perceive us. Are we a threat to them? I don't expect them to show up with an invasion force, at least not right away. That will come later."

"It's interesting," Eric said. "Your reply, that is. The Ovarrow seem to have a unified fear that the Krake will do just that—show up here and invade. At least, certain factions share that belief."

"That's the behavior of the Ovarrow that come out of stasis. Their soldiers come out ready to fight. I understand we're still learning more about them and observing them. We're also still analyzing the data we've taken from the Krake base. And then there's the group of Ovarrow we encountered on the other side of the continent that were guarding the Arch," Connor said.

Flint nodded. "Our recon teams couldn't find them. There were tunnels beneath the city that went on for kilometers. We had drones mapping the area, but we still couldn't find them."

"Who do you think they were?" Eric asked.

"They were different," Connor replied. "They used ryklars but in different ways. They removed the ryklars' auditory systems and relied on visual aids to control them. That kind of training doesn't happen overnight and means they must have some kind of tech base to work from. I wonder whether they were ever in stasis at all."

Eric's eyebrows lifted. "Never in stasis?" he repeated. "That means they'd have had to find a way to survive for over two hundred years in an Ice Age *and* avoid a superior enemy."

Connor shrugged. "It's not impossible. There was no power in that city, and they were keen to prevent us from using the Arch."

"I guess it shouldn't be too surprising. If the Ovarrow were strapped for resources and the stasis technology wasn't available everywhere, I guess it makes sense that there were pockets of them who tried to weather out the long winter. Why haven't we encountered them before?" Eric asked.

"We've mainly kept to our own cities and the surrounding

areas. The main supercontinent is huge, so I'm not surprised we haven't come across them. We haven't been on the planet that long, and if they were hiding and had limited transportation capabilities, why would they ever need to travel across the continent?"

Eric nodded. "I guess that makes sense."

"More than that," Samson said, "we should be focused on finding them. They might be the only group of Ovarrow worth allying with. They didn't bury their heads in the sand, hoping to wake up to a better world."

"That's a bit harsh," Eric replied.

"I've been called worse."

Eric shrugged. "It's easy to judge. There's a lot of evidence out there that points to a desperate situation they were facing."

They glanced at Connor for a moment. "We still need to learn all we can about them. Then we can judge them or not—I don't care. Remember, if it comes to a fight with the Krake, we'll need more than just us to face them. The Krake could have a population that numbers in the billions and all the resources that go with that. So, whether we agree with what the Ovarrow did or not, we might still need their help."

9

It was early afternoon by the time Lenora and Dash arrived at Sierra. The sky was thick with clouds, and it felt as if it was going to start raining at any moment. Sierra's proximity to a large river made for a more humid region than what they had at home. Sanctuary was closer to the foothills of an old mountain range, which generally gave them better weather, in Lenora's opinion. She found the drier region more agreeable, especially since she liked to be outside.

Dash walked beside her, and his mood seemed to have improved. She asked him about it.

"I'm happy to be working with you again, even if it's only for the next day or so," Dash replied. Then after a few moments, he added, "I do miss fieldwork. I like going into places no one's ever been before. It seems like now all I get to do are things related to the Ovarrow and translating their language."

"It's important work, Dash. You should be proud. You're becoming an authority in the area."

Dash smiled a little. "You're the real authority. You've been studying the Ovarrow since you got here."

"There's more to learn. Much more."

Dash nodded. "I know, and I'd like to get back to it."

"So, what's stopping you?"

They were walking across the garden path from the landing zone, heading into the governor's offices.

"Nothing is stopping me. There's just so much to do. I feel like I'm being pulled in a bunch of different directions, but I'm happy for all the opportunities. Mostly, I just want to help Connor as much as I can."

Lenora sensed that a "but" was implied. "I know he appreciates it."

"I even offered to join the CDF."

Lenora smiled and shook her head. "Why would you want to do that? Never mind, you don't need to join the CDF. Connor doesn't expect that from you."

Dash's face became grim.

"What happened to Noah wasn't your fault, Dash."

She understood Dash's feelings. He had a lot more in common with Connor than either of them thought. It was almost as if they were related somehow. Lenora had seen many people be drawn to Connor whether those people understood it or not. Some of those people, like Dash, were drawn toward Connor and rebelled against him at the same time. She often told Connor that he underestimated the effect he had on other people.

"I'm supposed to say that I know it's not my fault, but I was there."

"We'll find Lars and whoever he's working with. It doesn't have to be you, and it's okay if it's not you. Noah would never blame you for what happened to him. You need to let this go," she said. "Think of it like this: What if you *were* the person to catch Lars and bring him before the judiciary committee? What then? Do you think you'll feel satisfied?" Lenora asked.

Dash blew out a breath and lifted his chin. "I would. It would feel great. I'd love to see Lars get exactly what he deserves."

After years of dealing with Connor and other people from the CDF, she knew how to deal with what Dash was experiencing. "You might feel a little bit of satisfaction, but the anger would still be there. What you're really struggling with is forgiving yourself for something that isn't your fault, and that won't come from Lars Mallory at all."

Dash's eyes went cold. "What do you—"

He stopped himself from saying the rest, and his cheeks reddened a little bit.

Lenora arched an eyebrow. "What do I know about it?" she asked. "A lot. Do you know how long Connor blamed himself for not being able to help his friends Wil Reisman and Kasey Douglass? It's not just him, either. For a long time, Sean Quinn blamed himself for his father's death. It didn't matter to him that he was commanding all the ground forces engaging the Vemus. They were sacrificing entire cities to keep them from getting to us. And don't forget about Diaz. He's struggling with the same thing right now. Juan wants to do his duty, but he also wants to be there for his family. It's all different shades of guilt, and not all of it is healthy. I'm not saying you can escape feeling guilty about what happened, but you don't have to let it consume you."

Dash's eyebrows drew together, and his mouth hung open for a few moments.

"I'm also good at archaeology. Don't just stand there with your mouth hanging open. Come on, let's go," Lenora said and quickened her pace.

One of Governor Wolf's assistants met them and led them to the conference room. As they walked, Lenora glanced at Dash, and he seemed to be thinking about what she'd told him. She'd been meaning to talk to him about this for a while, but they could never quite get the chance.

Dash had the makings of a fine young man. He reminded her a little bit of Noah and Sean—probably Lars, too, if she really thought about it. She knew all three of them. They'd all been part of the early risers in the *Ark* program. Lars Mallory had always been as straight as an arrow, just like his father, and she couldn't begin to guess why he was doing the things he was. She and Connor had talked about it quite a bit, and he was less surprised than she was. At least Connor was able to rationalize it more readily than she'd been able to.

They entered the room and Governor Wolf smiled in greeting. She then introduced the other people who were in the meeting. "I'm sure there are some people here you already know and recognize."

Lenora nodded a greeting to Darius Cohen and then some of the members of his staff.

"Thank you for joining us at such short notice," Kurt Johnson said as he rose and came around the table to greet her.

Governor Wolf gestured toward a short woman with pale skin and curly brown hair. "Allow me to introduce you to Meredith Cain. She's the Director of the Colonial Intelligence Bureau."

Lenora had never met Meredith Cain before, but she'd heard of her. She gave Lenora a friendly smile.

"It's nice to finally meet you, Dr. Bishop. I've read much of your work on the Ovarrow, and I've found it very insightful," Meredith said.

"Also, we have a few of our interns sitting in on this meeting," Governor Wolf said and gestured toward the nearest young lady who had dirty blonde hair, brown eyes, and looked athletic. "This is my daughter Kayla. Next to her is Lynn Butler, and last but not least is Devon Sims."

"A pleasure to meet all of you," Lenora said.

"Dr. Bishop, it's so nice to meet you," Kayla said, and Lynn and Devon echoed the same.

Wolf smiled. "They've been excited to meet you since they first learned you were joining us. I think some of them are interested in attending the Colonial Research Institute at Sanctuary."

"It's the best place to be," Dash said and drew a few appreciative but shy glances from the two young ladies.

Lenora smiled at them and then looked at Governor Wolf. "We'd be lucky to have them."

"Thank you," Wolf said. "Back to the matter at hand. Let's bring you up to speed and we'll take it from there."

For the next half hour, Darius Cohen and Kurt Johnson went over their concerns about dealing with the Ovarrow. This was more of a strategy session for finding a way for the colony to form an alliance with them. They also highlighted the opinions of those who couldn't be at the meeting, including Connor's input. Lenora was no stranger to dealing with government officials, but it was usually over a matter of appropriating resources for her research.

"I'd like to hear your thoughts on the Ovarrow. We have the highlights from your research findings, but I'd like to hear your thoughts on how the archaeological record matches with the behavior we've seen from the Ovarrow," Wolf said.

Lenora sipped her water and then placed the glass back on the table. "For any archaeological record, we try to piece together everyday-life-type things. What makes that difficult with excavating any of the Ovarrow sites is that they've been sanitized."

Johnson frowned for a moment. "What do you mean by sanitized?"

"What I mean by that is that the sites weren't just left; they were cleaned. Evidence of the Ovarrow living in their cities was mostly erased. Some of that occurs naturally, but to the degree that we found . . ." Lenora shook her head. "There's also the purge protocol that summons the ryklars to attack and kill any living thing inside the Ovarrow cities. They could've been involved in removing all the evidence of what Ovarrow everyday life was like. I'm afraid mostly what I can speak to about this is something you already know. The wars the Ovarrow fought affected almost everywhere there was a city. We've theorized why they fought those wars, but when we introduce the outside influence that is the Krake, it just paints all their actions in a much different light. However, catastrophic events need to be taken into account. They could spur a civilization into doing the things they did—things like scrambling to get into a stasis pod. The archives that we've been able to decipher indicate there were a lot of events going on at the same time, and some of those things just spiraled out of control—a recipe for the perfect storm. I think what you're asking me is whether I think we can trust the Ovarrow. Isn't that right?"

"It wouldn't be fair to ask you that," Governor Wolf said. "Trust will be an ongoing issue until a baseline is established."

"From an archaeological perspective," Meredith interjected, "how would meeting an ancient species affect the perceptions of the archaeological record?"

Lenora thought about it for a few moments. "It would put things into context. I mean, just our interactions alone have enabled us to translate more of their archives."

Meredith pursed her lips in thought and then nodded.

"That makes sense," Governor Wolf said. "We're trying to find ways to compare the research that's been done with what we're observing now, and we're falling short. We can assign an AI to highlight some things, and it might give us some insight, but it's not the same as an expert giving us feedback, as I'm sure Mr. DeWitt can account."

Lenora glanced at Dash, and he nodded. "Being around them is different. I've observed them both in person and from video feeds from reconnaissance drones, and it's not the same. Being among them and interacting with them, seeing how they live—it just paints all the places we've explored in a new light."

"That's it exactly," Johnson said and pointed a sausage-sized finger toward Dash. "We need more of this."

Lenora frowned in thought for a few moments and then looked at Governor Wolf.

"Darius and I have spoken quite a bit about how best to deal with the Ovarrow," Wolf said. "We can try to be as diplomatic as possible, but the fact of the matter is we're still piecing this together as we go based on what we've learned. Any effort that can help this process would be a benefit to all of us."

"I understand that," Lenora replied. "I just don't know what else I can possibly say on the matter. You already have Dash working with you. I highly value his work and his observations."

"We do appreciate all of his contributions," Darius said. He gave a firm nod toward Dash and then turned back to Lenora. "I'd be curious to know whether you'd be interested in coming out to the Ovarrow city and seeing them firsthand. You've been studying them the longest of anybody in the colony."

Lenora felt as if all the eyes in the room were now focused on her. She'd been curious about Camp Alpha and everything they were doing there, but she hadn't ever been there. There was always something else getting in the way. She thought about Lauren for a moment. She loved being a mother, but it had made her change her priorities, which meant less time in the field.

"Is this something you would consider?" Governor Wolf asked.

"I hadn't thought about it, to be honest."

Wolf nodded. "One of the things Connor suggested is that we make an outward show of our support for the alliance with the Ovarrow. We rotate teams that go with the diplomatic envoys to the Ovarrow city, including interns," Wolf said and gestured toward her daughter and the other two interns. "If this is something that would interest you, then would you consider going with the next envoy? It would only be for a day or two. It could be longer if you decided you need more time, but I'd appreciate any insight you could give us. I really want the alliance with the Ovarrow to work as smoothly as possible. In a lot of ways, we're truly pioneering the effort. This is a first-contact-type scenario."

Lenora looked away from her and glanced from Wolf's daughter to Dash. His eyebrows raised, and he gave a slight nod.

"All right, I'll go."

"Excellent," Governor Wolf said.

"If you want," Darius said, "Dash and I can bring you up to speed about the Ovarrow we've been dealing with."

Lenora nodded. "That would be helpful. When do we leave?" she asked, knowing she also had to make a few calls herself before leaving.

"Not until tomorrow morning," Darius replied.

"Okay, that's fine. I'll need to make some arrangements. But right now, give me some more details about what you've learned so far," Lenora said.

This would be the first time Lenora would be away from her daughter, and she felt a slight tightening of her chest. She couldn't bring Lauren with her, but it would only be a few days, and Ashley wouldn't mind the extra time with Lauren.

They had food brought into the meeting room, which was good because Lenora was starving. She often forgot to eat when she was working. She actually didn't like being in meeting rooms all day, but they were necessary so the fieldwork could be done. It had been too long since she'd gotten into the field. This would be good.

10

Lenora stifled a yawn as she sat in the diplomatic envoy's civilian air transport vehicle. There were multiple types of C-cats used throughout the colony, but this was among the bigger ones she'd been on. Since the C-cat was designated to the colonial diplomatic effort, it also doubled as a mobile work center. She'd heard the CDF soldiers with them mistakenly refer to it as a command center.

Dash walked over carrying two cups of coffee and handed her one. Lenora thanked him.

"Are you still reeling from the crash course in Ovarrow diplomacy?" Dash asked.

Lenora blew on her coffee to cool it a little bit, then took a sip. It was delicious and not nearly as strong as Connor's experimental roasts he liked to try every now and then. "It's mostly common sense, but I don't know how they expect anyone else to remember all this. We'll have guides, of course," she said, glancing over to where she saw Kayla Wolf and Lynn Butler speaking quietly. They paused to look over at Dash. Lenora smiled and then leaned toward Dash. "I think you have a few admirers."

Dash made a point not to look over at them and shook his head. Lenora grinned. He was a handsome young man with his athletic physique, wide shoulders, and outdoorsman tan.

"That's all I need," Dash replied and sipped his own coffee.

"Mind if I join you?" Kurt Johnson said, a short man whose stomach bulged against his shirt. Without waiting for an answer, he sat across from Lenora. "Thanks again for coming along on this trip."

Lenora nodded. Johnson had sweat accumulating on his brow, and he dabbed at it with a handkerchief. His eyes were close together, which gave his face the appearance of being scrunched. She supposed it didn't help that he had one too many chins.

"Have you been to the Ovarrow city often?" Lenora asked.

"Only one time," Johnson replied and stuffed his handkerchief into his pocket. "Connor let me tag along with him a few months ago."

"He mentioned it," Lenora said.

Johnson's smile seemed more like a practiced response than one of sincerity. "We didn't always see eye to eye."

Lenora arched an eyebrow. "You think that's the case now?"

Johnson grinned a little bit. "Probably not, at least not on everything. But who does? Anyway, it gave me more insight into how the CDF operates. And more importantly, how Connor likes to work."

Lenora schooled her features. She knew Johnson was fishing for information or maybe just a reaction to his comments. "He's a tough nut to crack," she replied.

Johnson grinned, and Lenora felt that he was evaluating her. Perhaps being dreadfully obvious about it was how he disarmed a person into giving away more than they thought they were.

"What do you hope to see in the city?" Lenora asked.

Johnson pursed his lips in thought for a moment. "Their population has grown to over ten thousand, and we've expended a lot of effort helping the Ovarrow become independent. I guess you could say once the ball got rolling, we've certainly delivered on our promises to them."

"And now you're hoping they'll reciprocate."

Johnson nodded. "The Krake are as much a problem to them as they are to us. Something I'd like to get your opinion on after this trip is whether you think we can trust them."

That question had been implied multiple times by Governor Wolf. Even Darius Cohen had said they were looking for ways to better understand the Ovarrow so they could communicate in a more meaningful way. Darius was under a lot of pressure to get the Ovarrow to cooperate. Lenora understood the political bureaucrats of the colony. She had to work with them in order to get what she needed for her own work.

"Trust is a two-way street. Do they understand what we want?"

Johnson glanced at Dash. "I guess that depends on young Mr. DeWitt's translator."

Dash set his coffee cup down. "They understand."

"I hope they do because there are a growing number of people who want us to withdraw our support of the Ovarrow," Johnson said.

Lenora shook her head. "That's a bit shortsighted, isn't it? I mean, we just started helping them. That kind of thinking might make more sense a year from now if we've gotten nothing in return. My guess is that they never supported the alliance in the first place."

"Well that's another reason we're here, and we'll continue to send diplomatic envoys to the Ovarrow city. All our efforts will be in the public eye. This is part of our new ongoing effort to demystify the Ovarrow to the colony."

It made sense to Lenora, but at the same time the whole motion to withdraw their support of the Ovarrow was borderline absurd. It was quite simply too soon for people to even form an opinion about it, much less arrive at a conclusion. "Do you know which groups have been voicing the most objections to our support of the Ovarrow?"

Johnson's shrugged. "It's nothing new. Ever since we discovered . . ." he said, pausing for a moment to look at her, ". . . *Connor* discovered that the Ovarrow were in stasis pods in secret bunkers, it's been a concern."

A concern, Lenora thought with a flash of irritation. "Were these the same people who wanted Connor to be held criminally liable for destroying the military bunker?"

She saw Dash turned toward her and then look at Johnson. The government advisor hardly reacted at all, but his dubious demeanor seemed to melt away. "I can see why you'd asked that."

"Really? The first reaction to a life-threatening situation was that Connor and the other people with him were wrong to retaliate in self-defense. I believe the term used was 'warmonger.'"

Johnson held up his hand in a placating gesture. "I understand your frustration, Dr. Bishop. But we also denounced any wrongdoing for everyone involved."

"Only because there were no actual laws that forbade what Connor had to do to survive his first encounter with the Ovarrow."

"Perhaps it's best not to dredge up something that happened so long ago," Johnson said.

"I just wanted to know whether the same people who denounced Connor's actions in the past were now opposed to helping the Ovarrow overcome the devastation that has been visited upon them from their war with the Krake," Lenora said, her voice firm and unyielding.

The conversations going on in the C-cat's cabin quieted down, but she didn't care.

"I honestly don't know, and I didn't think to check out the sources of the objections under the context of which you've just described," Johnson replied.

"Well then, perhaps you *should* check it out. In fact, I'd look forward to hearing all about it once you do," Lenora said.

Johnson looked like someone who'd gotten his hand caught in the cookie jar. He hadn't expected to be handled quite that way. Lenora was sure he'd expected the conversation to go in a completely different direction, but she didn't care. There were some things that drew her ire, and this was one of them.

An audible chime drew their attention to the small holoscreen that powered on above them. It flashed with the estimated time of arrival, and the pilot announced that they would be approaching the landing zone in a few minutes. It was probably just as well because Lenora wanted to stretch her legs. Johnson made a hasty excuse to leave and went over to speak with Darius Cohen.

Lenora finished her coffee and could feel Dash watching her.

"What?" she asked quietly.

"I just haven't seen anyone handle Johnson quite like that."

"I'm tired of all the tiptoeing and beating around the bush. We —and I mean the collective 'we'—can't go around having a knee-jerk reaction to every bit of news that sweeps across the colony. It wastes time."

Dash's smile was a borderline smirk. "You have my vote, Dr. Bishop, should you ever run for office."

Lenora glared at him for a moment and then laughed. That was the last thing she'd ever do. She loved her chosen field, and she loved teaching. She had no desire to cater to the masses and said so.

"Well, you have my vote for that, too," Dash said.

"Oh please, what's with all the flattery?"

"Nothing. You were one of my two favorite teachers."

Lenora smiled widely. Over the years that she'd lived on New Earth, she'd had many students, and very few of them had stood out as having the potential to accomplish the things Dash had achieved. He was one of the good ones, even though he'd gotten off to a rocky start. "Who's the other one? The other teacher, I mean."

Dash looked at her for a moment. "You really don't know?"

Lenora shook her head. There were a lot of teachers at the Colonial Research Institute, and as far she knew, Dash had respected most of them. He really only bumped heads with— "Connor?"

"Who else could it be?" he replied right as Darius called him over.

Lenora leaned back in her chair and closed her eyes for a moment. There was no shortage of young men who idolized Connor. He underestimated his influence sometimes. It was one of his more endearing qualities.

"Excuse me, Dr. Bishop," a high voice said.

Lenora opened her eyes to Kayla Wolf, and she gestured for the young woman to sit next to her.

"I was hoping it wouldn't be too much trouble if we stayed by you while we toured the city?" Kayla asked.

"I'm pretty sure they'll want us all to stick together, but that's fine with me."

Kayla smiled, and it made a few adorable dimples appear on her face.

"So, your internship is at the governor's office?" Lenora asked.

Kayla nodded. "Thank you for that—not calling it my mother's office. I think sometimes she just wants me to follow in her footsteps."

Lenora nodded amiably. She couldn't wait for Lauren to be old enough to come to a dig site. "What are you interested in?"

"I don't know," Kayla said, her eyes gleaming with excitement. "Everything. My last internship was at the biomedical research institute in Sierra. I helped—more observed—the work done on the cure for the cellular degeneration disease that affected the Ovarrow. I loved what they were doing there. But sometimes I just want to take one of the rovers and head off in one direction and keep going."

"Well, if you're interested in leaving Sierra for a while, I'm sure you could get an internship at any of the other cities, including Sanctuary."

She watched as Kayla glanced toward Dash, her head slightly tilted, making her almost look a bit shy. She was just a girl with a crush.

"Ladies and gentlemen, we are on our final approach to the landing zone," the pilot said over the nearby speakers.

The C-cats had a soft landing that Lenora hardly felt. She supposed the large vehicle had better inertia dampeners than the smaller ones because a soft landing hardly ever happened, at least when she flew them. A flash of irritation climbed up her neck, and she scowled. She could fly a C-cat just fine and had landed them on some of the most challenging terrains on the planet.

Lenora stood up and reached behind her seat for her backpack. It contained basic survival equipment, along with a few extras she normally took with her when she went anywhere away from home. She grabbed her jacket.

Darius Cohen walked over to her and glanced at her backpack. "I'm pretty sure you won't need that while we tour the city."

"I'll bring it with me just the same. They're just some things I'd take with me to any remote site. I know there are Ovarrow living here, but this was once a site we would've excavated, so I just have some smaller handheld devices for that."

Darius nodded and walked away, heading for the nearest exit.

Dash came back over and retrieved his own backpack. He glanced at her. "How about that landing? I hardly felt it. It's almost as if that's the way they're all supposed to feel."

Lenora slipped one of her arms into her jacket and then the other, giving Dash a look of mock severity. "Is that some kind of sly comment about my flying?"

Dash smiled at Kayla and shook his head quickly. "Wouldn't dream of it. Whenever we've flown together, I'm just thankful to get on the ground safe and sound."

"I think I liked you better when you were quieter."

Dash glanced at her jacket and frowned. It was a dark brown field coat, but she wondered if he was going to notice. "Is that—"

"Yes, it is," Lenora said, cutting him off. "It's not the whole suit, just the jacket. It's a civilian version of it. Connor insists that I take it with me when I go out in the field. They're actually quite comfortable."

The material used to make her jacket was the same nanorobotic material used for the multipurpose protection suits. It could form a hood that would protect her head, but it wasn't meant for anything drastic.

"Looks good. I want one of those. My birthday is just around the corner," Dash said.

Lenora leaned toward him. "I know people, and besides, I thought you already had an actual MPS."

"I do, but sometimes it gets to be a bit much wearing that over my regular clothes."

They headed toward the door, and as soon as Lenora stepped down the loading ramp, she heard gusts of wind blowing outside. It died down after a few moments and then kicked back up again as she felt the slight tug of a few strands of her ponytail lifting off her neck. She followed the others around and got her first look at the Ovarrow city.

The midmorning sun reflected off the bronze metallic alloy the Ovarrow used in the construction of their buildings. The city had probably been home to several hundred thousand Ovarrow before the Ice Age, so the refugees had plenty of room to expand; however, there was a lot of restoration that needed to occur to make it safe. Scaffolding enveloped multiple buildings near the border. The taller buildings looked as if they'd been left alone.

With only ten thousand refugees, there wouldn't be a need to expand into those areas for the time being. There were several wind turbines placed throughout the city, as well as the open field area outside the city. There was enough wind here to keep those turbines turning and charging the power station the Ovarrow used to generate electricity.

Lenora shielded her eyes from the sun and saw dark shapes moving about the city in groups. She couldn't tell what they were doing, but she assumed they must have been work crews.

A squad of CDF soldiers came over to join the diplomatic envoy. One of the soldiers glanced at her for a moment and then began speaking to the others. Several more of the soldiers looked over at her.

"Dr. Bishop, I'm Lieutenant Scott Morgan. I hadn't been informed that you were among the visitors here today."

"Is something wrong?" Lenora asked.

"Not at all. You just weren't on the visitors list. If there's anything you need, please don't hesitate to ask," Lieutenant Morgan said and left.

She saw him speaking to one of the other soldiers, nodding in Lenora's direction. She supposed she was getting her assigned escorts for this trip—one of the perks of being a general's wife, she supposed.

They waited a short distance away from the C-cats, and a large group of Ovarrow came toward them. They wore dark chest armor and carried shock lances that were capable of delivering bolts of energy. Lenora remembered Connor being quite impressed with them since they still worked after being sealed for hundreds of years.

Lenora stood next to Darius, who gave her a nod. An updated program registered itself on her wrist computer. It was the latest version of the Ovarrow translator program, so at least they wouldn't have to type in every single line of communication. Their voice-recognition software would do its best at translating human language into the Ovarrow symbols that would appear on the holoscreen. The Ovarrow would still have to type in their replies, however.

"I've just sent out the latest translator updates to everyone here," Dash said to Darius.

"Good. Let's see who they send us."

"Do they rotate who comes out here to meet visitors?" Lenora asked.

"Yes, they do. They usually get representatives from different factions, which can be difficult sometimes, but it also allows us to interact with a variety of Ovarrow," Darius said.

Lenora watched as the Ovarrow soldiers approached them. They held their weapons with the same familiarity she'd seen among CDF soldiers. She looked for Lieutenant Morgan and saw him watching the Ovarrow approach as well. They appeared at ease, but Lenora knew that wasn't the case. If anything, the CDF soldiers were more alert than they'd been before. She couldn't blame them. There was a large contingent of Ovarrow soldiers—Mekaal— coming toward them who were heavily armed.

"Military escorts all around, I see," Lenora said.

Kurt Johnson stood next to her and watched the approaching soldiers warily. "It's one of their rules," he said.

"They'll assign escorts to guide us throughout the city. It makes them feel more secure," Darius said.

Lenora nodded. "Will they restrict us from going anywhere, or are we allowed to go wherever we want?"

Darius frowned for a moment. "You know, I'm not sure. In all my visits here, I've never been told I couldn't go somewhere, but I've always had an escort, which is fine. They don't deny us our weapons, so we do have some protection ourselves. Our presence here is hardly new, given that we brought these Ovarrow out of stasis. They've all seen humans before."

"Do they do the meet-and-greet here, or will they take us somewhere else in the city?" Johnson asked.

"They've done both in the past. Given that this is a larger group, they might want us to meet with their high commissioner, an Ovarrow named Senleon who's from the administrator faction," Darius said.

"High commissioner—administrator?" Lenora asked.

Dash nodded. "Yeah, our translators are based on the symbols we've translated from their computer networks. The translator might be off on the actual term, but it does give us the context of who we're dealing with. It beats referring to some of them as superuser or sudo. That would be awkward. Linguists are working on a better translator, but it'll take time. For now, at least, we have a foundation from which to communicate with them."

Lenora was familiar with the translation program they were using, as well as its limitations. It was all they had, and it had gotten them this far, but she hadn't realized Dash had used so much creative freedom with the Ovarrow reference. She looked at Darius Cohen. "How far is Camp Alpha from here?"

"Not that far. About fifty kilometers, but we don't have any permanent residents in their city."

"Why is that?" Johnson asked.

Darius arched an eyebrow. "Do you think Sierra is ready for an Ovarrow embassy? How about New Haven or Delphi, for that matter?"

Johnson looked at the approaching group of Ovarrow, considering. "I guess I hadn't thought of it like that."

"The Ovarrow are keen to be independent," Darius replied.

"Yes, but they do realize they need our help," Johnson pressed.

"There's a difference," Lenora interjected, "between knowing they need somebody's help and having it thrown in their collective faces. You have to remember that when they went into stasis, their world was crumbling around them. They had no idea what they were going to wake up to, and in some cases—a lot of cases—they thought they were going to die if the stasis pods didn't kill them by breaking down. Look at them," she said, and then added, "Not the soldiers, look at the city. They're working hard to get this place up and running."

Johnson frowned in thought, his expression unreadable. "Yes, I can see that they're working hard."

"You're missing the point," Lenora replied and glanced at Darius, who watched her shrewdly, waiting for her to continue. "There's probably a strong dose of survival instinct kicking in here, but we could also be dealing with psychological avoidance— meaning that if they were to slow down, they'd have to deal with the fact that the world they knew is lost to them. This is something we can all relate to, if you think about it."

Lenora looked around at the others. New Earth was a wonderful world to colonize, and even with all its dangers and nuances, it had become humanity's second home. What had haunted their proverbial footsteps was the fact that the old Earth they'd known was gone forever.

Darius nodded and smiled a little. "You make a very good point, Dr. Bishop. I think on some level I realized what you were saying just from being among the Ovarrow for months. But we've had so many other concerns that it's not something we've spoken about at Camp Alpha. We certainly haven't aligned the Ovarrow experience with what the experience of losing Earth was like for us."

"There are some similarities, I'll grant you that. Loss is a loss, I suppose," Johnson said.

"I was merely pointing out that we have some common ground. We've sent probes back to Earth that will one day give us a status," Lenora said.

Johnson shrugged. "I probably won't live to see that, given the distance to Earth. Won't it take the probe two hundred years to get there?"

"No, it won't," Dash said. "I remember this project. It's more like a probe swarm that's en route to Earth, and it can travel at near relativistic speeds. It will take them about seventy years to get there. They'll do an assessment and send the data back to us, and the fastest it can reach us is sixty years. That's how long it takes light to travel here."

Johnson gave Dash an amused expression. "Okay, fine. Not two hundred years, but a hundred and thirty years, give or take. Either way, I'll either be very old or not here at all," he said and turned back to the approaching Ovarrow.

Darius stepped in front of the others, but the CDF soldiers fanned out on either side of him, regarding the Mekaal. The Ovarrow were a tall species whose tawny skin tones were almost pebbled, like that of a reptile, but they were warm-blooded. Pointy protrusions stemmed from their shoulders and elbows. Their large, four-fingered hands were twice the size of a human's despite them being of similar size and weight. Thick brow lines framed their eyes, which were separated by a flat nasal cavity, giving their skulls a convex shape on top. Their wide mouths had frown lines that made them look aggressive.

Lenora watched as the soldiers regarded each other coolly. Darius made introductions, and she noticed that more than a few Ovarrow looked at Dash with open appreciation. Then she remembered that Dash had been instrumental in finding the medical cache they'd based the cure on for the rapid-aging problem the Ovarrow faced when coming out of stasis.

A comms drone hovered in the air, and a large holoscreen appeared above it so the Ovarrow translator could show the symbols of their language. It was a slow way to communicate.

She watched as an Ovarrow named Raylore entered his responses through the holographic interface.

"Welcome, human colonists. You are requested to see High Commissioner Senleon before any other activities in the city," Raylore said.

Lenora saw Darius hesitate for a moment and then reply. "Of course, we'd be honored to meet with the high commissioner."

Raylore turned and addressed the nearest Ovarrow soldier, and they all stepped back, making a path. The Ovarrow soldiers gave them plenty of room, but nevertheless, they surrounded the colonial diplomatic envoy.

Lenora looked at Darius. "Have you met the high commissioner before?"

"A few times. They usually have us meet with different faction leaders, but this time we're asking to have a look around. Sometimes that can put the Ovarrow on edge. This is their home, after all, and we must be respectful of that," Darius replied.

Lenora was quiet, and she noticed that one of the CDF soldiers had taken up a position to her right, matching her pace. The soldier looked at her and gave her a firm nod. His name appeared on her internal heads-up display.

"Ma'am," Sergeant Cook said.

"So, you're to be my personal escort, I take it?"

Sergeant Cook smiled. "I'm the winner."

"I'm quite certain I can look after myself, Sergeant Cook."

"Oh, I know that, Dr. Bishop; however, in the unlikely event that the shit hits"—he stopped speaking, realizing what he'd said —"uh, things go sideways, let's just say I'd rather report to General Gates that I did everything I could to help his wife."

"You do realize that the governor's daughter is several places behind me," Lenora replied.

"Make no mistake, I'll do everything I can to ensure the envoy's protection. I'm just choosing a strategic location from which to execute my duties, Dr. Bishop."

Lenora smiled and nodded. The military had a particular way

of phrasing their intentions in one of the most direct manners she'd ever encountered. She had long gotten used to it with Connor and all the soldiers she'd met over the years.

She looked around at the Ovarrow that surrounded them. These were the first she'd ever seen in person, which was much different than observing them through a live video feed from a reconnaissance drone. The way they walked seemed both familiar and foreign at the same time. She was glad Sergeant Cook was nearby, but she also knew it wouldn't make a difference with so many Ovarrow soldiers surrounding them.

Nothing is going to happen, she told herself. As they walked toward the city, she had to repeat the sentiment a few more times.

11

LENORA FELT as if she'd taken a trip back in time. Most of her time on New Earth had been spent exploring the alien ruins they'd found there. She'd spent countless hours trying to imagine what the previous inhabitants had looked like and how they'd lived. Now she was walking among them. Most Ovarrow they passed stopped what they were doing to watch them for a few moments. Their cinnamon-colored eyes had vertical pupils that looked more feline than reptilian. They were the eyes of a predator, and Lenora suspected that they were capable of razor-sharp focus.

As the Ovarrow watched them, Lenora wondered what they were thinking. Being around them would take some getting used to, and it was probably the same for them.

They walked down the main thoroughfare past groups of Ovarrow working to restore their living quarters. Darius continued to share what he knew as they entered the city. He was speaking in a conversational tone, and Lenora wondered if the Ovarrow thought it was rude because they couldn't understand what the colonists were saying.

"Why isn't there a team of linguists stationed here?" Lenora asked.

"They were too much of a distraction. The linguistic team is allowed to come here once every five days. They can stay for the entire day, but they have to leave in the evening," Darius said.

Lenora looked around and saw small colonial listening devices attached to the buildings, essentially hidden in plain sight. Her implants allowed her to spot them, but she wondered if the Ovarrow knew they were there.

Darius followed her gaze and then gave a slight nod in Johnson's direction. Lenora didn't think Dash approved, but perhaps the listening devices were a necessity. Improving communication capabilities with colonists was a lower priority to the Ovarrow while they started to rebuild their society.

"Do the wind turbines provide enough power to the entire city?" Johnson asked.

"No, not by a long shot, but they don't need them to power the entire city. Remember, there are relatively few of them here," Darius said.

"Yes, but at this rate of growth, won't there be a problem soon?"

"We've offered our assistance, but they haven't taken us up on it yet. They're working to restore their own reactors, but it's going to take some time. Possibly a few months to bring them back online, if they can."

"I remember working with the engineers for the geothermal taps the Ovarrow used at Sanctuary," Lenora said. "We had to replace almost all the components, but at least we had a tech base to work with."

"They're pretty good at salvage," Dash said. "I think they had a lot of practice at it before they went the stasis route. They don't appear to be surprised at the state of things," he said and shook his head. "Don't get me wrong. They're surprised when they come out of stasis, but I think they were prepared to do whatever they had to do to survive once they came out. None of them thought there wouldn't be a struggle."

Lenora glanced through the open door of one of the buildings as they walked past. There was an Ovarrow inside, attempting to use a console, and his finger had just poked through the mesh screen. The Ovarrow hastily tried to prevent it from disintegrating, but it was too late. Lenora had firsthand experience with trying to prevent the destruction of those consoles. She could help them out with that. She glanced at Dash, thinking he'd probably already offered them help, and wondered why the Ovarrow hadn't developed anything like a holoscreen but chose to instead project their interfaces onto a mesh screen. Sometimes the mesh was encased to protect it from deterioration, but all too often it wasn't. That was why Lenora had helped developed an interface so they could access the Ovarrow consoles through their wrist computers.

A group of Ovarrow gathered off to the side of the street. They were craning their necks, trying to peer past the Mekaal as if they were looking for someone in particular. Dash stuck out his hand and waved toward them. The Ovarrow brought their left hands to one of their brow ridges and then raised them.

"What are they doing?" Lenora asked Dash.

Dash stopped waving and looked a little uncomfortable. "They're thanking me for saving them."

Johnson harrumphed. "Don't they understand that it was colonial scientists who actually synthesized the cure?"

"I've told them. Believe me, I've told them many times."

Lenora smiled. "It doesn't matter. You were the one who found it for the scientists to synthesize."

The farther they went into the city, the more attention was drawn to them.

"Darius, I haven't been able to detect any ryklar-deterrent signals here. Why is that?" Johnson asked.

"They're using their own signal, and you're scanning for a colonial one. There aren't any ryklar in the vicinity of the city. In addition, the Mekaal patrol the perimeter of the occupied sections of the city. They also assign protection details for the salvage groups that go into the city, as well as to the farmland that workgroups manage. They're having trouble with some of their equipment, but they're making it work. We're monitoring it."

Lenora hadn't looked out the window as they'd flown toward the city, so she hadn't seen any of the farmland. She wondered what they grew for food. The sites she'd excavated contained only the equivalent of colonial rations, which was a mix of dehydrated carbohydrates and proteins.

"We do bring food supplies with us. In fact, there will be a shipment here tomorrow. Apparently, the Ovarrow enjoy eating gourds. In particular, the purple variety is highly valued, so we bring crates of it as a token of good faith," Darius said.

Lenora tried not to gawk at anything, but seeing even this small section of the city filled with Ovarrow was exciting. In her experience, the only beings that had frequented an Ovarrow city besides people like her were the ryklars. They'd had more than a few terrifying encounters with ryklars until they figured out how to reproduce the ryklar-deterrent signal. However, New Earth was home to other predators—perhaps not as dangerous as the ryklars, but there was always something new to discover. She glanced at the Ovarrow and wondered who'd created the watchdogs that guarded the Mekaal bunker Siloc had taken Connor to. She found that her mind was trying to bridge who she'd imagined the Ovarrow to be with what she was seeing in front of her, and she couldn't. At least not right now.

"Where are the children?" Lenora asked.

The question drew a few raised eyebrows, but after a quick look around, they looked at Darius for the answer. All the stasis pods Lenora had ever seen were of a standard size, so it was impossible to determine who was inside.

Darius glanced around to be sure they wouldn't be overheard. "Be careful. That's a sore subject. We haven't found any yet, and when we asked, we were told that the stasis pods wouldn't work for their younglings, although a juvenile nearing the end of puberty could survive just fine."

Lenora's mouth hung open for moments. "What?"

"The stasis pods wouldn't work for their younglings."

Lenora swung her gaze toward the Ovarrow. *Younglings*, she thought. "All the Ovarrow in stasis pods are adults?"

Darius swallowed hard. "No, but most of them were. The ones with their younglings . . ." He shook his head.

"Stop calling them that! They're children, Darius," Lenora said, her voice shrill.

Darius looked away, and she inhaled sharply. She couldn't believe it. She looked around as if seeing the situation of the Ovarrow in new light as her brain raced with all the implications. The Ovarrow had to go into stasis or they were going to die, but their children . . . Her throat thickened. She was being emotional, and she knew it, but she kept thinking about Lauren. There was no way she'd ever abandon her child. She'd rather die. But it couldn't be that simple. No parent who loved their child would ever leave them to die. As she looked at the Ovarrow, she wanted so much to believe they shared that sentiment, but what if they didn't? Lenora shook her head and sighed. What had happened to their children? Had they been abandoned? Had they been slaughtered? Didn't they care about them? How could they do this?

Lenora heard Kayla whisper something to Lynn and Devon. They gasped.

"Please, could everyone just calm down a little bit? Don't jump to conclusions," Darius said. "This is an extremely sensitive subject, and I'd urge you all to be cautious about whatever assumptions you're forming in your minds right now. The fact of the matter is that we don't know the entire story."

Lenora narrowed her gaze and looked over at the Ovarrow who was leading them, the one named Raylore. She wanted to storm right up to him and demand to know what had happened, but that was foolish, and she knew it. This was grim survival at its worst.

"He's right. We can't make assumptions," Lenora said.

"We might not be able to, but when the rest of the colony learns of this, they'll make their own assumptions even if we provide the facts," Johnson said. He shook his head and folded his arms in front of his chest.

"We need to get all the facts, but people are always going to judge. There's no stopping that," Lenora said quietly. She glanced at Dash, and the forlorn look on his face indicated that he'd known about this. She felt a flash of annoyance at the fact that he hadn't warned her. Then she realized it wasn't because he was hesitant to warn her but more that she needed to experience her exposure to the Ovarrow with a fresh perspective, and that meant not tainting it at all. Academic objectivity at its best. She didn't like it, but at least she understood.

Dash mouthed the words, "I'm sorry."

Lenora nodded. The main road took them further into the city and downward. There were bridges not far from them that connected different parts of the city. The Ovarrow architecture changed the farther they went. The buildings were taller, but they all had an overhang. It would be difficult for a ryklar to scale them onto the roof. They walked beneath footbridges that connected larger buildings to each other, and there were outdoor ramps that circled around the exterior of the buildings. The Ovarrow hadn't created stairs, which was the source of a lot of discussion among the colonists. The ramps looked to be well made, and in most cases, they were part of the actual building. The construction seemed solid enough, but she did see Ovarrow checking the supports and marking them with a black or white stripe. Lenora didn't know what that meant. She peered at the supports that had a white stripe, and they looked to have deteriorated much more than those with a black stripe.

They were led to a main square where there was a gathering of Ovarrow soldiers. Lenora glanced at Darius, who seemed surprised by the gathering.

"What's going on?" Johnson asked, his voice thick with concern.

"I'm not sure, but I believe they're taking us to the warlord and not the high commissioner," Darius replied.

Lenora looked at Dash.

"I've never met him," he said.

Lenora remembered from their conversation the previous night that the Ovarrow hierarchy was that of a shared political entity. There were faction leaders in addition to the high commissioner's office and also a warlord who was in charge of the Mekaal. Lenora glanced at the Ovarrow who were escorting them, and they didn't appear surprised at the gathering of soldiers. They were acting more like they'd expected it. The Ovarrow soldiers wore helmets, and some had a protrusion extending at the back, which Lenora supposed could be an antenna. Perhaps they had a way to communicate with each other that hadn't been in any of the sites she'd excavated. She looked at Lieutenant Morgan, who was stone-faced, but she could tell he didn't like the situation any more than they did.

Raylore led them to an armored Ovarrow who was neither heavily muscled nor extremely tall. There was no mistaking that this was the warlord because there was a general air of deference to him when he spoke.

Raylore gestured for Darius to come forward, and Lenora joined him. After a few moments, Johnson did as well. Sergeant Cook remained at her side, and Dash came forward, too.

The communications drone became active again, and a large holoscreen appeared above it. Lenora heard a banging sound from one of the tall wooden storage containers off to the side. There were Ovarrow soldiers all around them.

"Colonists, High Commissioner Senleon was unable to attend this meeting, but I present you to Warlord Vitory and the Warlord's First, Cerot," Raylore said.

Darius made the introductions, which also included a description of their roles. Lenora was introduced, and Darius described her function as someone who studied the ruins of ancient civilizations. Vitory looked at her and then stepped closer. Lenora saw the CDF soldiers become rigid next to her, but she didn't pay them any mind and kept her gaze fixed on the warlord.

"Your colony employs thieves?" Vitory asked Darius, keeping his gaze on Lenora.

"I'm not a thief," Lenora said and reminded herself that the translation might not be one hundred percent accurate, and the way the warlord was almost glaring at her led her to believe that that was the case right then.

The warlord considered her for a moment. "You raid our cities and take what doesn't belong to you. How is that anything but a thief?"

Lenora shook her head, becoming irritated. "There was no one else around. The Ovarrow weren't there."

The warlord drew his head up, and it made him look smug. "The Ovarrow never left. We were sleeping."

"Don't you mean hiding?" Lenora said. "Hiding from the Krake."

Several Ovarrow soldiers gripped their weapons tighter, and the warlord scowled.

Lenora didn't let up. She knew a bully when she saw one, and this was just for show. "If I'd found any Ovarrow, I would've been more respectful."

There was a deep rumble from the warlord's chest, and the Ovarrow soldiers immediately reacted. They gripped their weapons and slammed the ends of them into the ground. There were hundreds of them in the area, and the sound wasn't lost upon the envoy.

The CDF soldiers readied their weapons but didn't raise them all the way.

"Mr. Cohen," Lieutenant Morgan said, "this situation is getting out of control. Tell them to calm down or we will defend ourselves."

Darius spoke with Raylore and tried to reason with them. Lenora watched the warlord try to appear as if he wasn't listening, but she could tell that he was. He glanced at the holoscreen, reading every symbol that was translated. When he spoke, it was harsh, and Raylore winced. Then the Ovarrow cleared the screen and entered a few symbols.

"Visitation is over," Raylore said.

"Please forgive any offense we have mistakenly given. May we meet with the high commissioner?" Darius asked.

The translation appeared on the holoscreen. Raylore glanced at the warlord, who didn't utter a word. The answer was plain enough, but Raylore replied just the same.

"Visitation is over. You will be escorted out of the city immediately."

Darius turned toward them regretfully. "I'm afraid our visit will have to be cut short. We can try again tomorrow."

"I don't believe this," Johnson said. "How can they treat us like this? After all we've done for them," he said and then looked at the warlord. "You need to treat us better. You wouldn't be here if it weren't for us."

The warlord leaned over to speak with his second-in-command. Then he left, taking half the soldiers with him.

The warlord's first came over to them. "Please accept our sincerest apologies. The visit is over. Our projects are falling behind schedule and we cannot have a distraction at this time. That is the reason for the visit to be cut short," Cerot said. After he was sure they'd read the translation, he continued. "I will escort you back to your ship now."

Cerot took them on a different pathway out of the city, which Lenora found to be curious. As they made their way back, one of the Ovarrow came over to them. The designation on the Ovarrow shirt was for the healer's faction. The Ovarrow's skin was a bit more pebbled and had significantly more age lines than the others, but he still moved with agility.

"Jory," Dash said and walked over to meet him.

He turned on his personal holoscreen so the translation could be read. "I'm not able to stay around today," Dash said and gestured toward the Mekaal.

Lenora watched as Jory entered his reply on the holographic interface.

"I would like to show you something," Jory said and walked over to Cerot, speaking quietly to him. The Ovarrow language still sounded so foreign to her. It was a mixture of screeches and other sounds, as if they were speaking with more than one vocal cord. Lenora didn't think they'd ever be able to replicate the sound without help.

Jory gestured toward Dash, and the warlord's first considered him for a moment. There was another exchange between the two Ovarrow, and then Jory returned.

"You are allowed to accompany me for a short time," Jory said.

Dash glanced at the others. "I'll meet you at the ship."

He looked at Lenora and then gestured toward her. "This is my teacher. Can she come with us?"

Jory took a moment to read the question and then glanced at Cerot for a moment.

"It is not permitted."

"It's fine," Lenora said. "Go on, build bridges," she said and smiled.

Dash walked away with Jory and two Mekaal escorts.

Lenora heard Johnson blow out a breath, not trying to hide his irritation at all. Lenora walked over to Cerot and brought up her own personal holoscreen.

"You mentioned that the work being done is behind schedule. Is there anything we can do to help you?" Lenora asked.

Darius and Raylore stopped speaking, waiting for Cerot's reply.

"The work will get done. Having outsiders visit so frequently disrupts things," Cerot replied. The Ovarrow's hands easily selected the symbols to craft his reply.

"Perhaps if you let us help you, we wouldn't be such a distraction," Lenora said.

"The Ovarrow must become great. This will not happen with help from outsiders."

Lenora was quiet for a few minutes as they continued walking down the street, passing under several footbridges. An Ovarrow yelled nearby, followed by a loud thud of something slamming to the ground. Lenora spun toward the sound. A group of Mekaal soldiers were dragging two prisoners toward a storage container. They unlocked it and shoved the two prisoners inside.

Lenora looked at Cerot. "What happened? What did they do?"

"Punishment," Cerot replied.

"Punishment for what?"

Cerot glared at her, and Darius came over. "I think I can help here," he said.

More Ovarrow soldiers came with citizens in custody, who were hauled to another storage crate and forced to go inside. They hardly put up a protest, seeming resigned to whatever fate had been bestowed upon them.

Lenora turned toward Darius.

"Just hold on a second," Darius said and looked at the others. "Don't jump to any conclusions. We're the visitors here."

Lenora fought to keep her voice devoid of scorn. "I understand that. I just wanted to know what happened," she said, looking at Cerot.

The Ovarrow watched them, and their escorts waited on his next command.

"It might be best if we just moved on," Lieutenant Morgan suggested.

Lenora inhaled a deep breath and nodded, and they continued onward for a few minutes. She glanced back at the storage crates as the whole event played back in her mind. The prisoners hadn't put up much of a fight, and she wondered what they could have done. Perhaps they'd stolen something. Lenora glanced around, wondering what they'd steal. Food, maybe? There were other Ovarrow going about their business, and they didn't give the storage crates anything more than a passing glance.

They continued, heading toward one of the longer footbridges that was about fifteen meters wide. There was a lot of foot traffic going to and fro. Above them was a much larger bridge, which didn't look to be in use.

"I knew it would be different coming here, but I hadn't expected all this," Johnson said to her. Beads of sweat covered his head. The wind gusts blew harder for a few moments and then subsided.

"Neither did I," Lenora admitted.

She heard Darius speaking to Raylore as they walked, and Cerot walked in front of them at a quicker pace. The ramp inclined when they were almost halfway across it. The higher elevation gave them a stunning view of a city being brought back to life.

Lenora quickened her pace, heading toward Cerot.

"Maybe it's best to leave well enough alone," Johnson called out to her as she passed him. He was breathing heavily from all the walking.

Lenora ignored him. Sergeant Cook kept pace with her and gave her a nod.

She closed the distance to the Ovarrow soldier—the warlord's first, the second-in-command, and a step away from being in charge of the Ovarrow military. Lenora just stood next to him, looking out at the city. She didn't bring up her holoscreen or engage the translator, wanting to wait and see what the Ovarrow did. Cerot seemed to regard her for a few moments and then waited.

Lenora brought up her holoscreen and thought about what she wanted to ask. There were a couple of different ways she could open this conversation. The Ovarrow were just trying to survive, but she wanted to ask them questions. She looked at Cerot, and the Ovarrow glanced at her holoscreen and then away.

"You've done a lot with the city in the short time you've been here," Lenora said.

Cerot read the message and then replied. "More work needs to be done."

There was always more to be done. Lenora could relate to that.

Another strong gust of wind blew, and Cerot turned and ran toward the edge of the ramp. A few seconds later, Lenora saw several Ovarrow gesturing toward them from a tall building down below. She could hardly hear them over the wind. Suddenly, the bridge sank, causing her to adjust her balance. She turned and saw that the bridge above them was twisting in the high wind. There was a loud crack, and the ground split apart a few meters in front of them. Lenora heard someone scream and turned to look back the way they'd come. There was another jagged split farther from them. Then the bridge collapsed under her feet, and she sank into rubble-strewn darkness.

12

CONNOR GLANCED at the time and saw that it was early afternoon. His daughter, good food, and good company waited for him at the Salty Soldier. Victoria was watching Lauren, and he couldn't wait to get over there.

Major Natalia Vassar sat across from him in his office. Despite the considerable soundproofing of the walls, he could still hear the high-pitched whine of multiple Hellcats as they returned to the CDF base at Sanctuary.

"Sounds like the training exercise is over," Connor said.

Major Bethany Anders looked at her personal holoscreen and then nodded. "A bit ahead of schedule, but these are the 3rd and 7th Ranger companies."

Connor heard a bit of dismay in his operations officer's voice. The 3rd and 7th Ranger companies were led by Carl Flint and Samson.

"Is there anything I should know about the results of the exercise?" Connor asked.

"Negative, General. Efficiency scores are all at the top, as well as taking advantage of tactical awareness. However, it might be more constructive not to celebrate quite so much at the expense of the other participants in the training exercise," Anders replied crisply.

Connor smiled. At this stage in his career, he didn't have to hide it when he found the situation amusing. "Sometimes a little negative reinforcement is just what someone needs for their performance to reach new heights."

"I agree, General, but changing the names of the other units to include the word 'incompetent' in the name while they return to base might be a bit too far. In other cases, they revoked access to their designated transport vehicles, forcing the now-disgraced company to walk back to base. I had to send another team to undo the changes, and they were automatically assigned additional training—" She stopped speaking as a new message appeared on her screen.

"What kind of training?" Connor asked.

Anders looked at him squarely. "Potty training."

Samson, Connor thought and chuckled. Vassar snorted and attempted to cover it up with her hand.

Samson probably didn't have the technical know-how to accomplish all that, but he was making good use of the people under his command.

"General," Anders continued, "I think these actions are setting a bad precedent. This sort of behavior can readily get out of control."

Connor nodded. "I see your point, but at the same time, it can inspire a creative response. As long as no safety regulations were violated during the exercise, I don't see how any disciplinary action should be taken against those soldiers. What we have here is probably just a case of wounded pride. We're not in the business of coddling our soldiers."

Major Anders stiffened for a moment. "Understood, sir."

"Just to be clear," Connor began, "I'm not against retaliation, but it has to be in the right context. They have to beat them on the field. I suggest you inform their commanding officers of those options. Maybe a little reminder would go a long way in keeping things from getting out of control."

Major Anders's posture became a bit less rigid at that. "Thank you, sir. I'll make sure they know that."

"Good. Oh, you can go ahead and remove the new training item. Now, if that's it, ladies, I have another appointment that I intend to keep," Connor said and stood up.

"There's one more thing, General," Major Vassar said.

Connor remained standing and looked at her. "What is it, Natalia?"

"There's been another report from Major Alexis Brooks, the commanding officer at Camp Alpha. I think you need to see it, but in the interest of time you could probably just review the vid log," Natalia said.

Connor inhaled and rubbed his chin for a few moments. "All right, put it on the wallscreen over there and I'll take a quick look."

A few moments later, Major Alexis Brooks's head and shoulders appeared on the wallscreen in Connor's office. She was making her report from her own office.

"Major Alexis Brooks, Ovarrow report number sixteen-thirty-two. The population of the Ovarrow settlement has grown to ten thousand residents. Twenty percent of that number is from the Mekaal faction, which is the Ovarrow military designation. There have been increased instances of the Ovarrow distancing themselves from colonial support. They've also have been limiting access to their city. While the Ovarrow mannerisms could be considered terse by human standards, by Ovarrow standards, it seems to be the norm. Behaviorists advised that we should not rush to judgment. However, I thought it pertinent to include more detailed findings later in this report. On the highest levels, the reports I'm seeing from visitors to the Ovarrow city are ones of increasing Ovarrow isolation—"

"Stop the video log," Connor said. He looked at Natalia.

"She appended detailed accounts from various observers. I thought this was important enough to warrant making you aware of the situation, sir," Natalia said.

Connor frowned in thought for a moment and then opened a comlink. "Dr. Young, can I see you in my office, please?"

"Yes, of course. Right away, General Gates."

A few minutes later, Dr. Eric Young walked into his office.

"Have you seen this report, Eric?"

"I was actually just reviewing it. Major Vassar sent it over to me a short while ago."

Connor looked at Natalia and she smiled a little. His intelligence officer was exceedingly efficient at managing—well, him, to be honest. Connor smiled.

"All right, do I need to be concerned about this?"

"This behavior isn't entirely unexpected. It was observed when the Ovarrow were restricted to Camp Alpha. However, it decreased when we helped them establish themselves in the city. Now we're seeing it crop up again. My opinion is that this behavior is normal. The Ovarrow need to assert some control over their own world. I mean this in the sense of their immediate vicinity."

"Wanting control over their lives doesn't equate to pushing away their support structure," Connor replied.

"Yes, it does in some instances. Asserting control over your own environment is something we see in any intelligent society. We see it among humans, especially with teens on the brink of adulthood."

Connor shook his head. "Are you kidding me? You're equating the behavior of the Ovarrow with that of a rebellious teenager?"

"Just bear with me for a second. That's an oversimplification of the situation. Think of it this way: You did the same thing when you first woke up on the *Ark*. You created a niche for yourself in the colony as a way to assert control over your own world. This is the same thing," Eric said.

"I didn't push everyone away in some silly, rebellious tactic to assert myself."

"Different circumstances. We know the Ovarrow went . . . put themselves into stasis pods as a last-ditch effort to survive. Think about the motivations behind that. There had been a definite lack of control for who knows how long before they were reduced to those options. Now, they wake up and there's this invader. I mean that loosely, but from their perspective, we are the invaders. We're a powerful group who brings them out of stasis and are inserting ourselves into their lives. It's invasive no matter our own intentions," Eric said.

"But we're trying to help them," Major Anders said.

"Yes, we are," Eric replied. "But at some point, we should stop expecting to be allowed entry into their city and start asking for permission without the expectation that they'll say yes. The Ovarrow are merely asserting their independence."

Connor was about to reply when a priority comlink registered on the wallscreen in front of him.

"General Gates, I have an alpha priority message from Major Alexis Brooks," Lieutenant Sabatino's voice said over the speaker nearby.

"Put it through," Connor replied.

A video comlink came to prominence on the wallscreen, showing Major Brooks in combat attire.

"General Gates, there's been an incident at the Ovarrow city. Reports came in a few minutes ago about a catastrophic accident. At this point, we have colonial visitors unaccounted for. The Ovarrow are highly agitated and have expelled all colonists in the city. They're barring entry. The Mekaal faction has assembled at the city perimeter and is armed," Major Brooks said.

"Who's on site now?" Connor asked.

"There's a supply team, a diplomatic envoy, and the CDF squad who were their escorts. The supply team was attempting to access the city when the incident occurred. We still don't know what happened. I'm scrambling our alert force and heading to the city now. What are your orders, General?"

"As you were, Major. Get to that site and figure out what's going on. I'll be in touch, and I'll be sending support to you ASAP. Gates, out."

The video comlink went dark. Connor turned toward Anders. "I want the 3rd and 7th Ranger companies assembled and deployed to that site in two hours. Orders will come en route. They are to be combat-ready and expect hostilities. After that, I want the First Battalion assembled and ready for deployment. Get to it."

"At once, General," Major Anders said and hastened from the office. Connor heard her shouting orders as she opened various comlinks to her command structure.

"Lieutenant Sabatino, get me Governor Wolf, now."

A few moments later Governor Wolf's face appeared on Connor's wallscreen.

"General Gates, I've just been informed about an accident at the Ovarrow city."

"That's correct, Governor. The Ovarrow are barring entry to the city. We have an unknown number of colonists unaccounted for. I know diplomatic relations are a priority, but so are colonial lives. I need authorization to engage the Ovarrow if they're uncooperative," Connor said.

"You want authorization to kill them?"

"That isn't my first choice. I want authorization to protect colonial citizens. I need to get on site to do an assessment of the situation. My first priority is to get there and gain access to the trouble area."

"I can authorize you going to the area, but I cannot authorize the use of lethal force except in self-defense at this time."

Connor strangled his frustration. "Very well. I'll keep you apprised of the situation, Governor."

"General Gates," Governor Wolf said, "my daughter is among the colonists in the city."

Connor's mouth formed a grim line. "I understand," he replied.

The comlink was severed.

"I'm here. Put me to work," Eric said.

"You're coming with me," Connor said and looked at Natalia. "I want you to stay here and figure out what the hell happened."

"Do you suspect foul play, General?"

"A diplomatic envoy just happens to be at the Ovarrow city when an accident occurs? The timing's a bit too convenient, don't you think?"

"Understood, sir. I'm on it," Natalia said and left.

Connor left his office with Eric running to catch up.

"What are you going to do?"

"It might be time to remind the Ovarrow exactly who they're dealing with. They respect a show of force, and I intend to give them one if they don't cooperate," Connor replied.

Eric looked as if he were about to say something else but didn't.

Lenora had been intrigued about seeing the Ovarrow city. She'd been studying them for such a long time. Connor had made sure she had experienced soldiers there to protect her, so she should be in good hands, even if something bad happened. She was a survivor. Connor clutched onto that hope and stormed down the hall, bellowing orders.

13

Lenora woke to a muffled sound she couldn't identify. Her ears were ringing. She blinked several times, and her eyes slowly came to focus on a message in crystal-clear amber letters.

Impact detected.

Emergency protocols engaged.

MPS protection mode is active.

Power level near maximum.

Below that was a list of her vitals, which the MPS jacket was getting from her biochip. They were normal, so she cleared the message from her internal heads-up display. The MPS systems had engaged and a quick-response helmet had protected her head. She glanced around for a few moments, looking for anything that could hurt her. She was wedged between twisted metal and the construction material the Ovarrow had used for their footbridges. It was dark, but her implants adjusted her vision so she could see just fine. Lenora looked around for any sharp objects and then disengaged the helmet. She heard the faint coughing sounds of other people.

"Hello! Can anyone hear me?"

She waited a few moments. The air was thick with pulverized material, and she sneezed. She heard the deep groans of straining metallic supports, followed by clanging as some of them broke. She tried to move but was pinned where she was. A deafening rumble shook everything around her, and Lenora squeezed her eyes shut. It felt as if everything was pushing in. Lenora's lips trembled and her shoulders went rigid as she tried to worm her way free. She gritted her teeth and pushed.

"Dammit!"

The rumbling stopped, and she tried to calm down by taking several breaths. Both bridges had collapsed—the main one and the footbridge they'd been on. Her stomach attempted to slither out of her mouth when she tried to figure out how much debris was on top of her right then.

Not helping, she thought. She needed to get free.

Lenora had drawn in a breath to shout when she heard someone call out her name. "I'm here," she said.

"Dr. Bishop, it's Cookie."

Lenora was sure she hadn't heard him right. Why would someone offer her a cookie? "What?" she asked.

"It's me, Sergeant Cook . . . You know, Cookie. I'm below you. I can see your legs. Can you scoot downward? I'll catch you," he said.

Lenora tried to twist around but couldn't get enough leverage to push effectively.

"Can you work your way downward, Dr. Bishop?"

Lenora grunted, trying to move, and then cursed. "I think we can dispense with the formalities, don't you?"

"That's fine with me, Lenora. Are you able to move?"

"No, I'm wedged in pretty hard."

"Are you injured?"

"No, I'm fine. I have an MPS jacket on. It engaged and kept me from getting hurt."

"Good. That's good," he said, sounding as if he were looking around as he spoke.

Lenora grunted with effort, pushing as hard as she could to free herself. "I don't think I can do it," she said.

"Yes, you can. I'll talk you through it."

"No, I mean I don't think I can call you 'Cookie.' I can't think about cookies right now. What's your first name?"

"Benjamin, but my friends call me Ben."

"All right, Ben. I'm wedged in because my MPS is in protect mode. I think once I disable it, I'll be able to slide on down," Lenora said.

"Wait!" Ben shouted. "Make sure there's nothing around that can hurt you. The suit might be all that's supporting the pocket you're in."

Lenora glanced around and shook her head. "I think it's a little late for that."

She disabled the MPS and immediately began to slide downward. She felt something sharp scrape along her back, and she winced. The MPS had gone into passive protect mode, which prevented whatever was sticking into her back from penetrating the skin, but she'd still have a heck of a bruise. Her backpack got hung up on something and almost forced her face into a ragged wall of sharp edges. She unbuckled her backpack and felt strong hands grab hold of her feet. "Hold on," Lenora said and pulled her backpack loose.

Sergeant Cook set her on the ground, and she noticed blood from a gash on the side of his head.

"You're hurt. Let me take a look at that," Lenora said.

The CDF soldier leaned away from her and shook his head. "I'm fine. You don't need to do that."

"Don't be an idiot, Ben. You've got a head wound. Now let me see it," Lenora said and gestured for him to lean down so she could see his wound.

She took the first aid kit out of her backpack and then dabbed the wound with a piece of cloth. Next, she used medi-paste. She knew it stung, but he hardly reacted at all.

Men.

"You'll live," Lenora said. "Do you know where the others are?"

"I've only been able to find Green and Yemshi. I have them searching for other survivors. I haven't been able to reach anyone on comlink," Ben replied.

They were in a large pocket surrounded by wreckage from the bridge, clearly lucky to be alive.

Lenora glanced down. They were standing on a flat piece of the footbridge. Loud bangs were heard, followed by another deep rumble. They had to find the others and get out of there. She sent out a comlink broadcast but didn't get a reply, so she set the broadcast to loop while they got their bearings.

"I'm not able to reach anyone either. Not even Green or Yemshi," Lenora said and frowned for a moment. She shook her head and looked at Ben.

"That's because they must be on CDF comms channels. I'll let them know to monitor for civilian comlink chatter."

They picked a direction and headed off. As they climbed over the wreckage, the area became more cramped. Lenora could stand up straight, but Ben couldn't.

A comlink chimed, and Lenora smiled as she acknowledged it.

"Dr. Bishop, she's hurt." Lenora looked at the comlink ID and saw that it said L. Butler. "They both are. I tried to—she's hurt. There's blood. Oh God, she's bleeding so much."

Lenora shared a look with Ben. "Lynn, who's bleeding?"

"Kayla is. She had something sticking into her leg, and I pulled it out. Now I can't stop the bleeding. I need help! I need help, now! I have to help her! She's going to die!"

"Lynn, listen to me. I'm going to help you, but you have to calm down. Is there anything you can use to cover the wound? Anything at all—a jacket or a piece of your shirt? Just put something over the wound and then compress firmly with your hands. That will help staunch the bleeding. Can you do that? Find something to cover the wound and then compress it. Lean on it with everything you've got."

Lenora heard Lynn muttering half-formed thoughts to herself as she looked. "I found something. I've covered the wound. I'm pressing down, but it's soaking through. It's not stopping."

"That's okay, we just need to slow it down. Now, we're coming to you. Is your PDA working? Can you to activate the emergency beacon?"

Lenora waited and then she saw the beacon on her internal heads-up display. She glanced at Ben and he nodded.

"Good. That's great. We have your signal, and we're coming to you."

"Please hurry," Lynn said, her voice sounding strained.

They hurried to the end of the pocket they were in and the path narrowed.

"I should go first," Ben said. He'd just finished bringing Green and Yemshi up to speed.

Lenora glanced back at him. "Have you had any SAR training? Have you spent years crawling around Ovarrow ruins, including tight spaces? I didn't think so. Follow me."

Ben hesitated for a moment and then gestured for her to go first. They crawled through the debris for a few minutes. Lenora checked in with Lynn to assure her that they were coming. Green and Yemshi caught up with them. On their way, they found another CDF soldier, but he was unconscious. His name was

Philip Jones. Lenora checked Jones's injuries. He was just knocked out, and they were able to wake him up.

They found an open area that was an even larger pocket than the one they'd been in. Two Ovarrow soldiers were trying to rescue their comrades. The two Ovarrow were surprised to see them and didn't look too happy about it.

"This would be a good time to tell them we're here to help," Lenora said.

Ben brought up his personal holoscreen and engaged the Ovarrow translator. The two Ovarrow soldiers read the message and, after a few moments, seemed to accept that they were there to help.

"I want the three of you to stay here and help them," Ben said to the three CDF soldiers. "I'm going on ahead with Dr. Bishop."

The soldiers didn't look thrilled with their orders but walked over to the Ovarrow.

Lenora followed the emergency beacon. As they closed in on the source, they found that the area was blocked off. The beacon indicated that Lynn and Kayla were just on the other side.

"Lynn, can you hear me?" Lenora asked.

"I can hear you."

"We're just on the other side of this wall. Do you see any other way for us to reach you?"

"We're surrounded by debris. I can't look—I don't see a way."

Lenora heard a slight panic in her voice and didn't want to push her too far. "Is Devon with you?"

"Yes, he is, but he's unconscious. I haven't been able to check him."

"That's fine. It's going to be okay. We'll find a way to you."

"How? We're trapped in here. There's no way out," Lynn said, her voice rising.

"Lynn, I need you to calm down. Just give us a few minutes and we'll find a way to get to you. We made it this far," Lenora said.

While she was speaking to Lynn, Ben was looking for a way through the debris. She muted her comlink to Lynn.

Ben shook his head and stepped back. "I don't have anything that can get through this. My sidearm would just poke holes in it, and that's not going to help us. If I had some thermite, I could burn a hole through it pretty easily."

Lenora peered at the maze of twisted metal and found a flat surface that looked brittle. It must have been some kind of filler material similar to concrete. She couldn't reconcile what she was seeing in front of her with the bridge they'd been walking across. Jagged edges had burst through on the top, and she touched the flat surface. It was solid but looked brittle. She reached inside her backpack and pulled out a sonic hand blaster.

"What good is that gonna do?" Ben asked.

Lenora smiled and opened the handle. "It's been modified. I can crank up the output, but it'll deplete the power cell a lot faster. I think I can use it to shatter that wall, and we might be able to get through that way."

She raised the power output and Ben had squatted down, examining the wall she intended to use it on.

"If we're wrong, it might collapse on top of them. Maybe even us," Ben said.

Lenora nodded. "I don't think we have much choice. If we don't get in there, they'll die."

Ben turned away from her, looking for an alternative. Then he looked back at her and nodded. "Okay, let's do this. They're located over here," he said, gesturing to an area to the right of the wall. "If you angulate slightly upward, they might be able to crawl through here and then drop down."

Lenora came closer to the wall and put the end of the sonic hand blaster within centimeters of it. She adjusted some settings. Though the power output increased, it didn't unleash in one high-powered, concussive blast. This was a modified version of the sonic hand blaster Connor had used to escape when he'd been wedged in a ravine. He'd made it less dangerous.

Lenora squeezed the trigger and, at first, nothing happened. The acoustic resonance bounced off the wall, and the sonic waves increased in intensity. Dust billowed off the wall. Lenora pushed the blaster forward, and the wall shattered apart, opening a cavity inside. Lenora thrust her arm out and continued to angulate upward. She engaged her MPS jacket, and the helmet formed overhead. She peered through the dust cloud and stopped firing when she finally reached an open area.

Ben crawled up through the opening and into the cavity above, then reached his hand down and helped Lenora up. Lynn was hovering over Kayla. Both her hands were compressed over a wound in the girl's thigh. Lynn had tears streaming down her cheeks, but she wasn't injured.

Lenora went over to Kayla and took out her first aid kit. She told Lynn to take her hands away and then pulled away the blood-soaked shirt. There was a deep, inch-wide puncture in Kayla's thigh. Lenora slathered medi-paste into the wound and forced it closed with her fingers, holding steady while she waited for the medi-paste to work. A minute later, she loosened her fingers and the wound stayed closed. The bleeding had stopped. Lenora removed a syringe of medical nanites from the first aid kit and plunged it into Kayla's thigh above the wound, ejecting them into her system.

"Will she be all right?" Lynn asked.

Kayla's face was pale, but at least now she had a fighting chance. "You did just fine," Lenora said.

She turned toward Devon and saw that Ben was checking his vitals. He turned toward her and shook his head. "He's gone."

Lynn gasped. "No, he was fine. I spoke to him. He said he just needed to rest for a minute," she said and began moving toward Devon. Ben blocked her path, and she struggled to get past him.

"Let me see him. You have to let me see him. He was fine. He just needed to rest."

Ben remained rooted in place. "I'm sorry," he said, holding the young girl firmly. She struggled against him, and Ben leaned down so he was in front of Lynn's face. "He's dead. He had a wound on his side that he probably didn't even feel."

Lynn's face became ashen. "He couldn't have had a wound. He said he was fine. He told me . . . He told me to take care of Kayla."

Lenora's eyes tightened, but she forced her voice to remain firm. "We have to get Kayla out of here. We can't stay here. I need your help, Lynn. I need you to help me move her."

It took a little bit more coaxing, but they got Lynn to help them move Kayla out of the pocket they'd been trapped in. As Lynn and Ben worked to get Kayla out, Lenora looked down at Devon's body. Her throat thickened. He was so young, and his face looked innocent, as if he were sleeping. Her eyes became misty and she quickly wiped them, then followed the others.

They carried Kayla back to where they'd found the Ovarrow. Lynn kept talking about how she had tried to protect them both, rationalizing a desperate situation. Lenora tried to reassure her. Redirecting her attention toward Kayla helped.

When they finally reached the others, six Ovarrow had been freed. Lenora's eyes widened when she realized that the warlord's first was lying on the ground. He was conscious, but he looked as if he was in a lot of pain. The Ovarrow soldiers were agitated, and Green, Jones, and Yemshi stood off to the side.

Lenora tried to get closer to Cerot, but the Ovarrow soldiers wouldn't let her. She brought up her Ovarrow translator. "I can help him," she said and held up her medical kit. She looked at Cerot. "Let me help you."

Several Ovarrow soldiers moved to block her path. Ben was at her side, and the rest of the CDF soldiers came up behind her, ready to intervene.

Cerot growled an order, and after a few moments, the Ovarrow soldiers parted to let Lenora pass. She knelt down by Cerot and began assessing his wounds. There were more than a few of them.

"This might hurt a little," she said and waited for the translator to convey her words.

Cerot read the message and waited for her to begin.

14

Lars flew the Hellcat through a narrow ravine, winding his way back to base. Newer pilots found the route to be challenging, but Lars had done it so many times he could do it with his eyes closed. The Hellcat was a highly maneuverable aircraft. It flew at high speeds and carried a respectable amount of armaments. Larger models were capable of carrying heavy loads, but this was a lightweight version, capable of transporting just one squad at a time. It was difficult to detect, which was why Lars preferred to use it when searching for Ovarrow bunkers.

Martakis closed down her personal holoscreen and stretched her arms out in front of her. "It wasn't a total waste of a trip," she said.

Lars glanced at her questioningly. "We came up empty-handed. All three sites were a bust."

Maggie Martakis had been part of Lars's team for almost a year and believed wholeheartedly in what they were doing. She had a background in Field Ops Search and Rescue and could quickly adapt to challenges. Her dark, curly hair was tied back, and she had a larger-than-normal nose.

"That's three fewer sites we have to investigate in the future. Now we can focus our efforts somewhere else," Maggie replied.

"Those sites were based on new intelligence. I would've expected to strike pay dirt on at least one of them."

"Pay dirt?"

"No appreciation for old Earth sayings?" Lars countered.

"Touché."

They'd had to change their Ovarrow bunker missions to restrict them to parts of the continent that were infrequently monitored by the CDF. This was safer for everybody.

Lars decreased the Hellcat's altitude as they approached the LZ. A large group was gathered near another Hellcat, and Lars frowned. He hadn't authorized any other missions that day.

"Looks like we missed something," Maggie said.

He initiated the power-down protocols and lowered the landing ramp. "Or we found something," he said as he unstrapped his seatbelt.

He hastened out of the Hellcat with Maggie close behind. The group of people surrounding the other Hellcat was chatting excitedly.

Lars approached them. "Did I miss something? What's going on here?"

The crowd of people quieted down and stood aside. A path opened and he saw Colton Evans grinning widely. Next to him stood Dean Morris, who gave Colton a sidelong glance.

Evans walked over to Lars. "Great, you're back. I've got good news."

The Hellcat behind them had obviously been flown, which meant someone had disobeyed his orders. Lars held up his hand and looked around at the others. "Don't the rest of you have something to do? Clear the deck. Now. Evans and Morris, follow me."

Lars didn't wait for a reply; he simply turned and led them

toward the interior of the base, ignoring Morris muttering something behind them. Evans told him to be quiet.

They entered his office, and Lars nodded for Maggie to close the door.

Lars looked at Evans. "I hope you have a good explanation for disobeying orders. There were no scheduled missions today."

"A last-minute mission came in during your scouting run," Evans said.

Lars glared at the two men. "Bullshit. I would've been notified."

Evans and Morris stood motionless for a second.

"Excuse me, sir," Maggie said. "You need to see this."

She activated a nearby holoscreen, and it showed a news broadcast from Sierra. The banner at the bottom read: *Fatal accident at the Ovarrow city. Events are unfolding now. The Colonial Defense Force is on site, but the Ovarrow military is denying entry into the city.*

"That was the mission," Evans said, smiling.

Lars glanced at him and then back to the holoscreen. There was a video feed that showed that the CDF had gathered a sizable force outside the Ovarrow city walls. The video then switched to a surveillance drone feed that showed a collapsed bridge. Ovarrow were at the site, searching for survivors. Lars felt something cold sink to the bottom of his stomach, and he turned toward Evans. "What did you do?"

"The operation went off without a hitch. Now there's no way the colonial government can sit on its collective asses and do nothing about the Ovarrow. It was so easy, and we couldn't have had a better opportunity. You know who was down there—"

The rest of what Evans was about to say was cut off as Lars grabbed him by the shirt and slammed him up against the wall. "You're a god damn idiot! Who the hell authorized you to do this?"

he demanded, gesturing to the holoscreen. As he did so, he was distracted by a snippet of the report.

". . . A diplomatic envoy was on scene when the accident occurred. We've heard from Governor Wolf that her daughter, Kayla Wolf, was among the members of the envoy, as well as Dr. Lenora Bishop. The envoy is currently missing."

Lars growled and threw Evans across the room. Dean Morris attempted to intervene, and Lars twisted the man's arm behind his back and slammed his face into his desk, surprising him.

"You've put colonial lives in danger! They might be dead!" Lars bellowed. He withdrew his sidearm and pointed it at Evans.

"Wait! Wait," Evans said quickly. "We had authorization. Let me show you. I'm just going to show you the mission briefing." He activated his wrist computer and made a passing motion at the holoscreen. A second screen appeared, and Lars read the message. It had all the correct authentication codes associated with it.

Morris regained his feet.

"Get over there by Evans. Now," Lars said and looked at Maggie. "Watch them."

Maggie pulled out her own sidearm and covered the two men.

Lars initiated a secure comlink to his superiors and gave his authentication.

"Agent Mallory," a voice said through a vocalizer so he couldn't tell who he was speaking with.

"I've just read the mission briefing sent to Agent Evans. This was sent out to my team but not through me. I was kept out of the loop, and I want an explanation. This is a huge shitstorm. We've crossed the line. I have the two agents in custody now," Lars said.

"Release the agents immediately. They were following orders."

Lars clenched his teeth for a moment. "Sir, this isn't—"

"I said, release those agents now."

Lars glared at Evans and Morris, who actually seemed proud

of what they'd done. He jerked his head toward the door to his office. "Get out of here. I'll find you later."

As soon as they left, he looked at Maggie. "Keep an eye on them. Make sure they stick around."

"Yes, sir."

Lars took a few breaths, trying to calm down. The comlink was still active. "Sir, I need an explanation."

"An opportunity came our way, and I chose to exploit it."

Lars frowned. He was trying to figure out which superior he was speaking with, but he knew better than to voice their actual names, even on a secure comlink channel.

"You've served the cause well, never hesitating to do what had to be done. This was the next step. We had to do this. I've initiated Operation Burrow Down."

Lars winced. "They're going to come after us," he said at last.

"That was always going to happen. You don't have time to decide how you feel about this. There's work to be done, and you have to evacuate. There are hundreds of lives at that base depending on you. Get to it."

The comlink deactivated, and Lars snarled as he shoved everything on his desk crashing to the floor. He glanced at the news broadcast again and shook his head. His thoughts raced. *Colonial lives*, he thought and clenched his teeth.

He sighed in disgust and opened a broadcast channel to the base. "Prepare for immediate evac. First alert. Wheels up in one hour."

Lars shut down the broadcast channel, his hands shaking with rage. This wasn't how it was supposed to happen. They weren't supposed to put colonial lives at risk. The Ovarrow were the enemy. Feeling bile creep up into his throat, he growled and kicked the chair, sending it to the other side of the room where it slammed into the wall.

"Dammit!"

He'd always known Evans was a hothead. Lars didn't want to believe anyone else on his team could have done what Evans had. His superiors had known just who to order to fulfill this mission. They'd also known Lars would've refused. Evans had not.

His thoughts turned toward the group of people who'd been celebrating outside Evans's Hellcat. Had he been wrong? He'd gone through great pains to instill the mission objective into his team. The Ovarrow were the enemy. Lars swallowed hard in disgust. Who was the enemy now?

The door to his office opened and Tonya Wagner stood in the doorway. "I came as soon as I heard. We're evacuating ahead of schedule. What do you want done with the prisoners?"

He frowned for a moment as images of the news broadcasts flashed his mind.

"Lars, are you okay?"

Lars gathered himself. "The prisoners?" he repeated, his voice sounding grim. "We take them with us. Prep them for transport."

15

THE EDGE of the loading ramp clanged when it hit the ground and Connor stepped off. His boots bit into the dirt and a gust of wind howled. A few thick drops of rain pelted him as he registered the faint whooshing sounds of the wind turbines the Ovarrow used to power their city.

Major Alexis Brooks stood at attention and saluted Connor.

"Sit rep, Major Brooks."

"Three hours ago, two major bridges collapsed. The diplomatic envoy was on one of the lower footbridges when it went down. We don't know how it happened, but the Ovarrow are keenly suspicious. They've locked down their city and won't let any of us inside."

"We'll see about that," Connor said.

Major Brooks led Connor to the command area.

"Have we heard from anyone inside the city?" he asked.

"Negative, sir. The Ovarrow escorted the remaining colonial visitors out of the city. They weren't mistreated. You can speak with them if you want."

Connor nodded. "Who's speaking with the Ovarrow?"

"No one right now. Our diplomatic negotiator on site is Sebastian Crosby. After initial communications ceased, he elected to wait for you to arrive before trying again," Brooks said.

Connor went into the command area where Sebastian Crosby was waiting. Connor made it a point to study the dossiers of anyone who worked in the colonial diplomatic relations office, especially those stationed at Camp Alpha.

Connor looked at Major Brooks. "Where's Darius Cohen?"

"He was on one of the bridges that collapsed, sir."

Lenora had likely been right by him, which meant she was trapped. He put a stranglehold on his fear and focused on what had to be done.

"Mr. Crosby, why won't they let us inside the city?" Connor asked.

"They said they're searching for survivors. I suspect that someone high up in the Ovarrow hierarchy must have been on the bridge when it collapsed," Sebastian said.

"We have better equipment than they do. Did you explain that to them? I have a team of engineers ready to get in there and find the survivors."

"I did try to express our interest in helping them search for survivors; however, they refused to listen."

Connor glared at the diplomat, and he flinched, but Connor resisted the urge to chew him out. It wasn't his fault. "Who were you speaking with?"

"An Ovarrow faction leader named Wigren."

Connor shook his head in disgust. "Faction leaders have limited power. We need somebody who can actually negotiate with us. I want High Commissioner Senleon, the warlord's first, or the warlord himself. Speaking to anyone else is counterproductive."

"I'll get started, but I must caution you against making

demands of the Ovarrow," Sebastian warned, "if we hope to get them to cooperate with us."

Connor's muscles tensed and his tone deepened. "The window for their cooperation is closing. I'd rather have their support, but I'm prepared to do whatever I must to ensure the safety of the colonists trapped under that collapsed bridge. Convey that to them. I'll be with you shortly."

Sebastian's face went pallid, and he swallowed hard. Sensing his dismissal, the diplomat left the area.

Connor marched over to the operations center where he found Flint and Samson waiting for him. "Where are your men located?"

"About five clicks west of the city. Nearest the bridge our people are trapped under," Samson replied.

"We have recon drones scouring the area," Flint said. "We don't know how those bridges collapsed, but we do have a search grid to hand off to the engineers so they can find whoever's trapped."

"Are the Ovarrow searching in the right place?" Connor asked.

"They're all over the place," Samson said. "They're trying to be as thorough as they can, but the equipment they're using to reach any survivors will take them two or three times as long as ours would. If we want to save anyone, we need to get in there and take over the search effort."

Connor's lips formed a grim line as he considered his options. First Battalion was on its way there and would arrive shortly. The Ovarrow might let them into the city after First Battalion arrived, but Connor didn't have that long to wait. Lives were on the line. Flint and Samson waited for his orders. The 3rd and 7th Ranger companies could hold their positions, but they had to choose the right bridge.

Connor looked at a holographic model of the city. "How certain are we about the target?"

"The reports I've seen show that the envoy went down the main thoroughfare," Major Brooks said, gesturing at the model.

"Comlink check-in pings have them taking a different way out of the city that puts them on the path to this bridge, here. The second bridge that collapsed was farther away, and I can't think of a compelling reason why the envoy would go that way. I'm ninety-nine percent certain this is the target, General Gates."

Connor looked at the live video feed from the reconnaissance drone in the area, his mind already working on ways for the Spec Ops teams to take control of the area.

"Mission objectives, General Gates?" Samson asked.

"We need to get our engineers on site so they can use ground-penetrating scans to speed up the recovery. They also need medical teams on site. We need to rescue both the Ovarrow and the colonists," Connor said.

"They won't like us being there without their permission. This could get ugly real fast," Brooks said.

"If we can't get the Ovarrow to listen to reason, then we need to be prepared to push them back. We could focus on holding this area right here and then expand it based on what the engineers find," Connor replied, gesturing at the map of the city.

"Just give the order and we'll make it happen," Samson said.

Connor didn't doubt their capabilities, but he didn't want a confrontation with the Ovarrow. It felt like he was being backed into a corner, and his only recourse was to escalate the situation. It would be so easy for him to just give the order right then. The Ovarrow couldn't put up much of a fight, and Connor's teams could be on site and searching for survivors within fifteen minutes. Lenora would be safe if she wasn't . . . He wouldn't allow his thoughts to go there, but if she was hurt, he had to get to her as soon as possible. He could tell Governor Wolf and all the other people under his command that he was there to protect the colonists, and he was, but his wife was trapped under a bridge. He needed to find her, and he'd tear the entire city apart to do it.

They were all looking at him, waiting for him to give the order, but he still hesitated, considered the image on the holoscreen. She had to be safe. They had some time.

"Be ready to go when I give the order. First, I want to see if I can get the Ovarrow to cooperate. If not, we go in there."

"Yes, General," Flint said.

Both men saluted him and left. Connor looked at Major Brooks. "Come on, Major, let's see if we can talk some sense into the Ovarrow."

Connor headed for no man's land, which was an area just outside the Ovarrow city. CDF soldiers led the way in, but the real show of force would be there in a few minutes.

The Ovarrow had armed soldiers behind barricades at the entrance to the city, and Connor saw more soldiers on the rooftops of the nearest buildings. They had the area well covered.

Sebastian Crosby was speaking, and his words were being translated into the Ovarrow symbols that were showing on several large holoscreens. A drone within the city displayed the translation as well and was available as a user interface for the Ovarrow.

Connor walked over to Sebastian. "This is how you've been talking to them?"

"They've been on lockdown."

Connor shook his head and gestured toward the Ovarrow translator interface. He wasn't asking for Sebastian's permission to use it; he was informing him that he was going to use it. The Ovarrow knew who he was.

"This is General Connor Gates of the Colonial Defense Force. I want to speak with High Commissioner Senleon immediately."

Connor saw a brief commotion from behind the barricade.

"High Commissioner Senleon. I'd like to speak to you in person. Please meet me on neutral ground," Connor said.

The Ovarrow language was so different from anything that Connor had ever heard before that he doubted he'd ever be able to understand it. They'd always be dependent on some kind of translation device so the two species could communicate.

A message appeared on a small holoscreen in front of them, and Sebastian's eyebrows raised with surprise. "There's a group of Ovarrow coming out to meet us."

Connor walked toward the group. The Ovarrow were sensitive to certain hierarchies, and this was a meeting among leaders.

Two Ovarrow walked ahead of the Mekaal soldiers. One spoke to the other at his side, who began using the drone's holographic interface.

"I am Senleon."

"I want us to work together, High Commissioner. There are both colonists and Ovarrow trapped in the wreckage. We have the means to help rescue them quickly. Will you allow us into the city?" Connor asked.

"This is not possible. Colonial drones were spotted in the area when the bridges collapsed," Senleon replied.

Connor glanced at Major Brooks, who gave a slight shake of her head. Connor looked back at the high commissioner. "I don't know anything about that, but I assure you we'll look into it with the highest priority after we help those who are trapped."

Senleon regarded Connor for a few moments. Trying to anticipate what the Ovarrow were thinking or their intentions was extremely difficult, but Connor thought Senleon wanted to accept Connor's offer. Something was holding him back though.

"I don't know what happened here," Connor said, "but we can figure this out together. You just need to work with me. There are lives at stake."

Senleon glanced behind him at the Ovarrow soldiers for a moment and then looked back at Connor. "We are at a disadvantage. We must protect the Ovarrow."

Connor frowned in thought for a few moments. He glanced at

the Ovarrow soldiers, the Mekaal. They seemed more preoccupied with watching Senleon than they were with watching Connor.

Connor narrowed his gaze. "Where are Vitory or Cerot?"

He watched for their reactions as they read the message, and the soldiers seemed to stiffen.

One of the Mekaal said something to Senleon that Connor had no hope of understanding.

Senleon looked at Connor. "We are searching for survivors and will inform you of any new developments," he replied and began to walk away.

"Senleon, do you have the authority to grant us access to the city?"

The high commissioner read the message and didn't reply. Senleon didn't have the power. The warlord and his second-in-command were nowhere to be found.

Not needing their reply, Connor used his implants to recall the communications drone from the Ovarrow. He opened a secure comlink to Samson and Flint. "You're clear to go. Surgical strike. Try to intimidate them. I don't want to take them out if I don't have to."

Connor looked at Sebastian. "We need to send a quick message, and I want as many comms drones capable of projecting holoscreens as we can deploy so the Ovarrow know exactly what's going on. We're going into that city whether they want us to or not."

16

LENORA'S EYEBROWS pulled down in concentration. The warlord's first was severely wounded. Multiple metallic shards stuck out of his body, piercing his body armor. The largest shard, over a foot long, had speared into his abdomen. The jagged edges of the fragment had mostly sealed the abdominal wound, so Lenora left that one alone while she removed the smaller shards.

"Try to lie still," Lenora said.

Cerot read the message and gave her a slight nod.

The smaller shards were in nonlethal places on his arms, with others on his legs. She even found one on top of his shoulder. As she removed them one by one, she methodically cleaned and numbed the wounds. She then applied a variant of the medi-paste they used to heal their own wounds. Medi-paste would fill up the wound and begin binding the damaged flesh back together. However, healing the damage to an internal organ required the use of medical nanites, but her emergency stock of those was for humans only.

Once she'd finished tending to the least dangerous wounds,

Lenora glanced at the end of the metallic shard sticking out of Cerot's stomach. It was six inches across, and she hoped it had a pointy end like the others; otherwise, removing it might kill the Ovarrow. It still might kill him, even if the end of the shard narrowed to a point. She inhaled deeply and rolled her shoulders, stretching her neck. They couldn't move him like this or Cerot would die.

Cerot's gaze met hers. The Ovarrow's chestnut-colored eyes had bits of hazel to them that she'd never noticed before. They were two different species, but in that moment, there was understanding. She'd looked into the eyes of people who knew they were going to die many times. The last battle of the Vemus War had given her nightmares, but she had to try to save Cerot.

Lenora was no stranger to being watched while she worked. Years of teaching and fieldwork had provided an ample number of witnesses. She'd even been in quite a few survival situations. Technically, she was qualified as a field medic, but what Cerot needed was a real doctor.

The Ovarrow soldiers hovered around her, watching her with their feline eyes narrowed. It made their expressions fierce and a bit unsettling.

Cerot glanced down at the shard sticking out of his stomach and then looked at Lenora.

"It's the last one," she said.

Ben came to her side, holding a small canteen of water. He extended it and nodded toward her. Lenora sat back on her feet and gestured for him to come over. The Ovarrow soldiers allowed him to pass.

Lenora thanked him and took a long swallow from the canteen, then handed it back to him.

Ben looked down at Cerot's wound. "That could be messy."

"You've got that right. If I pull it out and it's damaged his internal organs, he could die. If we try to move him with that thing stuck inside him, he could die. If we stay here—"

"He could die. I get it. We can only do the best we can," Ben said.

Lenora sighed. "I'm sorry."

Cerot had watched their exchange and then uttered a few words. The soldier nearest her used the translator interface to input Cerot's words.

"Pull it out."

Lenora inhaled deeply and nodded. She looked at the soldier with the translator interface. "I'm going to need help. I need someone to hold down his arms, his legs, and his shoulders. He can't move at all, or it could make things worse."

Lenora knew the Ovarrow translator did the best it could with conveying the meaning of her words. Luckily for them, most computer programming languages required a subset of specific commands in order to tell the computer how to operate. So, the meaning of the message that the Ovarrow actually read might have said something like "stop motion or risk breakage." The context was conveyed through the unspoken communication of body language.

Lenora gestured the soldiers toward where she wanted them to go.

After reading the message, the Ovarrow soldiers moved into position around Cerot.

Lenora looked at Ben. "Grab his foot and hold his leg down."

She squeezed between the soldiers and peered at the shard for a moment. "Lynn, I need your help. Come over here, please."

Lynn hurried over and squatted down behind her. "What do you need me to do?"

"I need you to hand me these three things after I pull the shard out. I'll need to clean the wound with this pad. Make sure your hands are clean. Then, hand me the medi-paste, and last will be the compress to cover the wound," Lenora said.

Lynn cleaned her hands and exhaled a long breath. "Okay, I'm ready."

Lenora looked at the soldiers and gave them a nod. They put their hands on Cerot and held him in place. Cerot closed his eyes, waiting.

Lenora leaned in toward the shard. She needed to get the angle just right or she'd do more damage. She had to pull it out along the same angle it had entered Cerot's stomach. Reaching out with both hands, she took a firm grip of the end of the shard and held her breath. Then, she yanked hard.

Cerot growled in pain as the soldiers continued to hold him down. Lenora glanced at the end of the shard. It had a point. *Good*, she thought, dropping it to the ground.

Lynn already had the wad of pads ready, and Lenora began wiping around the area, careful not to press too deeply. Blood pooled out of the wound, and she couldn't see inside.

"Medi-paste," Lenora said.

Lynn handed it to her, and Lenora applied liberal amounts to the inside of the wound, as well as the outside. She squeezed the wound shut, and Cerot twisted in pain. Lenora leaned on top of him to keep him from moving. She had to give the medi-paste time to work. After a few minutes, it filled up the wound and the bleeding stopped. Lenora wiped the edges again and then covered it with the large bandage, which adhered to the skin.

She leaned back. "Okay, you can let him go."

As the soldiers removed their hands from Cerot, the lines of pain on the Ovarrow's face lessened, and he opened his eyes. He looked down at his stomach and then at Lenora. His breath came in small gasps but slowly returned to normal.

"Lie still for a few minutes and then you can move," Lenora said.

The Ovarrow soldiers watched Cerot for a moment and then looked at Lenora. One of them placed his hand on his own shoulder and pulled it across to his other shoulder. The gesture was mimicked by the other soldiers.

"It's a sign of gratitude," Cerot said.

Lenora looked back at the soldiers, and their gazes seemed less harsh. "You're welcome," she said and looked at Cerot. "How do you feel?"

Cerot sat up and winced. He slowly got to his feet, standing almost resolute and proud, if somewhat stooped all the same. He raised his large hand. The thick black nails at the ends of his long fingers touched his shoulder and gracefully glided across his chest to his other shoulder. It was a simple gesture, but it conveyed a lot.

"Good work, Dr. Bishop," Ben said.

There was plenty of light from the wrist computers the colonials wore, and the Ovarrow carried a bioluminescent stick with them. Clouds of dust swirled in the air.

"Hello?" a voice said weakly.

Lenora looked down and saw that Kayla had finally awakened. Lynn flew to her side.

"My leg hurts," Kayla said. She looked up at Lenora. "What happened?" she asked and looked around, her voice raising with alarm. "Where is everyone?"

Lynn began telling Kayla everything that had happened in a jumble of words that came out too fast to comprehend.

"Slow down, Lynn," Lenora said.

"Right. Of course, Dr. Bishop."

There was a subtle vibration that seemed to start all at once, and Lenora's eyes darted above her, afraid they were about to be crushed. She heard Jones whisper something to Ben, and the other CDF soldiers shared a look. The Ovarrow soldiers seem to mimic the gesture as well.

Lenora narrowed her gaze. "What is it?" she asked after a few moments. "Sergeant Cook?"

Ben frowned for a moment and looked away, glancing at the Ovarrow. He turned back toward her. "I don't know for sure, but it sounded like weapons fire. We felt the impact from it." He shook his head. "Again, I don't know for sure. It could be just another part of the bridge breaking apart and hitting the ground."

Lenora narrowed her gaze. "But you don't think so, do you?"

Ben met her steely gaze and swallowed hard, twitching a slight nod.

"We need to find a way out of here," Lenora said and looked at the Ovarrow. "Do you know where we are?"

They tried to review what had happened together. The way the bridge had collapsed had provided pockets, and some of them had been lucky enough to be dumped into them. Now, they needed to escape.

"I think we should pick a direction and angle upward so we're climbing out of the debris," Lenora said, gesturing toward the side.

"We can't get through. We already tried," Cerot said.

Lenora reached into her backpack and pulled out her sonic hand blaster. "I can use this to help make a hole," she said, gesturing toward part of the wall.

Cerot seemed to consider this for a moment. "How can we help?"

Lenora looked around. Nearby, several metal rods stuck out of the concrete. She pointed the sonic hand blaster near it and used the lower setting. The concrete seemed to dissipate into dust, exposing the rods. "Can we cut these into long shafts? We could use them to brace the ceiling if we need to."

She looked at Ben and the other CDF soldiers, but they didn't have anything that could cut through them. One of the Ovarrow soldiers produced a colonial-made handheld plasma torch, making quick work of the metal rods and passing them around.

Lynn helped Kayla to her feet, and she was able to stand, favoring her injured leg.

Lenora walked over to the wall. She looked around, trying to see if this was the best place to use the hand blaster. Everything looked the same, and it would be a roll of the dice.

"Here goes nothing," Lenora said and got started.

17

A BRUISE-COLORED sky covered the Ovarrow city in darkness. The only light came from the sections of the city they were living in. Connor had the First Battalion divided into three companies, and the first had taken up position two hundred meters outside the official city entrance. The other two groups were stationed farther away but within view of the Ovarrow soldiers. Connor wanted them to see the CDF troops. The ground forces were a mixture of infantrymen with standard combat suits and combat-suit heavies. Falcon Fighters Series 7s performed several flybys over the city as a reminder of CDF air superiority.

Nexstar combat suits could resist a direct blast of the Ovarrow particle energy weapons, but eventually it would break through. Connor's orders were to return warning shots in the event that the Ovarrow opened fire on them. If the Ovarrow engaged them directly, they were authorized to use deadly force.

The 3rd and 7th Ranger companies were on site by the collapsed bridge and were securing the area.

"How much resistance do you think they'll get?" Colonel Jason Rhodes asked.

They were gathered around a holographic display that showed a zoomed-in portion of the city.

"They took them by surprise, so not much," Connor replied. "I'm hoping the show of force will snap them out of it."

"It could antagonize them as well."

Connor nodded. "We need to get our people in there so we can start scanning the wreckage. The Ovarrow are no strangers to posturing."

A comlink opened from Samson. "They weren't expecting us, and we've pushed them back. Zero casualties, but I think they're going to regroup and try again."

"Understood. I'm sending in the first team of engineers now," Connor replied.

Before the standoff had begun, Connor had informed them of his intentions. The Ovarrow had had plenty of warning that the CDF wasn't going to sit idly by. He'd authorized a team of engineers, along with CDF Search and Rescue, to the location.

"General Gates, I've located the warlord," Lieutenant Davis said. "He's near the first collapsed bridge."

Lieutenant Davis put the drone reconnaissance video feed on a holoscreen.

"Why would their military leader not be with his soldiers?" Rhodes asked.

Connor frowned in thought for a moment. "I need to be there."

"General Gates, I have to advise against it," Rhodes said.

"Noted, Colonel, but I'm still going. Hold the position here and continue monitoring the situation."

"Yes, sir," Rhodes said. "Governor Wolf is due to check in. What should I tell her?"

"The Ovarrow don't do anything purely by chance. The warlord is at that bridge," Connor said, gesturing toward the holoscreen, "because there's a compelling reason for him to be there. I think it has to do with the fact that his second-in-command was at the location when the bridge collapsed. Tell her that. I'll be within comms range anyway."

"Very well, sir," Colonel Rhodes said.

Connor left the command area and sent a quick message to the Search and Rescue team waiting for him. Since he was heading into a hot zone, he put the MPS he was wearing into active standby status. Once they were airborne, he'd put it in full active mode. He reached the troop carrier and climbed aboard.

"General Gates, can I interest you in a pristine AR-71 for your use?" Captain Emery offered.

Connor nodded. "Thanks. I left mine at home."

The troop carrier rose into the air and flew towards the collapsed bridge with three Hellcat escorts. Within minutes, they were hovering over an LZ a short distance away from the target.

Connor engaged the MPS, and he suddenly appeared to the onlookers like he was wearing black armor with a gold stripe down the side. The helmet formed around Connor's head, and a heads-up display immediately came on.

"Nice suit. Any chance we can get some of those, General Gates?" Captain Emery asked as they walked down the loading ramp of the troop carrier.

"I'll look into that," Connor said.

Several CDF Rangers escorted Connor to the command area. Flint did a double take as Connor walked in.

"You look like you lost a bet," Connor said.

Flint nodded. "I did. Samson said you'd be coming along."

The engineers and the Search and Rescue squad immediately went to work deploying specialized drones equipped with ground-penetrating radar. They'd perform a soft-landing maneuver, scan the area, and then send the data back to the command center.

Connor heard Ovarrow weapons fire, then the CDF soldiers returning fire. The skirmish flared up in bursts of weapons discharge. Flint and the reserve platoon escorted Connor toward the fighting.

Several concussion blasts sounded, but the MPS system dampened the sound. The ground shook with each concussive blast that was used to force the Ovarrow soldiers back.

They reached the barricade and hunkered down. Samson saw Connor and grinned at Flint. "See, I told you." The grin quickly faded, and he looked at Connor. "They keep pressing forward, and we keep forcing them back. We took out a row of buildings, which convinced them to stay back, but I don't know how long that will work."

Connor nodded and opened a comlink to Captain Emery. "How much time do you need to get the scans done?"

"We've only just started. We can get the immediate area done within ten or fifteen minutes, but it's going to take awhile to do the rest of the area," Emery replied.

Connor look at Samson. "Is there a comms drone nearby? I want to send the Ovarrow a message."

"I can get you a few. They've been shooting them down," Samson said.

"We'll group them so we can create a large holoscreen. I don't want them to miss it," Connor replied.

It took a few minutes for the comms drones to get into position above the Ovarrow soldiers where Connor expected the warlord to be. The Ovarrow were gathering to press forward between the two buildings Samson had left standing. Connor took control of the comms drones, and a large, amber-colored holoscreen appeared above them. It was a giant square approximately fifty meters across and impossible to miss.

Connor activated the Ovarrow translator and began speaking. "Warlord Vitory, we're here to rescue the people trapped in the wreckage, both Ovarrow and humans. Cease hostilities at once. We have this position, and we're not going to give it up. Further action on your part will result in more soldiers dying, and you'll be putting anyone who's trapped in that wreckage at risk."

The Ovarrow symbols took up the entirety of the space for Connor's message. They hadn't charged yet, which was a good sign, but they hadn't replied either.

Connor stood up from behind the barricade, keeping his weapon pointed down.

"Hold your position," Connor said to Samson.

Connor walked toward the kill zone. He was in plain sight of the Ovarrow soldiers, and he saw them clearly through the enhanced optical feed of his MPS. "Warlord Vitory, it's me, General Connor Gates. I think it's time for us to talk. I'm right here."

There was a bit of commotion among the Ovarrow line and then a lone Ovarrow soldier walked toward him. The others glared at Connor and the CDF. If any of them fired their weapons, the CDF would obliterate every Ovarrow soldier in the area.

Vitory carried an Ovarrow weapon, which he held loosely in his hands. Connor had one of the comms drones fly down to them so they could speak without it being written in the sky.

Vitory came to a stop three meters from Connor.

"You attack us."

"You left us no choice. Our people are trapped in there, and we have the right equipment to rescue them," Connor replied.

"Your strategy was to attack us in order to force our cooperation. This does not speak well of the proposed alliance between us," Vitory replied.

"No, it doesn't," Connor said. "But my top priority is to rescue everyone who's trapped in the wreckage. I could do that much better if you'd stop attacking us. We don't have to fight."

Vitory read the message and seemed to consider it for a few moments. "We have the right to protect our city. We were trying to rescue everyone who's trapped as well. Your attack has set us back. Leave here immediately."

Connor shook his head. "That's not going to happen. If you continue to attack, I will authorize my soldiers to use deadly force. I don't want to do this."

Vitory's body went rigid and the end of his weapon seemed to stir. "I will order my soldiers to attack if you don't leave."

"What if we worked together to rescue the people trapped in the wreckage? You come in here with a team and we work together."

Vitory regarded Connor for a moment. The Ovarrow's face was almost a sneer.

"Once we rescue everyone," Connor continued, "I promise we'll leave the city, and we won't return without your permission to enter."

The warlord glanced at the CDF soldiers behind the barricades and then looked at Connor. "We don't trust you."

Connor met his gaze and put steel into his own. "There are many of us who don't trust you either, but there are people who are important to me trapped in that wreckage. The longer I have to contend with your attack, the less time I have to spend rescuing them. And if I have to choose between this alliance and their lives, I will choose them." Connor leaned forward. "Every time." He clenched his teeth and his muscles tensed. The next few seconds would decide just how bloody this conflict with the Ovarrow was going to become.

For some reason, the warlord looked more at ease than he had before. He wasn't happy about it, but he didn't quite look so suspicious of Connor anymore.

Captain Emery sent Connor the preliminary scan results of the area. It showed open spaces where people or Ovarrow could have survived the collapse. Connor sent the image to the holoscreen, and a secondary window opened with it.

"This is what we've found so far. Do you want to stand here and fight, or do you want to go rescue our people?"

Vitory peered at the holoscreen for a few moments, and his eyes widened as he realized what he was seeing. Then he looked at Connor. "Your proposal is acceptable," he replied.

The Ovarrow went back the way he'd come, and Connor returned to the others.

"We have a deal," Connor said to Samson. "Let's give them some room. They're going to help with the rescue effort. Send an update back to the command area. We need to get to work immediately. Some of them don't have much time."

Connor brought up the scan results again on his personal holoscreen. They were going to have to dig, and they had to be careful not to trigger any more collapses as they tried to reach the people trapped underneath. This was going to be a very long night.

"I notice you didn't show him the emergency beacons from the CDF soldiers who are trapped," Samson said.

"I will because that's where the people he most cares about are as well."

Samson arched a thick eyebrow. "How do you know this?"

"If he was more concerned about making a statement by rebelling against us, he would've stayed with the troops at the entrance to the city. Instead, he's here. There's someone here he cares about."

"I never would've guessed that. I can fight them, and they wouldn't have gotten closer to this area, but I never would've figured out what motivates them. You've changed, Connor."

Had he changed? He'd been moments from committing the CDF to firing on the Ovarrow military. He wasn't going to let anyone stand in his way of rescuing Lenora and the other colonists. He might have been able to figure out what motivated Vitory, but he wouldn't have hesitated to wipe them all out, and that must have been what convinced Vitory to cooperate. The warlord seemed almost relieved to at last measure Connor's resolve. He didn't know what that meant for the future of their alliance, but the warlord had seen something that gave him pause.

Connor pushed thoughts of the warlord out of his mind and went to oversee the rescue.

18

Jon Walker peered through the window at the Raven Class Scout Ship SR-01. He'd only been on Phoenix Station for seventy-two hours and was expected to depart soon, whether his crew was finalized or not. Colonel Cross had been adamant that she'd try to get his top pick for his XO but wouldn't delay the mission for it.

"You know, it's bad luck to take a ship out that doesn't have a name."

Jon snorted a little and turned around. "Lieutenant Oscar Rutland, you're late. We're shipping out, or hadn't you heard?"

Oscar glanced out the window, looking at the ship.

"Technically, I'm not late for anything. I haven't committed to going on this mission just yet," Oscar replied.

Jon rolled his eyes. "I figured this would be right up your alley —a somewhat prototype ship. It's never seen any action before and has hardly been through a shakedown cruise. And," he said, smiling wryly, "we get to take it into hostile territory."

Oscar folded his arms in front of his chest. "If you're trying to sweet-talk me into coming on this mission, you're not doing a very good job. And," he said, holding up one finger, "this mission is still voluntary. You're not going to strong-arm me into this like you did the last time."

Jon rolled his eyes. "Which time was that?"

Oscar stared at him for a moment, then turned and started to walk away.

"Hang on," Jon said quickly. "Hang on. I was kidding. Did you have a chance to look at the mission briefing?" he said in a more serious tone.

Oscar stopped walking and nodded. "Operation Sherlock. Who the hell comes up with these names?"

"That would be Colonel Cross. I think if you go far enough back in her ancestry, she's probably some kind of royalty. I do agree though. I don't know how some twentieth-century detective is going to help us with this, but I really don't care what they call this mission. They could call it Operation Finding Lost Kittens and it wouldn't matter. This is important," Jon said.

Oscar probably wouldn't believe that Jon had been just as reluctant as he was about this mission. Colonel Cross had brought him around like a bucket of ice water being poured over his head, but Jon had other ways to get Oscar on board.

"So, what can this ship do? What makes it so special?" Oscar asked.

"Well, for one, it was designed by the CDF. We didn't use any design specs from the NA Alliance Military, so you could say it's a bit of an original," Jon said, smiling. "It's designed for stealth recon; however, it can also run electronic countermeasure operations. She can jam transmissions, scramble signals of guided weapons, and assist Talon-V operations. Here, have a look at the specs."

Jon made a passing motion with his hand and sent the ship specs to Oscar's PDA. Oscar opened his personal holoscreen and began reading. "No weapons to speak of, just some countermeasures. Oh, here it is—some midrange hornet missiles."

"Our best weapons are stealth and speed. Believe it or not, that ship out there is one of the fastest ships in the CDF fleet," Jon replied.

"You do realize that the Krake ships are faster than ours. What if they detect us?"

"Impossible," Jon said, confidently. "Our cross section is much too small. If they could scan us with that much accuracy, they'd already know where we are."

"We don't even know what kind of scanners they have," Oscar countered.

Jon tilted his head toward Oscar. "Well, it's right here in the intelligence briefing summary on Krake ship capabilities," he said, sending the briefing over to Oscar. "It says 'don't get caught with your pants down or they'll eat you.'"

Another briefing appeared on Oscar's personal holoscreen. "For crying out loud, it doesn't say that," Oscar groused, peering at the holoscreen intently.

"You're right, it doesn't. It says they likely have similar scanning capabilities to ours. Their weapons are powerful, and they have faster ships, but they do have limits— What? I read the damn briefing. Don't give me that," Jon said with a bit of incredulity in his voice.

Oscar read the briefing for a few moments more and then looked at Jon. "Why did you ask for me? You could have had your pick of anyone."

Jon regarded him for a moment, allowing some of his bravado to slip. "I trust you, Oscar. We've been through a lot. And we've completed countless salvage runs on Vemus ships. Once the war was over, people seemed to forget all that wreckage in orbit nearby. We were among the crews to take care that. I just wanted somebody with me on the bridge that I knew and could trust."

Oscar pursed his lips in thought. "Bullshit," he said with a sneer and began to walk away.

Jon's mouth hung open for a few moments. "What do you mean 'bullshit'? It's true. I meant every word," he said, catching up to him.

Oscar glared at him. "That's not the reason, and you know it."

Jon inhaled deeply and sighed. "I need a good second-in-command just in case."

"Just in case what, Jon? Ever since your brother died on that ship, you've been keen to take on the riskiest missions. The only problem is, you're reckless about it. This time there's a crew of what," he said, glancing at the ship for a moment, "forty or fifty people?"

"It's forty-nine right now. You'd make fifty," Jon said. "And I'm not like that anymore."

"I'm tired of cleaning up your messes," Oscar said and was quiet for a few moments. Jon thought it was best not to say anything. "Do they know about you? Does Colonel Cross know about your record?"

"They came to me," Jon said. A flash of irritation made heat flush his cheeks. "They recruited me for this mission. Colonel Cross said she wanted somebody in command who had experience doing reconnaissance among enemy ships. She also wanted somebody who wasn't afraid to take some risks."

Oscar licked his lips and thought about it for a few seconds. "Oh," he said quietly. "I hadn't realized that."

Jon nodded. "You should probably know that Madelyn is part of the crew."

Oscar's mouth hung open a little. Then he shook his head. "You really are something else. Just to confirm, you're talking about *my* Madelyn, right? Madelyn Kniffin."

"This isn't my doing, Oscar. I wouldn't have done that to you. She was already assigned to the crew before I took command of the mission. She's the lead engineer on the ship."

Oscar closed his eyes and shook his head. Then, he took a few steps away with his hands on his hips and looked out the window at the ship. A long airlock tube connected to it from Phoenix Station, and docking clamps secured the ship in place.

"Oh," Oscar mumbled.

"Oh, *now* it's different. *I* ask you and it's all, 'No, Jon, you're just being reckless. Do they know about your record? They can't possibly have the right man for the job.' But if it just so happens that one Sergeant Madelyn Kniffin is serving on the crew, then one Lieutenant Oscar Rutland just can't help himself," Jon said grandiosely.

"Oh, it's not like that and you know it. I made a promise that I'd watch out for her," Oscar said.

"I've seen you in the room with her. This isn't just a mere promise," Jon said and quickly added, "but anyway, that's your personal business. What I need to know is whether you're volunteering for Operation Sherlock."

Oscar looked at him like a man who'd just lost a bet. "I officially volunteer for Operation Sherlock. And try not to look so smug about it."

Jon grinned. "I knew you were going to volunteer."

"I know you're my superior officer, but don't push me."

Jon's smile turned into a grin. After a moment, Oscar joined him.

"I'm glad to have you aboard. I mean that."

They walked together in silence for a few moments.

"Hey, I'm sorry for giving you such a hard time," Oscar said.

"You weren't all wrong. Some of that stuff probably needed to be said. No worries now."

"Where are we going?" Oscar asked.

"I need to take you to see Colonel Cross. She has the final say on the crew," Jon said.

Jon led Oscar through Phoenix Station, and before long, they were sitting in Colonel Cross's office while she read through

Oscar's record on her personal holoscreen. A few moments later, she made a swiping gesture and the holoscreen diminished.

"Lieutenant Rutland, I need you to confirm that you understand this mission is entirely voluntary, and that neither myself nor Captain Walker here have coerced you in any way to take this mission," Colonel Cross said.

"I understand the mission parameters, Colonel Cross. I freely volunteer and hope that my service will help achieve our objective," Oscar replied.

"Excellent. I'm glad we have that out of the way. Captain Walker will bring you up to speed en route to the space gate," Colonel Cross said.

"I thought we had another day, Colonel." Jon said.

"We're moving up the timetable. General Gates and quite a few others want this mission under way. The ship is stocked, as they say, gentlemen. Not much of a shakedown cruise, but we know it won't fall apart either." Colonel Cross paused and regarded them both. "This mission won't be by the book. It's one of the reasons I requested the crew I did. However, having said that, this is not an excuse to throw your lives away. I expect a certain amount of risk to be accepted by you and the crew, but do keep in mind that some risks are not worth taking. I'd much rather have you return with your ship intact than lose any of you to the Krake. It's not that kind of mission. Is that understood?"

"Yes, sir," Jon said, with Oscar echoing the same.

"Good. I'm glad we have that out of the way, too," Colonel Cross said and directed her gaze to Jon. "We have a space gate farther out in the system that you requested. At best speed, you should be able to reach that gate in a few hours. After that, we'll continue to operate the space gates at the predefined hours in the mission briefing. Make no mistake, gentlemen. We're sending you into hostile territory without a way to get home."

Jon sat up a bit straighter. "We understand the risk, Colonel. If it's all the same, I'd like to get to my ship. The sooner we can leave, the sooner we can get back."

Colonel Cross stood up and so did Jon and Oscar.

"Very well. Good luck and happy hunting. We're depending on you to get us some answers," Colonel Cross said.

They left her office, not saying anything as they walked down the corridor.

"I'll need to have my things sent aboard the ship," Oscar finally said.

Jon smiled. "I already had your stuff sent aboard."

"Is that so? Do you also offer a comfortable work environment and an afternoon turndown service? I like my morning coffee fresh."

"We can arrange all that. And you'll be bringing me *my* coffee," Jon said, arching an eyebrow. "With nothing extra, I might add. Don't need a repeat of—well, anything that might've happened before."

"I understand, Captain," Oscar replied. "If it's not too much trouble, I'd like to tour the ship once we get underway."

"That can be arranged. I think you'll find the main engineering section particularly interesting," Jon replied solemnly.

Oscar nodded. "I think you're right."

They grinned and hastened down the corridor. Jon sent a message on ahead to the tactical officer on duty to start the preflight checks before they got on board. He didn't want to waste any time now. The clock was ticking.

19

THE RAVEN CLASS scout ship only had one command bridge located amidships. Jon sat in the commander's chair of what could scarcely be called a bridge. They weren't quite crammed on top of one another, but it also wasn't what anyone would consider overly spacious. Both the pilot's and the tactical officer's workstations were set side by side. Oscar sat at the alternate tactical workstation to Jon's right. To his left was officially the operations workstation, but it was being manned by Specialist Amber Vandercamp. Amber was the resident expert on space gates. Jon hadn't wanted somebody who knew the theoretical concepts of how space gates worked; he wanted someone who'd actually worked with them. Thankfully, Colonel Cross had agreed and approved the transfer.

They'd put Phoenix Station behind them over an hour earlier and were heading to a space gate they'd positioned out near Gigantor's orbit.

Jon glanced at Oscar, who had his lips pursed and was nodding approvingly at the data on his holoscreen.

"Our engine output is at peak performance. We won't be at the space gate for another two hours, but we could cut down that time considerably if you wanted, Captain," Oscar said.

"It's tempting, but I don't want to thread any needles before we've had a chance to begin," Jon said. His comment drew a few chuckles from the bridge crew. That was a good sign. "Maybe on the way back."

The Raven may not have packed an offensive punch, but the stealth recon ship was jam-packed with some impressive equipment. They'd had to limit the number of crew serving aboard the ship because of advanced stealth recon systems. Jon reviewed the ship's systems, deciding whether he intended to alter the plan.

Jon looked away from his holoscreen to watch his crew for a moment. They were all quietly working, diligently going over their responsibilities, but there was very little they could do until they actually went through the space gate. The closer they came to it, the more he could feel the tension build. It could have been just him, but he doubted it. He'd never gone to another universe, but he'd led quite a few missions among hostile ships. Mostly, they'd been from combat shuttles or salvage ships with squads of heavily armed soldiers.

Jon stood up and stretched his arms overhead. He took in a deep breath and exhaled. Corporal Bruce Wente, a short man not much more than five-foot-nine, glanced at him from the pilot seat.

"It feels good," Jon said. "Go for it, Corporal."

Corporal Wente hesitated for a mere second or two and then stood up. He held his arms up over his head and stretched. Then he rolled his shoulder and stretched his neck from side to side. Jon could hear it pop and had to suppress a shudder. Hearing anything like knuckles or backs cracking had always bothered him.

"Am I right?" Jon asked and then added, "It gets the blood flowing."

"It does," Corporal Wente replied.

"Anyone else?" Jon asked, and even though he received a few speculative glances, no one else rose to their feet. "Come on Lieutenant Rutland, Lieutenant Watkins, up and at 'em," Jon said and turned toward Specialist Vandercamp, his eyebrows raised questioningly.

After a few moments, they got on their feet and did some in-place stretching.

"It's good to loosen up a little bit. I think we'll have plenty of time at our respective stations," Jon said.

"Perhaps this would be a good time to go over the mission objectives again, sir," Oscar said.

Jon nodded. "Sounds good to me. We're looking for Trident Battle Group. In the absence of any of the ships, we're supposed to figure out what happened to them. We also need to take a closer look at the NEC."

"What's the NEC, sir?" Corporal Wente asked.

"New Earth Candidate. It would be too confusing to travel to alternate universes and refer to anything like our home as New Earth. So, they'll receive designations with NEC, followed by a number that will be assigned. Since we haven't gone anywhere else yet, we're just calling this one NEC."

"Why do they want us to take a closer look? The reports from the planetary mission indicate that the Krake are no longer there, and General Gates hasn't received any signal from the Trident Battle Group," Specialist Vandercamp said.

"Therein lies the rub," Jon replied. "The drone reconnaissance from Phoenix Station through the space gates shows that the NEC doesn't match the planetary profile for the planetary missions General Gates was on. Believe me, I was just as surprised as you are. Regardless, it's our job to have a look."

Lieutenant Andy Watkins was one of his two tactical officers. His relief was currently off duty. Like most tactical officers Jon had ever worked with, Watkins had a highly analytical mind. His brows were often furrowed as if he was lost in deep thought.

"I've been going through the mission objectives, as well as the plans proposed to achieve those objectives, and there's something I'm struggling with," Watkins said. Jon nodded for him to continue. "It would take too long for us to fly and recon the whole star systems ourselves. I noticed that the briefing from CDF Intelligence wants us to assume there's some sort of Krake presence in the star system."

"That is correct. We are to operate as if there are enemy ships in the area," Jon replied.

"If we take a slow and measured approach, then we minimize the risk of being detected by the enemy, but you intend for us to move quite a bit faster than that," Watkins continued.

"I can see where you're going with this," Jon said. "We can't avoid the enemy. If they're there, as soon as we start poking around, at some point they're going to detect us—even this ship. What we *can* do is minimize the risk, and that's the plan I put forth. It's the plan we are going to execute."

There were about twenty seconds of enduring silence on the bridge and Jon continued. "The CDF spared no expense when they put this ship together. We have a lot of equipment on here that's going to be used, and much of it isn't going to come back with us. I intend to use everything at my disposal to achieve our objective. We're not going home empty-handed. One way or another, we're going to find out what happened to Trident Battle Group."

"I understand that," Watkins replied quickly. "Trident Battle Group would've gone straight to the planet once they'd gone through the space gate."

"We're going to do the same thing, but we're going to take a different route. My best guess is that they could've spent two or three days maximum before whatever happened to them happened," Jon said, enjoying the discussion. This was what got people working the problem instead of just thinking about it.

"So, the question is," Oscar said, joining the conversation, "where has Trident Battle Group been for the past three months? If they had communications capabilities, they would've responded to any one of the comms drones that've been sent through the space gate. I don't see how all communications capability across the entire battle group could malfunction at the same time, so we can rule out equipment failure."

"If they fought a battle with the Krake, we should be able to find wreckage," Watkins added.

"That's the idea. That's why we're going—" Jon began, but an alert appeared on the main holoscreen, indicating they were on their final approach to the space gate. "We'll continue this later. Right now, get back to stations."

There were three other space gates deployed throughout the star system in addition to the one at Phoenix Station. They were powered by their own reactors and had three CDF destroyer class warships along with missile-defense platforms just in case anything hostile came through the space gate while it was active.

Jon transferred his authentication to the space gate protection detail, and they activated the gate for him. Major Joseph Lovelace, commanding officer of the *Ardant,* sent them off.

Jon watched the live video feed on the main holoscreen. The space gate, even in its smallest iteration, was large enough to accommodate a CDF destroyer but could expand to accommodate a heavy cruiser. The CDF destroyer was about four times the tonnage that the Raven class scout ship was, so they had plenty of room to fly through.

Jon noted that the approach vector Corporal Wente executed would put them through dead center, and the pilot in Jon heartily approved. There was nothing quite like being dead-on balls accurate.

They transitioned through the space gate and beamed a transmission back through it. Jon switched the live video feed to the aft sensors, hoping to glimpse their home universe before the gateway was closed. He peered at the main holoscreen but couldn't find the gateway.

Jon had almost expected to feel something as he went through the space gate, but there wasn't anything. They were simply at one point in space and then were in another, much like walking through a doorway.

Jon turned his attention to the task at hand.

"Specialist Vandercamp, set Condition Two throughout the ship," Jon said.

An automated ship-wide broadcast was announced to all fifty crewmembers. Condition Two indicated that a threat was probable but not present. Although a certain amount of crew readiness was expected, it wasn't as much as full readiness in a combat situation. They would be at Condition Two until they left the star system.

"Lieutenant Watkins, I want passive scans of the system. Corporal Wente, plot a course for the NEC. Lieutenant Rutland, begin our deployment of the heavy decoys," Jon said.

The heavy decoys were equipped with a small scanner array that was capable of doing active scans. They'd been enhanced with a subspace communication module that would allow them to send and receive data in almost real time—at least within the three-to-five-minute window they had for a subspace communication channel to remain active. Jon planned to use the decoys' scanning capabilities as a way of getting an active blueprint of the star system much quicker than if he had to rely on only the ship's scanners.

Jon noticed Specialist Vandercamp watching him and bobbed his head in an unasked question.

"I finally get it, sir. The heavy decoys. You're going to use them to throw the Krake off our track," Specialist Vandercamp said.

"That's the idea," Jon replied.

"Sir, I realize my expertise is mainly around space gate operations, but would you mind if I asked another question, please?"

"No worries. Ask away."

"Our scanner array on the ship is much more powerful than on the heavy decoys. Wouldn't we just use our own scanner array and then, in the event that the Krake detect us, activate the heavy decoys' limited scanner array? With the subspace communicator, we can activate the scanners on the heavy decoys within seconds of the enemy detecting our active scan pulse."

Jon shook his head. "It would be too late by then. Even our own combat AI on any warship would advise us to focus on the first initial scan burst. I suspect the Krake would see right through it if we took that approach. What I intend to do is coordinate using the scanners in the heavy decoys. I want active data once we've deployed all of them."

Specialist Vandercamp frowned for a moment, thinking about what Jon had told her. "I see. That's much better than what I was thinking."

"Nonsense. You can't know what you haven't studied yet. Would you like to shadow Lieutenant Watkins at tactical?" Jon asked.

Her eyes widened and gleamed all at once. "I would appreciate that, sir," she replied.

"Captain," Oscar said quickly, "I'd be happy to have Specialist Vandercamp join me and go over some of the tactical approaches we've decided on for this mission."

"That's fine," Jon said, and Specialist Vandercamp scurried over to sit with Oscar.

Then, they waited.

THEY SPENT the next twelve hours making slow but steady progress toward the NEC. Their course wasn't a straight shot to the planet because they were deploying the heavy decoy drones. Once they were ejected, they'd travel to a predefined set of coordinates using corrective thruster capabilities and momentum from the Raven.

Jon had just gotten to the galley to have a quick bite to eat before heading to the bridge. Lieutenant Watkins and Specialist Vandercamp joined him.

"Sir, how'd you get selected for this mission?" Vandercamp asked.

Watkins closed his eyes and looked away for a moment, and Jon merely chuckled.

"Did I say something wrong?" Specialist Vandercamp asked quickly.

"Not every CO enjoys having someone ask how they got their current command posting," Jon said, smiling. "But I don't mind. I have a lot of experience."

"Salvage runs on Vemus ships," Watkins added quickly.

Vandercamp's eyes widened. Then she nodded. "Is that it? Meaning no disrespect of course, sir. But is that the only reason? I'm keenly interested in how the CDF selects people for their posts."

Jon leaned back in his chair and sipped his coffee. "Isn't that enough?" he asked and then set his coffee mug down on the table. "It wasn't just the salvage runs—at least that wasn't the only reason. Do you know how many people were assigned to the Trident Battle Group?"

Vandercamp frowned in thought. "Well, there were eleven ships—two heavy cruisers, eight destroyers, and one converted freighter that was used as a carrier. The crew was mostly CDF, but they did have civilian specialists on board." She paused for a moment and then shook her head. "A few thousand? I'm afraid I don't know."

"Two thousand, two hundred and ninety people," Jon said, and Watkins and Vandercamp went quiet. "Nearly twenty-three hundred, to make it easier. That's a lot of people. That's a lot of families and friends. Sisters," he said, his mouth going dry, "and brothers."

Jon swallowed hard. There wasn't a day that went by that he hadn't thought about his brother. If it hadn't been for Patrick, they might never have found a way to kill the Vemus. His brother had been all he had when he'd first come to the colony. He had close friends now, but he and his brother had been close.

"I suspect Colonel Cross was aware of this when she sought me out for this mission. After my brother died on the Vemus ship, I made sure no one else was left trapped on any salvage run. Granted, this is a bit different than those missions. I want to find them because if they did make the ultimate sacrifice, their families have a right to know what happened to them. You're part of that now," Jon said, and his two younger companions sat up a bit straighter. "It's time for us to get back to it. We'll be passing the NEC soon."

Jon stood up, and Watkins offered to clean up after them. He left the galley and headed to the bridge.

Oscar stood up from the commander's chair. "All clear, sir," Oscar said and went to his workstation.

He and Oscar were close friends, but on the bridge and while they were on duty, they followed CDF formal address.

"Thank you, Lieutenant Rutland."

The computing core on the Raven could rival that of a heavy cruiser. They had quite a bit of data storage, which would allow them to record the entire mission. The CDF had learned the value of going back over every piece of data they could collect that could potentially give them more insight into the Krake.

The image on the main holoscreen was of the NEC, and they could see the small cluster of an asteroid field that orbited the planet beyond the second moon. Jon had the high-res optics deployed so they could get detailed images of both the planet and the asteroid field. CDF intel suggested that the Krake space gate would be located near the planet.

"Anomaly detected," Lieutenant Watkins said. "The data analysis of the image shows what could be an enemy ship. It matches the profile of a Krake destroyer."

"Where?" Jon asked.

"Near the asteroid field. I'll put it on screen."

An image appeared on the main holoscreen. It was enhanced with the cyber warfare suite's AI analysis of the high-res optical feed. It could pick out the details much quicker than any of the crew could.

"Compare this image to what we have in our records and put it on screen," Jon said.

A sub-window opened on the main holoscreen showing the various profiles of a Krake destroyer. These images had been captured when the heavy cruiser *Vigilant* had engaged the enemy.

"A ninety percent match," Oscar said.

"Good enough for me. I want that ship designated as alpha," Jon said. "Has the computer detected any CDF ships?"

"Negative, Captain," Lieutenant Watkins replied.

Jon suspected as much but had to ask anyway. "Scan the data for any other ships in the area," Jon said.

"Yes, Captain," Lieutenant Watkins replied.

The two images minimized to a much smaller sub-window, and the main holoscreen went back to a star-field view with the NEC featured prominently. Jon's gaze drifted toward the current image of the enemy ship. All the reports he'd read indicated that the Krake destroyers had superior speed when compared with a CDF warship. The Raven was built for speed and stealth, but he didn't want to put it to the test against the Krake destroyer. If it came to it, the best he could hope for would be that they had enough of a head start to get away from them and escape the universe through an egress point.

Jon glanced at the others on the bridge and saw more than a few of them looking at the image of the Krake destroyer. Jon decided to remove it but left the designation and location highlighted on the main holoscreen.

For the next few hours, the Krake destroyer didn't move, remaining in orbit around the NEC. The planet was going through a severe Ice Age that reached almost to the equatorial line. Any living thing that couldn't adapt to the severe cold temperatures would likely die. Jon looked at it and shuddered. God, he hated the cold weather, but he loved working in space. He made a point to go to New Earth, but more than half his time was spent serving at the lunar base and Phoenix Station.

"Tactical, put a plot up on the main holoscreen, and I want to see the locations of the heavy decoys we've deployed," Jon said, then added, "Keep the alpha on the screen as well."

Less than a minute later, the main holoscreen showed a star map. Thirty blinking white dots appeared like a string of pearls across the star system from a distance of Gigantor's orbit, which was over seven hundred million kilometers from the star.

Jon peered at the main holoscreen. With the current deployment of the heavy decoys, they had just enough coverage for the star system's interior planets. However, if Trident Battle Group had had to retreat to the outer system of planets, they might still be able to scan them, but it would take longer and increase the risk of the Krake detecting them. If Trident Battle Group had fought the Krake here, then why would they have let the CDF retreat at all?

Jon pressed his lips together and furrowed his brow in thought. There was no sign of any CDF ships near the NEC, so he could pretty much rule out them taking any sort of refuge on the ice planet. Jon couldn't imagine Colonel Quinn abandoning all his ships without leaving any sort of comms drone out in the system. Whatever was there to find would be away from the NEC and probably wouldn't be beyond Gigantor's orbit.

Jon looked at Oscar. "I think we're ready to kick over a few stones. What do you think?"

"Agreed, Captain. We'll need just a few minutes to bring up the sub-comm network," Oscar replied.

"Very well. Do it."

Jon leaned back in the commander's chair, feeling his elbows push into the contours of the padded armrests. He opened a broadcast channel to the ship. "Crew of the *Raven*, this is the captain. Since we haven't found any sign of Trident Battle Group, we're about to execute the next part of our plan. There's one enemy ship located near the NEC. When all the scanner arrays are brought online, the active scan pulses will no doubt alert the enemy to our presence. That was always the plan. Our gamble is that the enemy will pursue the heavy decoys, giving us a chance to investigate anything we detect. If we don't find any trace of Trident Battle Group, we'll head to the nearest egress point and go home. Be ready."

He closed down the broadcast comlink and looked at Oscar.

"Ready to scan, Captain."

"Execute," Jon said.

Active scan pulses utilized a range of different detection methods by scanner array. Any intelligent species monitoring the system would be able to detect an artificial pulse such as the one occurring at that moment. What the Krake destroyer was no doubt detecting was the presence of thirty active scan pulses throughout the interior of the star system all at the same time. The Raven was the snake in the grass, slithering undercover.

"Tactical, have the new data points detected put immediately on the main holoscreen," Jon said.

"Yes, Captain," Lieutenant Watkins replied.

Jon fixed his gaze on the main holoscreen. All the while he hoped—well, he hoped they detected something, but it would be better for them if it was close to this position rather than across the star system. If they did detect something worth investigating across the star system, they'd likely have to return at another time, unless Jon was of the disposition to risk another trek across the star system, hoping the Krake would overlook them a second time. It was too soon to tell about that.

The advantage of leveraging the heavy decoys equipped with subspace comms was that it essentially gave them an entire scanner array network that delivered data in real time. This was a huge tactical advantage. With each passing second, the main holoscreen updated the star field with various detections, but they all seemed to be relegated to normal astral bodies, such as meteors with high metal content.

A second enemy ship was detected in the asteroid field near the NEC.

"Captain, we've detected another anomaly. It's a metallic mass that's not located near anything else. The AI has put together an image that looks like partial ship wreckage, but it could just be the angle," Lieutenant Watkins said.

"Does it match any of the known CDF ship signatures?"

"Negative, Captain. However, it appears to be our best lead," Lieutenant Watkins replied.

"Enemy ships are on an intercept course for two of our heavy decoys," Oscar said.

"Very well, kill the scans for now. Initiate thrust maneuver for the decoys and arm the self-destruct for the two the Krake are so keen on investigating," Jon said. His orders were confirmed. "Corporal Wente, plot a course to the anomaly. Best speed," Jon said.

"Course laid in. Thirty minutes to destination, Captain."

Jon nodded appreciatively. The Raven was fast. "Add it to the plot, Corporal."

Jon brought up the image of the metallic mass on his personal holoscreen. The AI was taking a few liberties with filling in some of the gaps, but it definitely wasn't a natural astral body. That, of course, didn't mean that it was a CDF ship either, or even the wreckage of one. They needed a closer look.

"Lieutenant Rutland, how long until the enemy ships reach the heavy decoys?" Jon asked.

"Best guess is thirty minutes. They're the closest to the NEC, Captain."

Jon nodded, doing some quick calculations in his head. "I want another active scan pulse from those two heavy decoys only. Their vicinity to the NEC should let us know if any other ships—scratch that. I want active scan pulse from every heavy decoy but not the Raven. Let's do it in fifteen minutes."

"Roger that. Active scan pulse from heavy decoys in fifteen," Oscar confirmed.

Jon had initially thought to only use the two heavy decoys with enemy ships heading toward them but decided against it. The enemy already knew they were there. He'd get a more complete picture of the current status of the enemy response if he utilized all the heavy decoys. Since the Raven was farther out in the system, he didn't need to scan in that direction anymore. There'd been no enemy detections that far out, and there was no reason to believe the Krake had stationed any warships out this far. They had the capability, but there was very little need for them to be out there.

Fifteen minutes went by in the blink of an eye. The active

scans still only revealed two Krake ships, but they were closer to the heavy decoys than they'd anticipated. The Krake destroyers accelerated at speeds within the known capabilities they had on file. That was something at least. The question still remained as to whether the commanders of those Krake ships would call for backup.

They closed in on the anomaly and Jon ordered a concise scan burst, which limited the scan to ahead of the ship. Unless there was something else in that line of sight, this active scan would go undetected.

"Put the scan results on the main holoscreen. I want a good look at this thing," Jon said.

They closed in on the metallic mass. It looked to have been a part of a CDF ship, but most of it was missing.

"Captain, this is the aft section of a heavy cruiser. That's where the engine pods are, but they've taken extensive damage," Lieutenant Watkins said.

"I see that, but where the hell is the rest of the ship? What kind of weapon could do this? There's nothing else left."

"Captain, this might not be a weapon at all," Specialist Vandercamp said.

"Go ahead," Jon replied.

"This ship has been sheared off. See how it angles away at forty degrees? This is because the ship was in motion when the event horizon alignment within the space gate got distorted. Alignment must be maintained in order for a ship to transition through. When the gate machines are misaligned, everything gets severed, quite literally cutting anything and everything off. There is no fail-safe or safety mechanism for this. I think we're looking at the tail section of one of the heavy cruisers that was part of Trident Battle Group."

Jon peered at the image, thinking that everything Vandercamp had just said was making a lot of sense. "Tactical, is there any way to identify which heavy cruiser it is?"

"I'm working on it. We'll know more as we get closer," Lieutenant Watkins replied.

Jon frowned. He needed to know which ship that was. He glanced over at Specialist Vandercamp, who was smiling. "Do you have something else, Specialist?"

"This is a good thing, Captain," she replied and shook her head. "Not good for anyone left in that section of the ship, but for the rest of the battle group it means they're not here. They had a space gate with them, and they could've all gotten through except the aft section of that ship."

Jon's gaze flicked to the main holoscreen, trying to imagine what had happened there.

"I think she's right, Captain," Oscar said.

"It would explain the inability to find Trident Battle Group, but what about this ship?" Jon said, jutting his chin toward the screen. "Doesn't look like there's any power, but that wouldn't have happened right away. One of the fusion reactors is located in that part of the ship. Bulkhead doors were closed. How do we know there isn't somebody trapped in there?"

"It's been three months," Oscar replied. "Field rations and survival equipment don't account for that length of time, even on escape pods, which we haven't detected."

"Captain, that ship is the *Douglass*. The designation numbers are on the far side of the hull," Lieutenant Watkins said.

"I want to take a closer look at it," Jon said.

"Yes, Captain. I'll slow us down so we can have a closer look," Corporal Wente replied.

The hull looked as if something had scraped off the outer layer of the battle steel alloy. Jon had never seen anything like it. He turned toward Specialist Vandercamp.

"Does the damage to the ship match with a misaligned space gate?"

She frowned for a moment in thought. "I don't know for sure, Captain. I wouldn't have the data here with me, but given the evidence, what else could it be?"

"Fair enough," Jon said.

He tried to think how many of the crew would have been trapped, wondering if anyone could have survived. How had this happened? Had Trident Battle Group fought the Krake here and, while fleeing, this disaster had happened? No other ships had been detected, not even the wreckage of Krake ships. There would surely be more wreckage if an actual battle had been fought here, but it had been three months. Where had Trident Battle Group gone?

The Raven circled around the remains of the *Douglass*, scanning the remnants of the hull.

"Captain, there's something—oh my God—there's an enemy ship attached to the hull. New class, smaller than a Krake destroyer," Lieutenant Watkins said.

Jon watched the main holoscreen, and his mouth dropped open as the enemy ship came online. It was using docking clamps that were attached to the hull.

"Pilot, best speed to nearest egress point. Go emergency!"

"Nearest egress nav point entered, Captain," Corporal Wente replied.

Klaxon alarms sounded throughout the Raven, and the crew strapped themselves in. Jon felt himself pressed into his seat despite the inertia dampeners compensating for the thrust of the powerful ship engines.

"Enemy ship in pursuit," Lieutenant Watkins said. "Attack drones have been fired."

Jon's first instinct was to launch countermeasures, but he waited. "Understood, Lieutenant."

"Captain, shouldn't we—" Oscar began to say but stopped himself.

"Tactical, ready countermeasures but wait to fire them until I give the order," Jon said.

Jon watched as the enemy combat drones raced to catch up to them. The Raven was fast, but the drones were even faster. The limiting factor of a spaceship's speed was the crew themselves. Ships without any life-forms on them didn't have to worry about keeping their crews alive. Also, the human body didn't react very well when approaching anywhere near relativistic speeds. The attack drones had no such limitations and would intercept them.

"Captain, we're not going to reach the egress point in time," Corporal Wente said.

Jon cursed and glared at the plot on the main holoscreen. His first instincts were those of a combat pilot, and that was to go as fast as he could. "Redo the calculations, Corporal, but don't slow down for the egress point."

"Captain, I don't think I can do that," Corporal Wente replied.

"Do you want me to fly the ship, Corporal?"

Corporal Wente's brows drew together and he looked to Oscar for help.

"Corporal, you can either thread the needle or you can't. If you can't, let me know so I can get someone who can, or do it myself."

Corporal Wente's face went pale and he shook his head.

"Lieutenant Rutland, take control of the helm," Jon said.

"Yes, Captain, I have control of the helm," Oscar said.

A few moments passed. "It's going to be close, Captain."

The plot on the main holoscreen updated. It showed Krake attack drones gaining on them, but the time to reach the egress point had decreased significantly.

Jon looked at Specialist Vandercamp. "Is the gateway there?"

"Not yet, Captain," she replied.

Jon cursed. The space gates in the home system were

scheduled to open at specific time intervals. He'd almost hoped that whoever was in charge of that space gate would open it earlier. Either they were going to overshoot the space gate, in which case the enemy drones would likely finish them off, or they could open fire while they were trying to transition, in which case they might not make it. They could end up in a worse state than that of the *Douglass*.

Close indeed.

"Captain, enemy attack drones are closing in," Lieutenant Watkins said.

"Wait," Jon replied. "A few more seconds. They've got to get closer," he said, almost to himself. He watched the main holoscreen with rigid intensity. The attack drones had just passed fifteen hundred meters. "Now! Launch all countermeasures!"

Lieutenant Watkins slammed his hand on his console. "Countermeasures launched."

Jon's gaze swooped to the space gate indicator on the main holoscreen, and it suddenly flickered to life. They raced through the gateway a half a second after it had been formed. They were going so fast that the CDF destroyers on the other side had scarcely acknowledged them.

"Fire braking thrusters. We need to slow down and report in," Jon said and transmitted his clearance to the CDF fleet so they wouldn't shoot them down. No doubt that they were targeting him, and no matter how fast he was going, he couldn't escape their missile-defense platforms.

"They've closed the space gate," Specialist Vandercamp said.

Jon blew out a long breath and laughed. "Good work, everyone," he said. Corporal Wente looked away from him. "Corporal, it's okay. You were doing what you were trained to do."

Oscar gave a nod and went over to Corporal Wente's workstation.

"Tactical, begin preparing all the data that was collected and upload to COMCENT," Jon said.

"Yes, Captain," Lieutenant Watkins said.

Oscar came over to him and Jon stood up.

"That was really close," Oscar said.

"You've got that right."

"I didn't think the gateway was going to open in time."

Jon glanced at Vandercamp. "Sometimes you just have to have a little faith. It was either that or we would've died. I'm happy with the current results."

Oscar regarded him for a few moments. "No one could have been on that ship."

Jon felt the smile drain away from his face. They'd gotten away, and that was a good thing. He met his friend's gaze. "We'll never know. They were waiting for us to come look for them."

"That may be, but they're not going to learn anything from us or from the heavy decoys we left behind. I set them all to self-destruct. There's nothing left of them."

Jon nodded and tried not to think about the CDF soldiers that had served on the *Douglass*. If any of them had survived, they were prisoners of the Krake. Who knew what was happening to them or had already happened to them? Vandercamp was right. At least they knew that Trident Battle Group had escaped the Krake. They just had no idea where they were now.

20

IT'D BEEN A FRUSTRATINGLY long night filled with planning, then hauling out debris while trying to prevent further shifts in the wreckage. Once on task, the Ovarrow worked with dogged determination whether soldiers or laborers. Vitory, after seeing how much faster they could reach the victims with the help of the colonists, had agreed to allow the CDF Search and Rescue team to help them at the other site. But tensions between the two species were still much too high. Connor didn't need to be an expert in diplomacy to understand that. He'd been receiving steady reports of Ovarrow soldiers gathering just outside the affected areas.

Connor glanced at the people they'd been able to save, seeing Lenora bob her auburn head in response to the medic's questions. She was covered in dirt and debris, and there were shallow cuts on her hands and cheeks. Someone else's blood was on her pants. She looked at him and smiled. The Search and Rescue team had only just managed to pull them out of the wreckage. Connor watched her and tried to temper his emotions, but his throat tightened. Her gaze was a mixture of relief and shock at what she'd been through. She'd saved lives down there. That's what he'd been told, but they'd lost a lot of lives, too.

Unable to wait any longer, Connor walked over to her.

The medic looked at him. "She's fine. Just a little bruised and scraped. A little dehydrated. Keep drinking that water. You were very lucky, Dr. Bishop."

Lenora thanked him, and Connor used his implants to access the MPS jacket she wore. He quickly skimmed the log entries of the suit's activities and his brows furrowed.

"I'm fine," Lenora said.

"I know, but you almost weren't. If you hadn't been wearing the jacket—why didn't you wear the pants?" Connor said and squeezed his eyes shut for a moment. "Never mind, I don't care. You're here. That's all that matters."

Lenora flew into his arms, and Connor gave himself this moment to forget everything that was happening around him. It didn't last long enough.

Lenora pulled away and looked around. "Who else were you able to save?"

"Darius and some of the people he was with. Not all of them. We've reached all the survivors we're going to reach. Now, we'll have to work on retrieving the people who didn't make it."

Lenora looked over at the other survivors. The Ovarrow had been taken to a separate location as soon as they were able. They'd pulled out twenty-one people, and eight more were unaccounted for.

Connor followed her line of sight. "Is that Kayla Wolf?"

Lenora nodded. "Yes, and the girl next to her is Lynn. There was another intern named Devon, but he didn't . . ." Her voice cracked.

"Hey, none of that now," Connor said soothingly. "You did everything you could and a good deal more. You saved that girl's life. You also helped the Ovarrow trapped with you. Lenora, I'm so proud of you."

Lenora's eyes became misty, and she hastily wiped away tears.

"Do you remember where Dash was when the bridge collapsed?" Connor asked.

Lenora shook her head. "He wasn't with us. He'd left the group before we even came to the bridge. He was with Jory."

Samson walked over and joined them. "The other SAR team reported in. The bridge collapse over there wasn't as bad as this one, but there were more injuries. There have been thirty-two casualties so far. The Ovarrow soldiers are insisting that the SAR team leave now."

"Understood. Did they get the scans they needed?" Connor asked.

"Affirmative."

"All right, get them out of there."

"I think someone wants to speak to you," Samson said, gesturing behind Connor.

Vitory was walking toward them, along with several soldiers. The Ovarrow looked at Connor for a moment in silent acknowledgment before looking at Lenora. A comms drone hovered near him, and he used the holo-interface.

"I've just learned that you saved the lives of my soldiers, including Cerot, my First. I was told he would've died were it not for you," Vitory said.

The Ovarrow waited for them to finish reading the message, and then all of them brought their right hands to their left shoulders and glided over their chests.

Connor had never seen the gesture before. He glanced at Lenora, who seemed to know what it meant.

"You're welcome," Lenora said.

A text message appeared on Connor's internal heads-up display.

D. DeWitt: *We need to talk.*

C. Gates: *Where are you?*

D. DeWitt: *I'm on my way to you. I don't want to send this over comlink.*

Darius joined them. Vitory and the others were watching Connor, and he looked at the translator interface.

"The rescue effort is almost finished. All of your people are accounted for. It's time for you to leave," Vitory said.

"We can help with the cleanup efforts. We will, of course, withdraw our soldiers from the city as agreed," Connor said.

"Your help will not be necessary. The terms of our agreement have been met," Vitory said.

The pre-morning gloom was giving way to a new day. There was a chill to the air, and Connor heard the wind turbines turning.

"I think we should respect their wishes, Connor," Darius advised.

Connor looked at the warlord. "We will leave now."

Orders were passed, and soon the Search and Rescue teams were being transported away. Within thirty minutes, Connor was boarding the last troop carrier to leave the city. Dash had joined them just a few minutes earlier. He hadn't said anything, and the Ovarrow had hardly reacted to Dash at all.

Connor walked to the front of the troop carrier and Dash followed him. Lenora was already on board, looking at one of the holoscreens.

Connor waved for Samson to join them, and after a few moments, asked Darius to come as well. "All right, where have you been? And tell me what you found out."

"Jory wanted to show me a new medical clinic he'd built. I was supposed to catch up with the others by the time they left the city. These bridges didn't just collapse because they were old. I went to the other site, and there were impact points indicating a sonic charge had been used, but there's also something else."

"Hold on," Darius said. "You're saying this wasn't an accident?"

Samson shook his head. "These structures have been here for hundreds of years through extreme weather. I'm surprised there aren't more accidents here."

Dash looked at Darius. "Yes, and I'll explain," he said and looked at Samson. "The materials they use in their construction are highly resistant to corrosion. The sonic charges targeted weak points in the support structure. So, someone did this, but they took advantage of someone else's work. The Ovarrow were already using their tools to weaken the support structure. I don't know why, but I've seen the results of their tools and have been in enough of their cities to know that the support structures would need some coaxing before a sonic charge would be able to finish the job."

Connor pressed his lips together for a moment, his thoughts racing. "I don't understand. Why would the Ovarrow do anything like this?"

"I don't know. Why would they send the envoy back through an alternative route rather than using the main thoroughfare?"

Darius shook his head. "This makes no sense. Cerot led us on that route. If he was involved, then why would he put his own life in danger like that?"

They were silent for a few moments. "Cerot couldn't have been involved, and Vitory seemed relieved that Cerot was okay," Connor said.

"That makes sense," Darius said. "Cerot is second-in-command of the Mekaal. Hierarchy is deeply respected among the Ovarrow."

Connor felt his mouth forming a grim line. "Unless we're dealing with someone like Siloc, a faction of Ovarrow that's loyal to the Krake. Who benefits if our alliance collapses?"

Dash nodded. "It's not just the Ovarrow. The sonic charges were colonial-made, which means—"

"That our rogue group of criminals was involved," Connor finished.

"This is something that Lars could do," Dash said.

"Yes, Lars Mallory has the skill set to do something like this, but we don't have any evidence that puts him there. I won't let this become a witch hunt, and Lars Mallory isn't working alone," Connor said, quickly quelling an accusation that could spiral out of control.

"It does mean they're changing their tactics," Samson said.

Connor shook his head in disgust, and Darius looked confused. "The rogue group's efforts hadn't put colonial lives in danger before." Dash started to say something, but Connor gestured for him to wait. "This is something different. This is more aggressive. They *wanted* a death toll with this. We need to analyze the scans and try to recreate what happened in a virtual environment. We need an official investigation, which means we need to get the colonial government involved."

Connor shared a look with Samson and Dash, but Darius frowned.

"I think I'm missing something here," Darius said.

"There are some of us who think this rogue group has been acting against our alliance with the Ovarrow, and anything related to it has support from someone high up in the colonial government."

Darius's eyes went wide. "It can't possibly be Governor Wolf."

"I agree. She's not my first choice. And the fact that her daughter was here pretty much rules her out, unless we're all underestimating her."

"Who do you think it is?" Darius asked.

"I'm not sure. I don't think it's a 'who,' but more of a 'they'— a group, a conspiracy if you will," Connor replied.

Darius sighed heavily and his shoulders slumped.

"You should go get some rest, Darius."

Darius nodded. "I will. I just can't believe this. They might've succeeded. This disaster is a major setback for the alliance."

"They still need our help. They don't have the transportation capabilities to retrieve the stasis pods to increase their population, but I agree it doesn't look good all around." Connor rolled his shoulders and stretched his neck.

Darius left them, and Samson cleared his throat.

"We should do our own investigation and then allow the data to be accessed by the governor's office," Samson said.

"Agreed, but we don't have much time," Connor replied.

"We don't need that much time—probably just a few days at the most. Mind if I borrow your protégé here?" Samson asked and nodded toward Dash.

Connor smiled a little. "Yeah, just be careful not to break him."

Dash snorted. "Protégé," he said and stood up to follow Samson.

"Hey, Dash, you did good. Keep it up."

Dash smiled and then turned around and left.

Lenora bounded over to him with a wide grin.

"Did you just see Lauren?" Connor asked. He wanted to see their daughter, too.

"I did see her, and she's fine. Ashley is with her, but I have news," Lenora said, brimming with excitement. She put her hand on Connor's arm and squeezed it. "Noah is awake."

Connor was sure he hadn't heard her right. Lenora repeated herself. Of all the things she could've told him right then, that was by far and away the least likely. He looked at her. "Awake," he said. "How?"

"She didn't say."

"Who didn't say?"

"Ashley. She was home, and she just got the call when I was speaking to her," Lenora replied.

Connor felt his lips curve upward in a genuinely heartfelt smile. Noah had awakened from his coma.

21

CONNOR WAS FINALLY HOME. It had taken another twelve hours to withdraw the CDF troops from outside the Ovarrow city. They'd also evacuated the camp just outside the city but left a colonial communication console for the Ovarrow to use if they wanted to contact them.

Connor heard Lenora and his daughter in the other room and resisted the urge to join them. He had a scheduled call with Darius and Governor Wolf. Listening to his daughter's squeals of delight, followed by Lenora's laugh, he knew that if he went into the room, he'd likely miss his call.

Lenora had stayed with him until he could return home, and they'd been home for less than a day, just the three of them. He kept watching Lenora, firm in the knowledge that he'd come dangerously close to losing his wife. Lauren had almost lost her mother. The thought still made him clench his teeth.

Lenora make a cooing sound, and Lauren's giggles became a full-on belly laugh. Connor stood up, thinking he'd just go in there for a minute. He had time before his meeting. He hastened over to the bedroom, but a warning chime appeared on his internal heads-up display, indicating that his call with Darius and Governor Wolf was about to begin.

Connor sighed and stepped outside his home. It was early afternoon, and thick clouds blanketed the sky with the promise of rain later on, perhaps sooner.

Connor activated his personal holoscreen and it split into two images. Darius Cohen appeared on one of the holoscreens and Dana Wolf appeared on the other.

"I wanted to make both of you aware of some of the evidence we've found," Darius said.

"Is the colonial diplomat's office involved with the investigation?" Connor asked.

"Of course we are. There's more going on here than simple relations with the Ovarrow," Darius said.

Connor glanced at Governor Wolf, who gave a firm nod. He had the CDF analyzing the scan data of the wreckage, and they were recreating a virtual model of what they thought happened with the two bridges based on empirical evidence.

"This evidence has already been shared with CDF Intelligence," Darius said, anticipating Connor's line of thinking. "We've been monitoring the Ovarrow since we helped them establish their settlement in the city. What we have is video surveillance evidence that supports Dash's theory that the Ovarrow had a hand in weakening the structural integrity of the two bridges that collapsed."

"Can you show it to us?" Governor Wolf asked.

Connor could still see the lines of worry on the governor's face. Her daughter had been there, too, and he could tell she wasn't in the mood for extending tolerance for half measures.

"Absolutely. I have three instances, but it's no—I'll let you look at it first, and then we can discuss it," Darius said.

A sub-window appeared on Connor's personal holoscreen, showing three video surveillance feeds. It looked like the stealth recon drones were making a routine patrol of the city, and the first video clip showed a group of Ovarrow gathering and working near the main support structure for the bridges.

"They could have been reinforcing it," Connor said.

"We've reviewed all the surveillance data, and this group of Ovarrow only came to these bridges in the middle the night. And only to the two bridges that collapsed," Darius replied.

"Do we have anything better that shows exactly what they are doing?" Connor asked.

He didn't want to jump to any conclusions. It was important that the facts led to a logical conclusion free of conjecture. At least, that was what Connor wanted to have happen, but things seldom worked out that way.

"No, the physical evidence is currently cut off from us, but we should have enough scan data of the area to make an accurate theory of how the bridges collapsed."

"So, the theory is that there was a group of Ovarrow who were weakening the supports to the bridges. Then, someone else comes along and uses a sonic disrupter to finish the job?" Connor said.

"Do you think these two groups were working together? The Ovarrow"—Governor Wolf's gaze became hard—"and the rogue group of miscreants that murdered eight colonists and twenty-two Ovarrow?"

Darius hesitated for a moment and then looked at Connor.

"I don't think so," Connor said. "I think the rogue group happened upon the weak points of the main support structure for the bridge. A simple integrity scan would reveal it, even from a reconnaissance drone—well, CDF reconnaissance drones and probably Field Ops as well. A civilian monitoring drone wouldn't have that amount of sophistication."

"Unless it's for research and development," Darius replied.

"Why would the Ovarrow do this to their own people?" Governor Wolf asked.

"We can't answer that. All we can do is speculate," Connor said. "We need to share this information with High Commissioner Senleon and Warlord Vitory. They'll conduct their own investigation and let us know the results. We can at least keep the lines of communication open with them."

"This needs to be handled delicately. They've cut off communication with us, and we shouldn't force this information on them; otherwise, it will seem like an intrusion," Darius said.

"He's right," Governor Wolf said. "We can't just dump this evidence in the Ovarrow's laps right now."

"Why would we wait?" Connor asked.

"The Ovarrow are trying to sever ties with us. Their last message indicated that they were content to wait to bring their people out of stasis, but not all Ovarrow feel that way. However, they're not convinced that we can stand against the Krake," Darius said.

"They might *think* they can sever ties with us, but they need us. I think waiting to tell them what really happened is a mistake in the long run," Connor said.

"Our own investigation isn't complete, so sharing anything with them at this point would be premature," Governor Wolf said, and Connor had to agree with her.

"But you do intend to share our findings with them, right?" Connor pressed.

Governor Wolf regarded him for a moment. "That decision will be made once the investigation is complete."

Connor shook his head. She was angry with the Ovarrow, and worse than that, she was afraid. She'd almost lost her daughter. Pressing his point at this moment wouldn't be smart.

"Why don't we just give them some space for a few days? Vitory will do his own investigation," Darius said and paused for a few moments. "If anything, this experience has taught the Ovarrow that they are vastly inadequate when it comes to a conflict with the Colonial Defense Force. This is a tough lesson for them to learn because they're trying to assert their independence."

Connor agreed with Darius. Maybe they all needed to take a few days to digest what had happened. The whole situation was a mess, and his own temper flared at the thought of it. The real stink of it was the fact that all the people involved—colonist and Ovarrow—had a part in it. He clenched his teeth for a moment and then forced himself to calm down.

"I've authorized the release of all the Ovarrow from Camp Alpha, and all further Ovarrow stasis retrieval efforts have been put on hold," Governor Wolf said. Connor looked at her sharply and she continued. "It's time the Ovarrow started holding up their end of the bargain. They need to provide credible intelligence about the Krake."

"Yes," Connor said, "but they've also awakened to a world they don't know, and the threat they'd hoped to avoid is still imminent."

"I understand that, but the Ovarrow will simply need to learn how to cope. Right now, I feel like they're taking advantage of what we have to offer—from the treatment of our diplomatic envoys to the events that took place during this disaster. They really thought they were going to keep us out of there," Governor Wolf said.

It would've been so easy for Connor to take the hard line of thinking regarding the Ovarrow's behavior, and that would have been extremely dangerous. Something he'd always known was that once they fired their weapons, they could never take it back. It was too easy to be angry with the Ovarrow.

"Are we asking so much from them that they're simply shutting down?" Darius asked and then added, "It's only been three months. We brought ten thousand of their population out of stasis. They must have had protocols for bringing their own people out, but we didn't know what they were. So, nothing about this entire situation is comfortable for the Ovarrow. Maybe 'comfortable' is the wrong word here, but everyone needs time to adapt, including the Ovarrow."

They were quiet for a few moments.

"I know firsthand what it's like to wake up and not be where I thought I was going to be," Connor said quietly.

He glanced at the others to see that his comment had had an impact on Darius and Governor Wolf. They knew what had happened to him. Connor wasn't supposed to have been on the *Ark*, but he was here—a two-hundred-year journey and sixty light-years from home. There was no going back for him. It had taken him a long time to come to terms with that.

"We'll table this discussion for the moment," Governor Wolf said and looked at Connor. "The Colonial Defense Committee will be reviewing a motion to give the CDF authorization to hunt down the rogue group responsible for the terrorist act in the Ovarrow city."

This was the first Connor had heard of this, and he said so.

"I expect the motion will pass. Nathan will attend in your stead. I thought you wanted to spend some time with your family," Governor Wolf said. "I need to thank you and Lenora. She saved my daughter's life," she said and paused for a few moments before continuing. "We need a plan to locate this rogue group as soon as possible."

"Dana," Connor said, using the Governor's first name, "we can locate their operations outside colonial cities, but I won't order anyone in the CDF to conduct an investigation inside any colonial city. That isn't the purpose of the CDF. You should also be aware that this is likely to get worse before it gets better, depending on who's involved."

Governor Wolf looked away for a moment. "They hurt my daughter," she said and looked at Connor. "They hurt her. She wasn't involved in this at all. She's innocent. There were a lot of innocent people who got hurt and others who died."

Connor met her gaze. "There were. We'll find who's responsible."

Governor Wolf leaned back from the video feed and gave a nod. Then the comlink to her office shut down.

Darius sighed. "Tempers are still pretty hot right now."

"I know, and I'm one of them. We can't keep going like this," Connor said.

"What are you going to do?" Darius asked.

Connor took a deep breath and exhaled. "I'll start doing some planning, but for the next few hours, I'm going to see a friend."

"I'd heard. Noah Barker has come out of the coma. That's amazing," Darius said.

"It is. He just started waking up on his own, is what I've been told. Darius, he always had a level head about this stuff. We need more of that right now," Connor said.

Darius gave him a long look and then nodded. The comlink closed. Connor was about to shut down the holoscreen when a new comlink registered on the screen. It was Savanah Cross.

Connor activated the comlink and took the call.

"General Gates, I'm so glad I caught you," Savannah said with a smile. "I have something to share with you that I knew you'd want to hear about right away. We found evidence that Trident Battle Group is no longer in the alternate universe. In fact, they went to a different universe altogether, which is why we haven't had any contact with them."

"Where are they?" Connor asked.

"We're not exactly sure, but we know that most of the ships made it through the space gate, which means they're still alive."

Connor had to stall his racing thoughts and process exactly what she was saying. He felt a tightening of his skin. "Okay, take me through this one step at a time."

22

CONNOR WALKED to the medical center. Lenora had more or less chased him out, claiming Lauren for her own, and gone off to do her own thing. It had been a few days since the attack at the Ovarrow city, and nothing regarding that incident required immediate attention. Connor knew that their own investigation into the collapse of the two bridges was complete; however, no report had been sent to the high commissioner of the Ovarrow. If it were up to Connor, he would've sent it over immediately

As the time went on, Connor became increasingly agitated. He could handle the pressures of command and even the standoff with the warlord, but these events had hit close to home. He wondered if it had all been orchestrated as a personal attack on him, and he also couldn't help thinking they'd been hoping to prevent an alliance with the Ovarrow. They might have delayed it, but what would they do next, and how many lives would it cost?

He could've gone to the CDF base. There was plenty of work to be done, but Nathan had insisted that he take a few days off. He'd decided to take Nathan's advice, but Lenora had her own ways of dealing with things. She was still shaken up over the whole thing. Being trapped under tons of wreckage was enough to rattle anyone's cage.

Connor walked up the large staircase that led to the Colonial Medical Center and went inside. He made his way to the long-term care wing, giving a friendly nod to the people he recognized, and went to Noah's room, but his friend wasn't there.

"Mr. Gates, if you're looking for Noah, he's out walking on the garden trails," the nurse said to him.

Connor thanked her and headed outside. There were other patients outside who were also recovering from whatever injuries they'd sustained. He spotted Noah walking in plain hospital attire, marking him as a patient. Noah saw him and waved.

Connor caught up to him. "Look who's up and about."

"That's me, making leaps and bounds. Couldn't stand being inside anymore," Noah said.

"I thought they wanted you to rest," Connor said.

"This is therapy—not physical therapy. My muscles don't need it; they didn't atrophy while I was in the coma. This is therapy for my brain," Noah said, tapping the side of his head. "They want me to get up and do things to help with my recovery."

"Makes sense, I guess," Connor said. After a few moments, he asked, "Do you remember anything that happened?"

"Bits and pieces. I remember fighting with Lars and falling off the cliff. People screaming . . . Dash. Kara filled me in on what happened after."

"We took out the archway," Connor replied.

Noah grimaced for a moment and then nodded. "I still can't believe how much time has passed. Ten months. It's hard for me to remember things, and what I do remember is fuzzy. I remember hearing your voice and Kara's. Lenora too. But it's weird—similar to a dream, or like I had something stuck in my ears. It's kinda hard to explain."

"We all came to see you. Do you remember sending me a message? A video log file before you found Lars?"

Noah frowned in thought, and then his eyes widened slightly. "I do . . . I remember making the video," he said and regarded Connor for a few moments. "It's funny because it was one of those last-minute things. I almost didn't do it." He rubbed the back of his neck and looked at Connor. "Did you do it?"

"Are you asking if I prayed for you? Yeah, Noah, I did. We thought you were dying."

Noah grinned, intrigued. "You actually prayed for me," he said, as if he couldn't quite imagine it.

Connor shook his head. "What do you take me for? A friend's last request—of course, I did."

"Yeah, but you . . . Well, you know."

It was no secret that Connor wasn't the most religious person. "I figured it couldn't hurt."

"Well, I appreciate it," Noah said.

They were quiet for a few minutes as they walked along the path. Connor noticed that Noah's shoulders were slumped just a little bit.

"Maybe we should sit down. Take a break," Connor suggested.

There were benches along the path, and they sat down on one.

"It's all right to pace yourself, you know. Three days ago, you were at death's door," Connor said.

"I feel like I've slept enough," Noah said with a bit of an edge to his voice. He looked away from Connor and shook his head. "I'm afraid to sleep. I'm worried that I won't wake up. Ashley told me that was normal—well, normal under the circumstances— but when I start to fall asleep, my mind races. What if I slip back into a coma and never wake up again?" Noah shivered at the thought.

"You've been through a lot, Noah. It's enough to shake anybody up. It'll just take time."

"And lots of rest and recovery," Noah said as if quoting the people who'd been telling him that. "Believe me, it's all I keep hearing about, but I don't want to rest. I want to do something. Go back to my work. I just want to go back to the way things were."

Noah was scared. That much was obvious, but Connor wasn't sure what to say. He decided to stay quiet and listen.

Noah arched an eyebrow. "No speeches about how I should make a full recovery or anything?"

Connor pursed his lips and bobbed his head to the side. "If there's anyone who could do it, it's you."

"That's the thing. It's like having a bunch of things at the edge of my thoughts, and I can't get to them. I want to think of them, and I feel like I should be able to do—well, anything really. What if that's the way it is now?"

"Then that's the way it is. You'll learn to live with it, but I think you're being a little too hard on yourself. You said it yourself. Your brain needs time to wake up."

Noah swallowed hard. "For me, it feels like it's only been a few days since the accident."

The muscles in Connor's shoulders went tight. "It wasn't an accident."

"Yes, it was. Lars didn't throw me off that cliff. He didn't mean to do it. We were fighting," Noah said.

"Give me a break, Noah. He may not have physically thrown you off the cliff, but he definitely created the situation where you fell."

Noah closed his eyes for a moment and looked as if he was trying to remember. He gritted his teeth and shook his head in frustration.

"Why don't we go get some food? Are you hungry?" Connor asked.

Noah opened his eyes and nodded. "I guess."

They headed back into the medical center and went to the cafeteria. As they got their food, many people greeted Noah and wished him well. Noah took it in stride. Connor thought his friend looked tired despite his assertions that he wasn't.

"Connor, can you do me a favor?"

Connor took a bite from his sandwich and put it down. "Sure. What?"

"Tell me what's been going on. Nobody really talks to me. Kara keeps telling me I need to rest and not worry about it. Ashley pretty much says the same thing. I did get to meet Lauren. She's cute. So, you're a dad now," Noah said.

Connor smiled. "Yes, I am, and dammit, Diaz was right about it."

"I hear he has a restaurant now."

Connor nodded. "The Salty Soldier. I'll take you to it when you're out of here."

Noah shook his head and smiled. "The Salty Soldier. Sounds about right for Diaz."

Connor began telling Noah what had been happening since he'd been in a coma, from reverse engineering Krake technology to what they'd learned about the Ovarrow.

"So, the NEIIS are the Ovarrow. That will take some getting used to. No one has been able to find Lars?"

"He moves around a lot, and he's actually pretty good at covering his tracks. We've come close a few times. Dash had a run-in with him about three months ago."

Connor paused, deciding whether he should keep talking.

"Don't do that," Noah said.

"Do what?"

"Treat me like a sick person."

"You almost died, Noah. You're going to have to be patient with all of us, especially Kara."

"I swear to God, if you start telling me that I need to rest, I'll start screaming and . . ." Noah clenched his teeth for a moment.

"Well, if you scream too much, they'll give you a sedative," Connor said dryly.

Noah grinned a little and then sighed. "You're right about that, but seriously, I can still do things. Can you restore my system access? Is there anything I can help with?"

"I thought you were being discharged in a day or two. You'll have access to all your things then. Your lab and all that."

Noah snorted derisively. "Like Kara is going to let me do anything. She'll no doubt have some kind of lockout in place so I can focus on recovery. But I can't just sit around. I *have* to do something."

Connor leaned back in his chair and regarded Noah for a few moments. "You want to do something?" he asked.

Noah's brow wrinkled. "Yes."

Connor gestured toward his empty cup. "I could use a little more coffee."

Noah frowned for a moment and then looked at the empty cup. He squeezed his eyes shut, shook his head, and laughed. "I think I can handle that."

Noah got them both a refill and sat back down. "I guess I walked right into that, didn't I?"

"I had to take a shot. It was a target-rich opportunity that I couldn't walk away from," Connor said.

Noah sighed and slumped back into his chair.

Connor had seen this behavior before with wounded soldiers. They wanted to get back out there and prove that they hadn't been affected by their injuries. Sometimes it was better to just let them push their limits.

"I don't think there's any harm in you reading a few reports or looking at some stuff. I'll make sure you have what you need," Connor said.

"Thank you, Connor. That means the world to me," Noah said

and paused for a moment. "I haven't heard you mention Sean. What's he doing these days?"

Connor drank his coffee and told Noah about Trident Battle Group. "We just completed a reconnaissance mission, and they found part of a ship's wreckage, but it was from retreating through the space gate. We think there was a battle and they were leaving. If they'd been destroyed, there would've been more wreckage to find. So, it's safe to say there's a good chance that Sean and the rest of the battle group are still alive. We just don't understand why they haven't come home yet."

Noah looked at him with a bemused expression. "You really don't know why Sean hasn't returned?" he asked and then added. "You?"

Connor frowned for a moment and shook his head.

"The mission. Sean's objective. He won't come home until he's accomplished whatever his mission was. You guys are so much alike in that respect. That's why he hasn't come back," Noah said.

"Maybe," Connor agreed. "They were fighting a battle, and there could've been damage to the space gate. It's been ninety days though. I would've expected some kind of contact. But I understand what you're saying."

They left the cafeteria, and Connor walked Noah back to his room. Noah paused outside the doorway, looking as if he didn't want to go in.

"You know," Connor said, "I could probably get you out of here. Have someone pick us up on the roof. They'll never find out."

Noah smiled and grinned. "Kara would find out, and then I'd have hell to pay."

"Maybe they can give you a different room," Connor suggested.

Noah glared at the empty hospital room. "I have nowhere else to go," he said quietly.

"Why don't we go back outside then?"

Noah shook his head and rubbed his eyes. He walked over to the bed and more or less collapsed onto it. Rolling over to his side, he was soon asleep. Connor watched him for a few moments and then closed the door as he left the room.

23

SEAN ENTERED THE GALLEY. It was midmorning, standard time, and technically they were still in the middle of the shift, so it wasn't as crowded as it would be later. Since it was between breakfast and lunchtime, there was a sandwich-making station for those who were coming in on their off-hours. Sean grabbed a couple of slices of rye bread, put some egg salad on one end, a few pieces of the lettuce, and topped it off with a few slices of bacon. He pushed the top slice down with his hand and walked over to the gleaming coffee station where he found a freshly made pot that smelled like a medium roast blend with hints of vanilla and caramel. He filled his mug and added some cream and sugar. There was no shortage of open tables, and he saw Oriana sitting by herself. Her back was to him, but there was no mistaking her long, velvety black hair. She was tall and slender, and her science team uniform hugged her subtle curves in all the right ways. He walked over. She was peering at the technical specs of the space gates.

"Want some company?" Sean asked.

Oriana looked up at him. Her face was sweetly angelic, sort of girl-next-door pretty. She smiled and gestured for him to join her.

Sean sat down. The remains of her own breakfast were evident —a healthy mix of fruits and vegetables with the remnants of eggs —and he wondered why she never finished everything on her plate. His plate would be devoid of even a crumb when he was finished.

"I didn't hear you leave this morning. Sneaking away in the middle the night?"

Oriana glanced around to see if anyone had heard. Then her gaze narrowed. "We decided to be discreet."

The words stung just a little bit, but Sean nodded. They'd been casual for almost the entire time they'd been in this universe. "Word travels fast, and we're old news."

"I doubt we're news at all. Regardless, people talk no matter what," Oriana said and tilted her head to the side. "It bothers you that I left."

Sean shook his head a little too quickly. "No, I was just surprised, is all."

"Uh huh," she said, sounding unconvinced.

"What were you working on?" Sean asked, deciding that changing the subject would be best.

"I was looking at the space gates design spec again."

Sean took a bite of his sandwich and nodded. "I'm sure you could see it with your eyes closed."

Oriana smiled and gave a slight roll of her eyes. "Probably," she agreed. "I just don't know how the Ovarrow could reverse engineer anything like this on their own."

"We don't know how long the Krake had been around to influence them."

"No, I understand all that. But still, I think they must have had help, or maybe they found the Krake technical manual of all things related to the space gate."

Sean raised an eyebrow. "Just one volume, or the whole set?"

Oriana smiled and shook her head. "Okay, maybe not that, but I still think they had help."

"Like who?" Sean asked, finishing his sandwich.

Oriana pressed her lips together. "I don't know."

A short distance away a group of soldiers was sitting together, and their discussion was becoming heated. Sean couldn't hear the specifics of it, but the tone was enough. Fuses were running short. A few glances in his direction were enough to prompt the others into quelling the argument before it had a chance to get out of control.

"There's been a lot of that lately," Oriana said.

"Tensions are always higher before a major operation," Sean replied. But he knew it was more than that. Three months of hiding from the Krake while they repaired their ships and the space gate were taking their toll.

Oriana glanced at the soldiers for a few moments and looked back at Sean. "My brother is a bit of a hothead, always letting the pressure get to him. He wouldn't like being on a ship like this."

Sean leaned forward. "I didn't know you had a brother."

"Colton. He's my younger brother. I've never brought it up before."

"Why not?"

"You never seem to want to talk about family."

Sean frowned. "I guess I never gave it much thought." He hated how that sounded as soon as he said it. "I figured you'd bring it up if you wanted to talk about it. It's just me and my mother now."

"Do you think she'll remarry and have more children?"

Sean's mind went blank. "My mother? I have no idea." He'd never really given it much thought. It was his mother, after all. "I suppose she could if she wanted," he said and looked away from her, shaking his head.

Oriana grinned. "You do realize that your mother was a

woman before she was your mother. She has a long life ahead of her. You can't expect her to be alone."

Sean reached for his coffee and almost knocked it over. "No, of course not. I just never—Do we really need to talk about my mother?"

Oriana's eyes twinkled with amusement.

Sean held up his hand. "I do acknowledge that my mother is a woman, and she certainly has the option to live her life as she wants. It's just not something I ever talk to her about."

Oriana smiled, pleased with herself, and he liked seeing it. "See? That wasn't so hard, was it?"

"Your brother," Sean began. "What does he do back at the colony?"

"He studied field biology but decided he'd rather work for Field Ops and Security."

Sean drank some coffee. "You don't approve?"

"He doesn't work well under pressure."

Sean shrugged. "Maybe he'll outgrow it."

Oriana shook her head. "He's always been that way. High strung. I don't think Field Ops is the best place for him."

Sean finished his coffee and they were both quiet for a few moments, each in their own thoughts. He didn't have any siblings. The closest people he had to brothers were Noah and Lars.

"There really isn't any other way, is there?" Oriana asked.

The operation they were about to execute was on everyone's mind. "We've done all the repairs we can do, and we've studied the Krake operation in this universe. It's strange that they had so many ships coming to where we are in this universe, but I guess since it's an industrial complex, it would make sense that there was some protection here. However, it doesn't explain why that same level of protection isn't maintained."

"Maybe they got called away to deal with something else," she said. "There's a lot we don't understand about them."

"Do you think you have the targeting figured out?" Sean said.

They hadn't been able to go back to New Earth because of the damage to their space gate and the fact that there'd been a serious flaw in how they'd targeted their home universe. Oriana and the rest of the science team had run themselves ragged trying to figure it out.

"The calculations work, but without an actual field test, we won't really know," Oriana replied.

"We talked about this before. I can't risk the Krake learning that we're here."

"I know, I know. We don't have enough space gate cubes to make a large enough gateway for the entire battle group to get through. If the Krake detected our test, then they'd come here and we'd be cornered," Oriana said.

"It's as good a tactical assessment as I've heard. I'm glad—" Sean began to say but then stopped. He'd almost said he was glad she'd been paying attention, which wouldn't have been smart. "So, the issue is with time. That's why we couldn't go back home before. Time is another layer that needs to be accounted for in the calculations used for targeting a universe."

Oriana looked at him with a dubious expression. She hadn't been fooled. She might not have known exactly what he was going to say, but she decided to let it go. "We based the new calculations off the Krake data we got from that base of operations. To put it in layman's terms, the math works. If the gate machines hadn't sustained as much damage as they did coming here, then we might've been able to get home by now."

Escaping to this universe had been a very close thing. They'd lost the *Douglass,* which was the sister ship of the *Vigilant.* Right now, only the *Vigilant* and the *Yorktown* could provide enough power to the space gate for the entire battle group to escape. Hundreds of lives had been lost, but thousands had been saved.

"I wish there was a better way," Oriana said.

"We can't minimize all risk. At least this way we won't have any surprise reserve fleets showing up," Sean replied.

"Unless they have arches on the planet."

"Even if they did, they wouldn't be big enough to accommodate ships. We'd still get the most valuable commodity, which is time—time for us to test the new targeting protocol you put together. Hopefully, we can put this place behind us."

Oriana eyed him for a moment. "You never talk about going home."

"No need to dwell on it. My time is better served by focusing on more immediate things."

"Do you *want* to go home?"

Sean frowned. "What kind of question is that? Of course I want to go home."

"You just never talk about it."

"Would it make you feel better if I did?"

Oriana's expression became one of bemusement, and Sean was pretty sure it was at his expense. He glanced around to be sure they couldn't be overheard and leaned toward her. "I don't think we have enough information to go home. We've learned a few things, which is great, but it's not enough. And we haven't learned nearly enough about the Krake to make any difference."

Oriana looked away for a few moments, considering. When she looked back, she also leaned in until they were less than a foot apart. "We don't have to do this by ourselves. You push yourself too hard."

"We're hardly alone. There're over two thousand of us here. At some point, the Krake are going to learn where we come from— our target universe, if you will. Based on our interactions with them, that wouldn't go too well for us the way things stand right now," Sean said.

"I understand what's at stake."

"You make a good point about not being in this alone, and

you're not the only one who feels that way. That's why, if this operation works, we'll be returning home."

Oriana smiled and looked relieved, but then she frowned. "What happens then?"

There were a number of ways Sean could've taken that question, and he had no doubt she'd phrased it in such a way as to have multiple meanings for him.

Gabriel, the ship's AI, had just sent them both a request to come to the bridge.

"We'll finish this later," Oriana said.

They stood up and took their dirty dishes to the racks for washing, then headed to the bridge.

24

MAJOR LESTER BRODY stood on the bridge of the *Yorktown*, the CDF's only carrier vessel in the fleet, currently a part of Trident Battle Group. He'd just returned from an inspection tour of the ship.

The *Yorktown* had been his residence for the past three months. Since losing the *Douglass* when they'd escaped the Krake, he'd lost a third of his crew. The surviving crew of the *Douglass* had been spread out among the other ships in Trident Battle Group, with the majority of them on the *Yorktown*.

Major Christopher McKay looked over at him. "We're almost home," McKay said quietly enough that only Lester could hear.

Lester nodded and looked at the crew on the bridge. "They know it, too. All their hard work is about to pay off."

"If you'd told me we'd be launching an operation to steal Krake space gate cubes, I would've thought you were crazy," McKay said.

"It *is* crazy, and desperate, but we need them if we're going to get out of here," Lester said.

The main holoscreen showed the eight Talon-V Stormer class vessels, along with a complement of Lancer and Stinger escorts, heading to the Krake space gate. The *Yorktown* remained at a safe distance, along with two CDF destroyers. The *Babylon* and the *Acheron* were in position, with orders to decimate anything that came through the gate.

Lester looked at the tactical display on his personal holoscreen. They still had over four hours before anything was scheduled to come through the Krake space gate.

"It would be an unfortunate turn of events if the Krake decided to change their schedule today," McKay said.

Lester nodded. "Unfortunate indeed."

They had four hours to disable the space gate, and they'd achieve that by stealing eight of the space gate cubes so they could be retrofitted to their own gate. This op would allow them to hit two birds with one stone. They'd disable the Krake space gate while regaining their own mobility. They couldn't just use the gate to go home because of the risk of the Krake learning where their home universe was. Despite Dr. Evans' assertions that she'd cracked the targeting issue, they needed to test her solution. There was too much risk in testing and going home in one operation. The Krake would learn that there was a hostile force here, but their reinforcements would be delayed.

"Are you all right, Major?" McKay asked.

Lester looked over at McKay. "Yes, it's just been a . . . long deployment."

Most of the crew Lester had spoken with were eager to return home. The months they'd spent in enemy territory had been fraught with the risk of the Krake discovering them, which was enough to wear away the nerves of even the most stalwart, including the seemingly indomitable will of Colonel Sean Quinn. Even now, Lester could sense that Sean was reluctant to go home, and he agreed, in part. The more they learned about the Krake, the more they realized how much more there was to learn if they were to have any hope of engaging them from a militaristic standpoint. The Krake were a very grave threat, like a looming hurricane in the night.

It was the waiting that was the worst part. All Lester could do was to make sure the crew remained focused on the task at hand.

THE MASSIVE SPACE gate cube loomed in front of the Talon-V Stormer.

"Beginning final approach," Sergeant Carl Reeger said.

"Acknowledged," Harper replied and checked the progress of the other ships.

The Talon-V Stormers were designed for sending an assault force to an enemy ship; however, that wouldn't occur on this day. There was a crew of twenty aboard the ship, but they were made up of combat engineers and salvage experts. Their mission was to decouple the space gate cube and utilize the ships to tow the cubes toward the *Yorktown*.

The Krake space gate cubes each had a single flat surface area of three hundred meters. They were to try to decouple the cubes first, and if that didn't work, they were to use strategically placed explosive charges to do the job. Harper hoped they wouldn't have to use the charges because of the risk of damaging the delicate machines that allowed them to transition between universes.

"Send an update back to Major Brody," Harper said.

"Yes, Captain," Sergeant Reeger said. A few moments later, Reeger said, "Update has been sent. Now we just hope the Krake don't show up."

That was an understatement, but they had a job to do.

"Spec Ops is on it," Harper said.

Reeger nodded. "There's a whole lot of sneaking around going on."

"That's right, and the Krake won't know we're here until it's too late."

"I know I said this before, but I still can't believe the lapse in security protocols the Krake have established here," Reeger said.

Harper frowned. "Do you mean for the space gate or the industrial complex?"

"Well, both of them, to be honest. Why would they leave the space gate unguarded? It's as if they don't expect anyone to ever attack them."

"Well, why would they? They'd be cutting off their own escape as well. Plus, we haven't been to the surface of the planet, but they probably have archways there."

Reeger shook his head. "You couldn't pay me enough to go to that planet. It looks like hell. There's hardly any atmosphere and no signs of life."

"Yeah, but it's mineral-rich, which is why they have a salvage yard here, as well as a major fabrication center utilizing all the raw materials. It would be much worse for us if this was an inhabited world with a significant military presence," Harper replied.

They reach their designated landing zone and deployed the landing gear. Since the cubes didn't have any artificial gravity, they had to deploy tether hooks to secure them in place.

Harper stood up. "Time to get to work."

"THIS IS CRAZY," Sergeant Benton said.

Boseman smiled and shook his head, but there was no way Benton could see it. The Spec Ops platoon was wearing Nexstar combat suits, hitching a ride on an asteroid that was heading to a preprocessing area to be broken apart before going to the main Krake industrial complex.

"You said the same thing before," Boseman said.

They'd been on plenty of combat drops both in space and on New Earth. The training regimen for Spec Ops required a certain amount of crazy, and Boseman found it fun, as did most other Spec Ops team members. They trained hard to be the most physically fit and deadly of any CDF soldier. That kind of training required a certain amount of tenacity that not everyone had, plain and simple. Most of the soldiers who tried to join Spec Ops failed. They didn't have what it took. Those who made the cut were the reason Spec Ops was the best at what they did. It was why the riskiest of missions were given to them. When failure wasn't an option, they didn't. No matter the cost, the objective was everything.

"That was before I realized just how high we'd be jumping," Benton replied.

"Well, if you do it right, you'll live to talk about it. If you don't, you'll bounce off into space and we won't be able to get you back," Boseman said.

He wasn't kidding. They had no air support. They were the distraction. They were there to cause destruction and mayhem, but in such a way that they didn't impact any Krake civilians that may or may not have been working in the industrial complex.

The asteroid the Spec Ops platoon was hitching a ride on closed in on the gaping maw of an automated crusher. That's what they'd dubbed it anyway. Asteroids of a certain size went inside, and through some function they had no information about, came out the other side in smaller, bite-size pieces so the industrial complex could get at the mineral-rich ores the Krake used. This particular asteroid was composed mainly of nickel and iron.

Boseman activated the command comlink, which patched him into the entire platoon. "Max suit thrust on my mark," he said. The distance and telemetry appeared on his helmet's internal heads-up display. "Mark!"

Boseman and the rest of them engaged their suit thrusters,

breaking free of the little bit of gravity the asteroid had. They then engaged secondary thrusters that would carry them over the crusher.

Boseman monitored the progress of the rest of the soldiers. All fifty of them had cleared the rim of the crusher. He looked over to the side and saw that Benton was a bit off kilter. He'd angled his jump and now was in a slow tumble that he was trying to get under control. After a few moments of using maneuvering suit thrusters, he stabilized, and their momentum carried them over the crusher.

The Krake industrial complex was a huge network of spindly arms the broken-up asteroids were fed into that then went into the main complex. It was like a giant spider in space, only this spider had hundreds of arms. The industrial complex was a vast network of these structures that spoke volumes of the Krake's salvaging efforts. Reconnaissance missions had revealed that they utilized automated processes to do the actual work, but there was still a Krake presence here. They'd selected their targets based on the minimum Krake presence they expected to find.

Boseman opened the command channel again. "Reverse thrusters on my mark. Engage."

Their Nexstar combat suits were able to use specialized attachments based on the mission. They each had an individual flight unit attached to the back. This turned upside down and, in conjunction with the maneuvering thrusters, stopped the Spec Ops soldiers from ascending and put them on an intercept trajectory with the asteroid fragments coming out the other side of the crusher.

They were breaking up into smaller teams, targeting every other shaft the asteroid chunks were heading towards. Twelve teams of four headed for their targets. Boseman had Sergeant Benton and Corporal Brentworth, as well as Private Jing on his team. Jing carried the payload.

Boseman switched to the team channel. They'd maintain comms blackout unless there was a general alert with the other teams. They had to get within close proximity to the asteroid chunks so they didn't draw notice from Krake sensors. This was a gamble because they weren't exactly sure about the capabilities of the Krake sensors. They were guessing they couldn't be that finely attuned because in all their reconnaissance, everything that was heading into the industrial complex at this point had gone inside to be processed.

"Captain, one of my main suit thrusters is faulty," Sergeant Benton said.

Boseman looked over at him and glanced down toward his feet. Given the speed they were coming in at, Benton needed both of his main thrusters in order to make a soft landing; otherwise, he'd bounce off the industrial complex.

"I'll help him with the landing, Captain," Corporal Brentworth said.

"Negative, Corporal. Stay with Jing. We need that payload. I'll take care of Benton." He switched to a private channel with Benton. "I'm going to ease over to your side."

Boseman used maneuvering thrusters to angle toward Benton. If he came in too fast, he'd knock Benton off course, so he kept his approach slow and steady.

"Dammit," Benton said. "I clipped part of the crusher on the way up. I think that's what broke it."

"I think you just couldn't stand not being close to me. Is there something you want to tell me, Sergeant?"

"Well, I've been harboring these feelings for you, sir, and I just can't keep them to myself anymore," Benton said, playing along.

Everyone knew Benton was an unabashed womanizer. It had gotten him into trouble many times, but when he was reined in, he was a good man to have in the squad.

"I knew it, but you're just not my type," Boseman said.

He slowed down and engaged his personal tether, which adhered itself to the back of Benton's combat suit.

"We're locked," Benton said, switching back to business.

"Copy that. Hold on," Boseman said.

The tether pulled them together back to back. "I'm taking over your suit functions," Boseman said.

Benton chuckled a little. "You know, if you were Delilah, I might enjoy this."

Boseman updated the calculations so the suit computer could handle the soft landing with the additional load. "Sergeant Payton? I think you're aiming too high. She's got standards."

"The higher the peak, the sweeter the reward," Benton said and laughed.

The connection points along the shaft that led to the industrial complex made it difficult to target their landing area. Boseman found an area that looked promising and had the suit computer target it.

"All right, three, two, one . . ." Boseman said.

He heard Benton grunt in anticipation. There was nothing like being in a combat suit and having no control of it, and Boseman wouldn't have liked it any more than Benton did right then. Maneuvering thrusters fired together on one side with the equivalent of a ship's braking thrusters, slowing down their approach as they angled downward toward the LZ. They were coming in fast. The main suit thrusters fired, slowing their descent, and they touched down.

Their mag boots engaged and they stopped. Boseman detached the tether, and full suit capability was returned to Benton.

"Oh God, let's not do that again," Benton said and sighed heavily.

Boseman did an internal systems check, and his combat suit was intact. He brought out his AR-71 and checked it. Benton carried a heavy plasma cannon, and he connected it to the main power source in his suit. Jing and Brentworth had landed a short distance away.

"Deal," Bosman said. "Let's catch up to the others."

Brentworth was checking the two specialized lightweight but high-yield missiles they'd been carrying.

"Both the missiles and the explosive charges check out, Captain," Corporal Brentworth said and closed the case.

"Good. We're on a tight schedule. Let's get moving," Boseman said.

Boseman and Brentworth took point while Benton and Jing stayed behind them. Their mag boots were engaged and, with the help of the Nexstar's combat suit computers, they were able to run much faster than they ever could have without a combat suit. In no time at all, they made it to the first junction that connected the shafts. It was a structural weak point that their explosive charges would do a great job of tearing apart.

It took a few minutes to set the charges and configure them for remote detonation with a fail-safe timer. Either way, these charges were going to explode on a schedule. The fail-safe only worked if comlink connectivity to Boseman's combat suit was disconnected. Then, it would do a quick calculation so the explosion happened on schedule.

They continued moving away to a minimum safe distance. Boseman sent out a signal that they were set and ready. Jing and Brentworth readied the mobile missile launcher while Benton covered them.

As far as Boseman could tell, no alarms had been raised. It was quiet right then, but in a few moments, all hell was going to break loose.

Boseman waited until all twelve teams had checked in and then sent back his authorization.

The lightweight hornet missiles raced across the span of five kilometers to the next intake shaft. The target was the end of the shaft where the asteroid chunks first went inside. They aimed for the adjacent shaft, with each team doing the same to maximize the destruction they were about to cause.

The missiles raced toward their target with rigorous fury, and twelve seemingly simultaneous explosions occurred at the end of the intake shafts. Boseman detonated the explosive charges at the first main junction. Eleven more explosions occurred, and the shaft shuddered beneath their feet. Roughly a quarter of this spider's legs had been destroyed. The crusher still spat out asteroid chunks, which continued to pelt the industrial complex, only now instead of going inside the intake shafts, they were bouncing out of control to impact other parts of the complex.

"Time to go," Boseman said.

They continued to the extraction points, and Boseman signaled for the combat shuttle to come pick them up. Six shuttles were deployed and would have to make two stops in order to extract the Spec Ops team.

"Contact!" Benton cried.

They all took cover and watched as Krake soldiers approached. Hulking figures three meters tall ran toward them.

Their extraction point had just become a hot zone.

The Krake response had been quick, and Boseman hadn't counted on that. They'd picked this target because it appeared to be lightly defended. The other CDF teams checked in. Krake soldiers were closing in on them, too.

"Let's draw them in. Wait for them to get closer," Boseman said.

They aimed their weapons at the approaching soldiers.

"Now," Boseman said.

Benton fired his plasma cannon, and a molten bolt of fury blazed into the Krake soldiers. They hadn't staggered their approach, and seven of them were blown off into space in various conditions of melted fury and pain.

Boseman configured the nanorobotic ammunition to use explosive penetrating rounds and then fired his weapon. The heavy slugs pierced the Krake armor and exploded, leaving massive holes.

The element of surprise was used up as more Krake soldiers arrived. They approached cautiously, each taking shots with their own weapons.

"Jing, keep an eye on our six," Boseman said.

The combat shuttle had picked up the other team and was heading toward them.

"Enemy contact, Captain," Private Jing said.

Dammit, Boseman thought. They were pinned down, and the enemy was closing in all around them.

The combat shuttle arrived and opened fire, first taking out the primary group and then the secondary group. The shaft rocked beneath their feet with the impact of the combat shuttle's weapons.

"Now's our chance," Boseman said as the combat shuttle swung around, presenting the loading ramp to them. They jumped and engaged their suit thrusters to clear the loading ramp.

"We're all on board. Get us out of here," Boseman ordered.

The loading ramp had just closed, and Boseman felt the shuttle lurch forward. He ran toward the cockpit.

"We're taking fire," the pilot said.

"Combat drones?" Boseman asked and peered at the shuttle's main holoscreen.

"Negative. They have automated defense turrets. Captain, you can take the aux seat behind me. Things are going to get a little rough."

Boseman sat down and auto-straps secured him in place. The tactical display showed multiple video feeds. Auto-turrets fired at them while the pilot executed evasive maneuvers. The pilot flew the combat shuttle as close to the industrial complex as he could, making it difficult for them to be targeted.

A comlink opened from another combat shuttle. "Krake ships inbound. Destroyer class vessels."

Boseman's stomach sank. "Alert the battle group. Use subspace comms."

"COLONEL, we're getting reports of Krake automated defense turrets coming online," Specialist Irina Sansky said.

Sean swung his gaze toward the tactical workstations. "What's the status of the Spec Ops evac?"

"They're under enemy fire. The alert squadron is en route. They're ten minutes out, Colonel," Lieutenant Jane Russo said.

Jade squadron appeared on the tactical plot on the main holoscreen. Talon-V Stinger class fighters were blazing a path toward the fleeing combat shuttles.

"Very well," Sean replied.

This was only the beginning of the Krake response to their attack. The auto-turrets had been concealed within the complex. Sean had two destroyers in reserve at a midway point between the space gate and Trident Battle Group's current position. The *Vigilant*, along with three other destroyers—the *Dutchman*, the *Burroughs*, and the *Albany*—were in position where Sean had expected the Krake response to be.

"Colonel, seven Krake destroyers are coming from the planet," Lieutenant Russo said.

"On screen," Sean said.

The Krake destroyers appeared on the main holoscreen. Active scans showed a staggered deployment. "Tactical, I want a firing solution on the three destroyers on point. Designate them priority alpha."

"Yes, sir," Lieutenant Russo said.

The CDF destroyers' combat AIs were patched into the *Vigilant's* onboard systems. Gabriel, the *Vigilant's* AI, would take the data from their computing core and transmit it to the rest of the battle group. This quickened their response times in an enemy engagement.

They hadn't done any reconnaissance of the planet below. Instead, they'd focused on the Krake industrial complex and the nearby space gate activity. Sean expected that the Krake had shipbuilding facilities in this star system, but they hadn't found them. It appeared they constructed their ships planet-side.

"I have a firing solution, Colonel," Russo said.

"Fire," Sean replied.

HADES Vs sped out the *Vigilant's* missile tubes, along with those of the CDF destroyers. Sean authorized five more volleys before they'd evaluate the damage they'd done to the Krake fleet.

"Helm, keep the industrial complex between us and the enemy ships," Sean said. Krake attack drones could fly around the industrial complex easily enough, but it would take them time.

"Third volley is away. No combat drones detected," Russo said.

HADES V missiles closed the distance to the enemy ships, and they hadn't returned fire yet.

The plot on the main holoscreen updated and showed that the first group of HADES Vs had detonated. Sean's jaw tightened in grim satisfaction.

"Krake destroyers are staggering their approach. Their course indicates they've deduced our approximate position," Lieutenant Russo said.

It was difficult not to remain in motion while ships operated in space, and a heavy cruiser was no different. The Krake might have figured out where their attack had come from, but there was still guesswork involved, and they hadn't detected any scans from Krake ships.

"Understood," Sean replied.

He glanced at the combat shuttles on the plot. They were still a few minutes out, but they were on an intercept course with the *Vigilant*.

"Ops, what's the current status of the space gate operation?" Sean asked.

"They've retrieved four of the cubes. The other teams were delayed," Lieutenant Davis Hoffman replied.

"Gabriel, how are we on time?" Sean asked.

"We're behind schedule, Colonel. Recommend holding off the Krake response here for as long as we can to give the retrieval teams enough time to secure the minimal number of cubes required," the *Vigilant's* AI replied.

Sean's gaze flicked to the tactical plot on his personal holoscreen. Another active scan pulse was about to happen. The tactical plot refreshed and showed that new Krake contacts had been detected. Two more Krake destroyers appeared on the plot. Their trajectory put them on an intercept course with the previous group of destroyers they'd already detected.

Sean frowned in thought. Why wouldn't those ships be heading toward *them*?

"Krake attack drones detected," Lieutenant Russo said.

The number of attack drones appeared on the main holoscreen, and the count quickly jumped past several hundred.

"Tactical, prepare missile-defense screen," Sean said.

During their other encounters with the Krake, they'd learned that detonating a HADES V missile blinded the attack drone's guidance systems momentarily, putting them into disarray. The missile-defense screen would coordinate the launches of HADES Vs, along with targeting the mag cannons of the *Vigilant* and the other CDF destroyers.

"Confirm, missile-defense screen protocol has designates in tubes seven and eight, Colonel," Russo said.

The Krake attack drone count on the main holoscreen climbed past three hundred, and Sean's mouth formed a grim line. That was too many drones. At the rate the Krake were launching attack drones, their defenses, even with the updated protocols, would soon be overwhelmed.

"Ops, what's the status of the combat shuttles retrieving the Spec Ops teams?" Sean asked.

"They're still a few minutes out, Colonel," Lieutenant Hoffman said.

That wasn't good enough. "Emergency landing protocols authorized. They need to get here ASAP. Helm, ready the rendezvous coordinates with the *Yorktown.*"

Sean's orders were confirmed, and then the tactical plot refreshed again on the main holoscreen. Their new defensive protocols were working. The numbers of attack drones detected had ground to a halt. The Krake must have fired everything they had at them, keeping nothing in reserve.

"Colonel, recommend beginning our withdrawal," Lieutenant Russo said.

She was right and Sean knew it, but he wasn't leaving the Spec Ops team. "Helm—" Sean began to say but was interrupted by an audible chime sounding as the number of attack drones skyrocketed to over four hundred. Sean's mouth went dry, and the bridge crew seemed to hold its collective breath. The new group of attack drones had come from the Krake reinforcement ships.

"Colonel," Lieutenant Russo said, her voice a bit higher than normal, "the new detection of attack drones is on a . . . Sir, they're shooting at their own ships!"

Sean peered at the plot on the main holoscreen. It refreshed again, showing the new salvo of Krake attack drones on an intercept course with the first group of ships they'd detected.

Why would the Krake fire their weapons on one another? Scanners showed that more than half of the attack drones that had been heading toward the CDF had changed course, heading toward the two Krake destroyers.

"Colonel, combat shuttles are all aboard and accounted for," Lieutenant Hoffman said.

They couldn't afford to get caught up in whatever Krake conflict was going on here.

"Helm, get us out of here. Best speed," Sean said.

The *Vigilant* and the accompanying CDF destroyers retreated from the Krake industrial complex. Roughly a third of the complex had been impacted by the attack, and Sean hoped it had been worth it.

"Comms, open a comlink to the *Yorktown*. Get me Major Brody."

A few moments later, Major Brody appeared on Sean's personal holoscreen.

"Colonel Quinn, the Krake space gate has been disabled and we have the cubes. We're making our way to the rendezvous point, and engineering teams have already begun retrofitting the Krake space gate cubes to our existing gate."

"Excellent! Convey my congratulations to the team," Sean said and told Brody what had happened.

"They attacked each other! Are they pursuing you?" Brody asked.

"Negative. Our missile-defense screen took out the attack drones coming after us," Sean replied.

"What do you think it means?"

"Well, for one thing, the Krake aren't as unified as we'd thought."

"And this other group just happened to show up when the attack began?"

Sean nodded. "We've stumbled onto something here."

"Yeah, but now the Krake know we're here. We need to leave. We'll be ready to test the space gate in just a few hours," Brody said.

"Excuse me, Colonel Quinn," Specialist Sansky said. "We've received a data burst from the Krake."

Sean frowned and Brody went silent. "Tactical, can you detect exactly where that message came from?"

"One moment, Colonel," Russo said.

"Colonel, should I try to translate it?" Specialist Sansky asked.

"No. Standby," Sean replied.

"It's from the secondary Krake attack group, the ones that fired on their own ships," Russo said.

"Gabriel," Sean said, "I want you to seal off the Krake data in a closed system and cut it off from the rest of the ship's systems."

"Done, Colonel," Gabriel said. "Preliminary analysis indicates that there are several space gate coordinates in the data burst. I would need more time to do a full analysis."

Sean rubbed his chin for a moment.

"Colonel, did I hear that correctly? You received some kind of communication from the Krake?" Brody asked.

"It appears that way. We need time to do a thorough analysis of it though."

"I'm sure we can do that once we get back home," Brody replied.

Sean shook his head. "Hold off on testing the space gate. I'm going to send you secondary rendezvous coordinates and we'll meet up there."

"But Colonel—" Brody began and stopped himself.

"You have your orders, Major," Sean said. "*Vigilant*, out."

Sean closed the comlink. "Tactical, is there any sign of the Krake coming after us?"

"Negative, Colonel. We stopped using active scans when we began our withdrawal."

Sean nodded. "Without their space gate, we have some breathing room. Helm, update course rendezvous coordinates to bravo. We're going farther out in the system."

"Yes, Colonel. Updated our course and have sent the new coordinates to the rest of the battle group," Lieutenant Edwards replied.

The Krake were fighting among themselves, and at least some of them wanted to help the CDF.

"Colonel, our last scans indicated that almost all of the Krake ships were destroyed," Russo said.

"Understood, Lieutenant. Ops, set Condition Two," Sean said.

He opened the comlink to the secondary bridge on the *Vigilant*. "Major Shelton, I assume you've been following along?"

"Yes, Colonel," Major Shelton said.

"Excellent. Report to the bridge. We need to figure out what the hell just happened," Sean said.

They needed to go over all the data they'd collected and do a thorough analysis of the Krake message.

25

NOAH WAS in his lab at Sanctuary. A few days had passed since his release from the medical center. He didn't need to follow up with Ashley because she was tapped into his biochip, which sent her regular updates regarding his health. It had been part of his agreement for release from the hospital. Since then, Kara had been watching him like a hawk, as if he was going to suddenly disappear. To Noah, it had only been a few days with patchy memory loss, but for his wife, it had been over ten months of constant worry. Noah kept having to remind himself of that, but he was getting tired of everyone telling him what to do and being hypersensitive to the slightest mishap. Physically, he was fine, but his mind needed time to heal, and he wasn't going to get that sitting at home.

He wasn't at his main laboratory at Sanctuary. He was out along the outskirts of the city in a mobile lab he'd set up before he'd been injured. He glanced around at all the equipment and checked the logs. Dash had been in there from time to time, doing his own work. Noah hadn't seen Dash yet. The young man was working out of New Haven, but they'd had a chat via video comlink. Dash promised to come back to Sanctuary as soon as he could, but he was needed with everything that had been going on with the Ovarrow. Noah envied him. It was as if the world had kept going on just fine without him, and he didn't like how it made him feel—insignificant. There was so much more for him to see and do.

Despite the bit of isolation at his mobile lab, he did have a window to the outside. It was currently open, and a breeze was blowing in. Echoes of soothing wind chimes sounded as the breeze increased. The solitude was peaceful. It was quite a bit of work for him to be around a lot of people, and it felt almost overwhelming. Because of this, he'd taken to long periods of being alone. He couldn't escape Kara and he didn't want to, but she was being overprotective.

A live video feed came to prominence on the main holoscreen, and Noah glanced at it.

"Think of the devil, and she will appear," Noah said quietly, and then berated himself for being too harsh. Kara wasn't the devil. She was his angel.

Kara had found his little hiding spot, and he readied himself for what was sure to be an unpleasant conversation. He closed down the work he'd been doing and went to the door. It opened before he could get there, and his wife's cornflower-blue eyes narrowed suspiciously at him. She glanced behind him at the blank holoscreens for a moment.

"So, you shut down your work before I got here. How nice," Kara said.

Noah sighed. "I was just getting some fresh air, and I thought I'd come to check these things out."

Kara nodded, then walked into the work area. "How many of these things do you have?"

Noah eyed her for a moment. "You should know. You have access to all of them."

Kara crossed her arms in front of her chest, but she looked oddly vulnerable at the same time, as if her shoulders had narrowed and she was hugging herself. "Why do you keep trying to shut me out?"

Noah's eyebrows squished together, and he frowned for a moment. "I'm not . . . I'm not trying to keep anything from you. I just needed some time alone."

"I've been giving you space, but you need . . . All I can think about is how you were lying in that bed at the medical center, hooked up to all those machines that were keeping you alive. I thought you were going to die. I've been *trying* to give you space, but do you understand what this has done to me? It wasn't just a few days sitting by your bedside. It went on for months!" Her shoulders shook for a few moments and she looked away from him. "I know you didn't mean for this . . ."

"I know exactly what happened," Noah replied. He knew this whole ordeal had been rough for her. He couldn't imagine what it must have been like not knowing whether he was going to live.

Kara narrowed her gaze, her eyes glistening with anger. "Do you? Do you really? Do you know how many different methods Ashley and all the other doctors tried to bring you out of that coma? How much time and effort . . . and I needed to approve them all. Some of the things they tried hadn't been done in years, and in the end, none of it worked. You just started to slowly come out of it. First, you started breathing on your own," she said and paused, tapping her head. "But you wouldn't wake up. Your brain activity was slightly above that of a vegetable."

Noah backed away from her. He wanted to ask what she expected of him. Instead, he said, "I know. None of you let me forget everything that was done to save my life. I didn't know any of this was going to happen, and I don't know what to say. I'm sorry. Does that make it better? I'm still struggling with that and —" His thoughts scattered, and what he'd wanted to say flittered away to nothingness. He tried to recapture what he'd been thinking, but it was just gone. It was as if his mind had slammed into an invisible wall that he didn't know the limits of. Then, a sudden headache lanced across his head and went down his neck like white lightning. He swayed on his feet.

Kara rushed over to him and placed her hand on his arm. "Noah, are you okay? You look like you're in pain."

Noah squeezed his eyes shut and clenched his teeth, trying to force the pain away by sheer force of will alone. It wasn't enough.

"Here, sit down," Kara said, guiding him to a chair. "I'll get you some water."

Noah shook his head. "I don't want any water. Why does everyone keep trying to bring me water? It doesn't help. I'm not thirsty. I'm not dehydrated," he said and winced at the pain.

He felt Kara's fingers rubbing his temples. Her fingers moved behind his ears to the base of his neck and then came back again, massaging all the pressure points, relieving the tension. The pain lessened. Her fingers felt warm against his scalp, and it was heavenly.

"Thank you," Noah whispered.

"Are the headaches coming less frequently?" Kara asked.

The headaches always came. He'd been out of the hospital for barely a week and they always came. It didn't matter what he was doing. The headaches just kept coming.

"I'm not sure. You can check the logs from my biochip."

"I know I can do that, but I wanted to know if you know. Are they worse, less, or more frequent?"

"They just catch me off guard. One moment I'm fine, and the next thing, I feel like I'm spinning. The more I try to focus, the worse it gets. Then it goes away as suddenly as it came."

Kara regarded him for a moment. "All right, Noah. I won't offer you water anymore. From now on, if you're thirsty, you can get your own damn water."

Noah grinned a little. "Thanks. I didn't mean . . . I know you're trying to help."

"It's going to take a little bit of time. Maybe more than a little, but you can't expect to jump right back into things.

"Why not? Haven't I slept enough?"

Kara's gaze became unyielding. "That's enough of that right now. I'm not going to let you feel sorry for yourself. You don't have to make up for lost time. You're the victim here, and you're just going to have to learn what your limits are, Noah."

He was no stranger to his limits. He'd been pushing against them for his entire life. The thing was, it seemed like everything he was ever good at had been taken away from him.

The holoscreens came back to life, along with the information Noah had been working on. Kara swung her gaze to him. "I can't believe this. What are you doing looking at all this stuff?"

"Trying to make sense of it."

Kara scowled. "Did Connor send this to you?"

"I asked him to."

Kara made a disgusted sound. "He should know better. I'm going to send a comlink to him right now."

"No, don't do that," Noah said quickly. "I—he—he delayed sending it to me, and I kept insisting. I already have access to the data. I'm just trying to get up to speed."

Kara was quiet for a few moments. "They're still hunting down Lars."

"They're getting closer."

"I hope he gets what he deserves when they catch him."

"Don't say that. It's not right."

"Not right!" Kara cried. "Look what he's done to you. Look what he's done to the Ovarrow. He almost killed you. When are you going to admit that to yourself?"

"You make it sound like he was working by himself. He wasn't."

"He's leading them. Dash said as much and Connor confirmed," Kara replied.

Noah waited for his wife to look at him. "It's not his fault," he said and raised his hands in front of his chest. "I know what you're going to say."

"That it's bullshit," Kara said, almost snarling. "No. You wouldn't've been on that cliff if it wasn't for Lars."

"He was trying to get me to understand what he was doing," Noah said.

"Yeah, and you tried to free the Ovarrow from what he was doing to them. You knew it was the right thing to do. You decided Lars was wrong, and you needed to do something about it. Lars didn't like that. He chased you down. Your *friend* was chasing you down, and he hurt you. I know you don't like to admit it, but that's exactly what happened."

"It was an accident!" Noah shouted. "An accident," he repeated.

Kara blew out a breath in disgust. "Lars doesn't deserve you. He doesn't deserve your friendship. Don't you think he should answer for what he's done?"

Noah considered it for a few moments. "I do. I'm not condoning what he's done. He has a lot to answer for, but I just don't want to see him killed for it."

Kara stepped away from him and shook her head. "I'll never forgive him for what he's done to you. Lars has crossed the line. When are you going to understand, Noah? Some people can't be saved. Lars cannot be saved."

Noah's gut tightened. "You're wrong," he said. "You're wrong. He's walking a thin line; I'll give you that. He's done despicable things, but that's when you need your friends and your family the most. We can't just write him off. I'm not going to give up on him."

His wife's eyes watered and Noah's heart broke. There was anger and frustration in her gaze, but that wasn't what hurt the most. She pitied him, and he hated it.

"I'd like to be alone now," Noah said, his voice sounding cold.

Kara didn't say anything as she left the lab. Noah's throat became thick and he clenched his teeth as he went back over their conversation in his mind. He, Lars, and Sean had grown up together. They'd been among the first to be woken up on the *Ark*, and they'd also been among the first colonists to set foot on New Earth. What the hell had happened to all of them? All Lars had to do was come home. Why couldn't Lars just come home? He kept seeing Kara's pitying gaze, and his shoulders went rigid.

Noah felt another headache begin to come on and he snarled, looking for something to kick. There wasn't anything, and that made him angrier. He tried to calm down, but his breath was coming in gasps. Noah sank to his knees and tried to clear his mind, halt his racing thoughts, but the headache lingered on the fringe like a looming storm about to blow.

He needed to focus on something, so he brought up a new report on the space gate and glanced at the author. Dr. Oriana Evans. Noah recalled seeing that name before. He checked the space gate reports and found her name associated with many of them. Maybe she'd talk to him about her research. He looked her up and felt his shoulders drop. She was missing. She was on the mission with Sean—another thing that had happened while he wasn't around. Noah glared at the report, and the name "Evans" became bleary. He'd been at this too long, and maybe it was time he took a break. He didn't like admitting it to himself. It was okay to push against his limits and maybe even break them a little bit, but sometimes taking a little step back was what he needed in order to take a giant leap forward.

26

Trident Battle Group had reached the rendezvous point, which was three hundred million kilometers away from the Krake. Sean had just left the bridge and was heading to the conference room to meet with his senior officers for the battle group. He walked in the room to find that Major Shelton was already there, as well as Oriana. Captain Chad Boseman was there to provide updates regarding what the Spec Ops team had observed during their mission. The rest of the attendees were virtual, which included all the commanding officers of the ships of the battle group. There were several holoscreens active over the main table.

Sean sat down. "I want to thank you all for coming. This is a meeting to go over what we've learned from the Krake message. But before we get into that, I need to know the status of the space gate."

"All space gate cubes are in the process of being connected. Initial diagnostics indicate that they are ready to be used. The next step is that of an actual test. I've conferred with Dr. Evans, and she's satisfied that the physical test is the next logical step," Major Brody said.

Sean glanced at Oriana, and she nodded.

"Technically, that's correct," Oriana said. "We believe the cubes will work, but there are some differences in their construction that we need to analyze. Also, we're not sure if it will alert the Krake when we use them."

"It just needs to work once," Brody said.

"At minimum, it needs to work once, but we need a reliable solution," Sean said and glanced around the room. "Let's table the space gate discussion for now. I want to go over what the science team and Gabriel came up with during their analysis of the Krake message we received. Go ahead, Gabriel."

"Thank you, Colonel Quinn," Gabriel said. "The message is a data burst that included our first contact protocols. These were the protocols that were transferred from this ship in the previous universe where we first engaged the Krake. I'd like to highlight the paramount importance of this. It indicates that the Krake have been spreading this information around."

"Why would they include our own first contact protocol?" Brody asked.

"Presumably to establish credibility that they want to communicate with us," Gabriel answered.

Sean nodded. "Makes sense. Our first contact protocols have been around for hundreds of years. We just never had to use them back on Earth. Our first contact message always included a way to talk back to us. I agree with Gabriel's assessment, and so does the science team. Gabriel, please continue."

"The other interesting part of the data is that it includes Ovarrow symbols. We also believe that whoever sent the message had knowledge of this and didn't communicate with us in their native Krake language, which we would have trouble understanding. However, we do have one advantage—the three Krake prisoners. They could provide insight into this, if we choose to share the message with them."

"I haven't made a decision on that yet," Sean replied.

"The message also contains a reference—this is a translation based on the Ovarrow language— calling themselves the overseers. They appear to be leaders in Krake society. However, there's another part of the message that indicates there's some faction, or what we'd refer to as a fifth column. At the end of the data packet is the set of space gate coordinates, along with the actual timing for using them. The time is twenty-four hours from the initial message."

"That sounds like an invitation to me. What do the rest of you think?" Sean asked.

Major Brody went first, which Sean expected since he was his second-in-command. "This is extraordinary and gives us more insight into the Krake and what their motivations are. Gabriel, you said the set of coordinates were to be used in the next twenty-four hours. Is that right?"

"That is correct, Major Brody. That means we have about twelve hours left to decide whether we follow those coordinates," Gabriel replied.

"Excuse me," Oriana said. "We've checked the data against the new calculations we've been using, and the temporal calculations do match up. This is another indicator that the next time we use the targeting coordinates to return to our home universe, they'll work. I just wanted to point that out."

Sean glanced around at the people in the room and on the holoscreens. They wanted to go home. Heck, *he* wanted to go home, but he just wasn't sure if this was the right decision.

"We have twelve hours, ladies and gentlemen," Sean said.

"This could be a trap, Colonel," Major Brody said.

"I disagree," Major Shelton said, speaking up for the first time in the meeting. Sean gestured for her to continue. "They attacked their own ships. Why would they then send us a message and invite us into a trap? I agree with Colonel Quinn that this is an invitation. The Krake had enough firepower to take us out. This other group showed up and sacrificed themselves so we could get away."

"Anything the Krake do is suspect," Major Brody replied. "There's a degree of risk with anything we do. Colonel Quinn, what do you intend to do?"

"We delay going home. We need . . ." Sean paused for a moment, noting some of the reactions, and then continued. "Our mission objective is to learn all we can about the Krake, finding their weaknesses and bringing that information back home so we can exploit it. This is worth exploring. We have twelve hours. I suggest you make all the necessary preparations."

There was a collective, "Yes, Colonel," and then the meeting ended.

"Colonel Quinn," Oriana said. They used formal address since there were others present. "I'd like to go to the *Yorktown* with my team to do our own analysis of the space gate. I just want to double-check that everything is working properly."

Sean frowned. "We have the data from the engineering team. Do you think something's wrong?"

"No, not exactly. I'd just like to double-check."

"All right, I'll have a shuttle take you guys over there, but we'll be transferring the space gate cubes over to the *Vigilant*," Sean said.

"That's why I want to run my own diagnostic before it comes here."

"Understood. Let me know the results of your analysis," Sean said.

Oriana left the room. Shelton and Boseman had stayed behind.

"Well, they weren't happy to hear about that," Major Shelton said.

"To be honest, I'm not happy about it either, but I know this is the right thing to do," Sean said and paused for a moment. "Which is another reason I told them now. Give them some time to let it settle."

There'd been a lot of tension and stress since their recent operation. While it had been a success, it could have gone terribly wrong. They needed to find a way to more effectively deal with the Krake attack drones.

"I want the simulation of our recent engagement with the Krake uploaded to the tactical computers and distributed among the fleet. Have our people go over it. See if we can improve upon our response."

"Understood, Colonel. I'll get it done."

MAJOR BRODY LEANED back in his chair. The meeting had just ended, and only he and Major McKay were left in the room. A comlink opened, and it was Captain Ryan Ward from the *Babylon* and Olaf McGee from the *Archeon*.

"Major Brody, we wanted to speak with you."

Brody narrowed his eyes and said, "What's this about?"

"We conferred with the other destroyer captains, and we were hoping you could speak to Colonel Quinn again about his decision on not going home. I'm not sure if he's fully aware of the state of the space gate. We could only have a one-time use of it."

Major Brody frowned. "You heard the colonel. We have our orders."

Captain McGee pressed his lips together and swallowed. "Permission to speak freely, Major."

Brody didn't like where this was heading, but if there was a problem, he'd rather meet it head-on than let it fester. "Okay, I'll allow it, but be careful, Captain," Brody warned.

"Thank you, Major. I'll be brief," McGee said. "I don't think chasing down this lead is worth losing the entire battle group. We've been out of touch with COMCENT for over ninety days now. We need to check in. We also need to resupply. We have ships that aren't fighting at full capacity, and we're at overcapacity for passengers. We just don't think this is the best time to chase down whatever this Krake fifth column group is," McGee said, finishing.

"I realize I gave you permission to speak freely, but what you're suggesting is—"

"Major Brody," McGee interrupted, "I just want to be clear. We request that you speak with Colonel Quinn to make him aware of the situation with the battle group. I respect the chain of command, but Colonel Quinn has a reputation of seeing nothing but the objective."

Brody had to agree with that estimate of Sean, but he wouldn't admit that to the destroyer captain. "What makes you and the other captains think he's not aware of the situation?"

"Major, we heard your comments during the meeting. This isn't just a group of captains questioning the orders of our superior officers. Certain members of our crews have voiced their concerns up the chain of command on our ships as well," Captain Ward said.

Lester inhaled and considered the two officers on the holoscreen. "Very well. I'll take your comments under advisement, and I'll let you know if anything comes from it. In the meantime, you have your orders," Brody said and killed the connection.

Major McKay sighed heavily. "This isn't good if they're coming to us. I've been hearing the same kinds of things. At some point, it's not the crew just blowing off steam. I think we need to bring this to Colonel Quinn's attention right away."

Brody felt like he'd just swallowed a mouthful of vinegar. "I'll bring it up with Sean. Better if I do it alone," Brody said.

"Are you sure, Lester? I'm here if you need me," McKay offered.

Brody thought about it for a moment and then shook his head.

"It could be nothing. There's a lot of fear going on, and considering what just happened, I'm not too surprised. But we need them to focus and keep working. I've got it," Brody said.

McKay left the room and Brody sent Sean a message asking to speak to him in private. Fifteen minutes later, Sean appeared on the holoscreen in Brody's office aboard the *Yorktown*.

"I figured you'd be contacting me," Sean said.

Brody smiled a little. "To be honest, I hadn't planned on it, but some things have come up that I think you need to know."

Sean's gaze didn't quite narrow, but it definitely hardened as he braced himself for yet another thing to deal with.

"I didn't want to bring this up again, since you've already given your orders. I want you to reconsider. A couple of the . . ." Brody paused for a moment. "Never mind. We need to check in with COMCENT. I understand that this lead with the Krake is worth investigating, but we need to go back and resupply. We're at overcapacity with limited food and water. We can keep going for perhaps another sixty days, but still it's something to be aware of. I just think that if we contact COMCENT and apprise them of the situation, we could get resupplied with ammunition and go at this fresh."

"I've been hearing the complaints here too, Lester, but we can't do all that in the timeframe the Krake have given. This is a way to contact them. We have less than twelve hours."

Lester waited for Sean to continue.

"I agree in part, and you have a point. There's the risk of staying out here, and that last battle was a pretty close thing. I'd still do it again because we got the gate components, so at least somebody can go home to report back to COMCENT."

"Thank you," Lester said. "We don't know who this fifth column is, and all we do know about the Krake is that they like to manipulate an intelligent species. What if we're just next on the list?"

"We *are* next on their list," Sean said with a bit of an edge in his voice, "and we're not going to win this thing by playing it safe. We don't have any reason to trust them, but we should go out there and at least meet them. We can take the necessary precautions. They know we have a mobile space gate; otherwise, the data burst the Krake sent us doesn't make any sense. But they don't know exactly where we'll come in from. This gives us an advantage." Sean paused for a moment. "I know this isn't coming just from you."

"You're right Colonel, this—"

"Well, I don't agree with them. While they might not like my orders, they'll follow them, as you will. Is that understood, Major?"

Brody stiffened and narrowed his gaze. He'd been on the receiving end of a tongue-lashing from Colonel Quinn more than once and was getting just about tired of it.

"It's crystal clear, Colonel. Will that be all?"

"That will be all, Major. Carry on."

The comlink closed and Brody found that he was clutching the arms of his chair. His teeth were clenched, and he felt like molten fury was blazing in his gums. He needed to calm down. His thoughts were going a million kilometers an hour in the wrong direction.

Brody stood up and pounded his fist on the table, crying out in rage.

"Son of a bitch," he said between clenched teeth.

27

CONNOR'S secret office was a small combat information center isolated from access by external systems. Only one-way communications were allowed and had to be initiated from inside the room only by people with the clearance to do so. Connor had designed the system this way, hoping he'd never have to use it. The level of access he had to colonial systems would've violated even the most basic privacy restrictions.

Lars had circumvented colonial laws to achieve his goals. Connor had tried to operate within legal parameters to find him and whoever was involved with the rogue group's activities, but he'd failed. He'd also given Field Ops and Security the tools to do the job, and they'd come up short. Both Lars and whoever he was working with operated at a level above what passed for law enforcement in the colony, and this was something he couldn't allow anymore—especially now that they were willing to sacrifice colonial lives to achieve their objectives.

Few people knew about this office and what he could do there, but he was still within the secure confines of the CDF base at Sanctuary. Major Natalia Vassar stood on the other side of the room with several floating holoscreens surrounding her. She looked over at him.

"All platoons of Ranger 7th company have reported in from the three primary target zones."

"Understood," Connor replied and regarded her for a moment. Natalia had good instincts for intelligence analysis. "What is it? I can tell you want to say something."

Natalia made a swiping motion with her hand, and the holoscreens became opaque. "I was just thinking of the post-op review and the shitstorm that's going to come of this. You know it's not going to go unnoticed that we didn't have an Ops here at Sanctuary."

Connor shrugged. The trail to the rogue group hadn't implicated anyone who lived at Sanctuary. "That's just the way it happened. Anyway, are you surprised? We're going where the trail leads us."

Natalia didn't reply. Instead she re-engaged the holoscreens and frowned for a moment. "Are you aware that Captain Samson is outside the door, looking for a way in?"

Connor brought up the security video feed and saw Samson looking up at the hidden camera. Samson's position was with his back to the door, and he'd deduced where the hidden camera was. Connor chuckled a little. "No, I wasn't aware."

"I still find it odd that he doesn't use a last name."

"Oh, Samson *is* his last name. He just doesn't like to use his first name."

"I've searched the colonial records, and I can't find it. Even the records from the *Ark*," Natalia said.

"That's because he deleted them."

Samson pounded on the steel door, and Connor shook his head.

"Should I let him in?" Natalia asked.

"I've got it," Connor replied and sent his authorization for the door to open.

Samson walked in, scowling at Connor. He looked over at Natalia and tempered his scowl just a little bit. Then he looked back at Connor. "Major Vassar, I want to speak to General Gates alone," he said, his gaze never leaving Connor's. "Please," Samson tacked on at the end.

Connor looked over at Natalia and gave her a nod. She closed down her holoscreens and left the room.

"You know, if you were anyone else, no major worth his salt would've allowed you to speak to them that way, Captain."

"I think we can dispense with the ranks for a few minutes. You're so far off the map that if we were to include ranks, you'd be in a lot more trouble."

Connor regarded him for a few moments. "What is it that you think you know?"

"Where's Carl Flint and the 3rd Ranger company?"

"They're on a training mission."

"A training mission," Samson repeated. "That's bullshit and you know it. Spec Ops doesn't conduct training missions in Sierra, Delphi, or New Haven. Are you conducting an operation in colonial population centers?"

"I'm assuming you're here because you tried to access the whereabouts of Flint's company and were denied."

"Please," Samson said sharply. "It's easy to track where they went. The mission objectives might be classified, but they didn't classify the method of travel they used to get there. Nor the check-in intervals, although I doubt most people would notice that."

"Field Ops can't deal with Lars Mallory and the rogue group. They're succeeding at all their objectives, while we're being merely reactive. The status quo must change," Connor said.

"You're doing it again," Samson warned.

Connor frowned. "I'm doing what again?"

"You're playing fast and loose."

"Hardly. I've been piecing this together as we've gone along. The events at the Ovarrow city merely forced my hand."

"Is that a fact? I wasn't talking about this. You played fast and loose before, or have you forgotten? Millions of civilians paid the price."

Connor glared at Samson. He'd never forget that. "This isn't a hunt for the Syndicate."

"Call it whatever you want. This rogue group is a symptom of a larger problem. If you back them into a corner, you're risking lives," Samson said.

"Are you going to stand there and tell me you care about colonial lives now?" Connor asked.

"I didn't want to be here. I didn't ask for it. I came back to help you protect these people. Well, who's going to protect them from you?" Samson said and walked toward Connor. "It's necessary. I can already hear the argument you're about to make—'I have no choice.'"

"I don't have a choice, and you don't even know the particulars of this operation."

"You cut everyone off, and you've also failed to inform the people with the rank to stop you," Samson said, jabbing a finger toward Connor.

"No one is going to stop me from finding them. This has gone on long enough. I didn't start it, but I'm going to finish it. Are you going to stand in my way?" Connor asked.

Samson was a giant of a man, as if he'd been carved from stone, and he was much bigger than Connor. He was more heavily muscled and probably just as dangerous as Connor was, but there was no way in hell Connor was going to let anyone stand in his way.

"If I have to. You of all people should know that once you open that box . . . this operation you're doing. It will be impossible to stop what's going to happen next," Samson said.

"You don't need to lecture me about the laws of unintended consequences. I'm well aware of them. But at some point, we have to draw the line, and this is where mine is."

"You're too close to this. You've moved on with your life, started a family, and I respect that, but now this group has put your wife in danger. They hurt some of your closest friends, and you'll do whatever you have to do to stop them," Samson said.

"That's right," Connor said, not bothering to hide it anymore. "You think it was an accident that Lenora happened to be at the Ovarrow city when all that crap happened? They made this personal, and they picked the wrong person."

"You're right; this is personal, but did you ever stop and think that maybe you're playing right into their hands?"

"Did you ever stop and think that perhaps they're going to get more than they bargained for?" Connor replied.

"Give me one good reason why I shouldn't inform General Hayes and Governor Wolf what you're up to. You're not the only one who can put in fail-safes," Samson said and held up the secure comlink.

The suppressors Connor had in the room wouldn't work against it. Connor knew that because he had several of his own.

Connor smiled a little. "Did it ever occur to you that maybe I wanted you to be here right now?"

Samson frowned. "What do you mean?"

"I need your help. I'm going to find all the hideouts. This rogue group operates away from colonial population centers, but the way to find them is by tracking the leads at our major cities. I don't have Flint's platoons conducting a clandestine operation armed to the teeth. This is an inform-and-observe operation, and they have instructions to coordinate with Field Ops and Security. So yes, I'm opening Pandora's box, but it's with limitations. And I know there'll be repercussions for doing this, but I'm going to do it anyway," Connor said.

Samson inhaled swiftly and sighed. "Not armed to the teeth but armed with suppressors and shock sticks. Either way, you're executing CDF operations inside a population center. That isn't going to go unnoticed when this is all said and done."

"I know."

They were quiet for almost a full minute. Technically, there were legal loopholes to justify what Connor was doing, but that would only get him so far.

An alert sounded and a live video feed showed on the nearest holoscreen. Noah and Dash were standing outside. Noah was staring right into the camera feed while Dash kept a lookout.

"It looks like I'm not the only one who found your secret operations center," Samson said dryly.

Connor knew there was no way Dash could've found this place, but Noah was another matter.

"Connor, I know you're in there. We have to talk," Noah said.

28

SAMSON ARCHED AN EYEBROW TOWARD CONNOR. "Is this part of the plan?"

Connor frowned and walked over to the door, then opened it.

Dash's eyes widened. "Wow, what is this place?"

"How did you get in here?" Connor asked.

Noah smiled. "I'd be happy to tell you about it once you let us inside."

Connor didn't move.

Natalia was heading down the corridor toward them. She didn't look surprised to see Noah.

"I think I figured it out," Connor said and stepped aside to allow them in.

He narrowed his eyes at Natalia as she came in.

"Leverage every asset we have," she said, reminding Connor of what he'd told her in the past.

The door closed and Connor stood next to Samson. "Plan change," he said so only Samson could hear. Samson grunted in reply.

"All right, Noah," Connor said. "You've got my attention, but before you begin, I need to ask something. Is a certain tiny but fierce blonde wife going to come hunt me down because you're here?"

The self-satisfied smile on Noah's face blanched. "I think she'll be hunting us both down. She might even recruit Lenora."

"Great," Connor said dryly. "We can get an apartment together. But I know you wouldn't be here if it wasn't important . . . Well, you wouldn't have contacted me if it wasn't important. You're here because you want to come along."

Noah met his gaze for a few moments. "I know where Lars is."

Connor tapped his fingertips against his thigh and regarded Noah for a few moments. "You have my attention, Noah."

"I know you're angry, and you have every right to be," Noah said and paused for a moment. "I'm going to tell you what you need to know. You know that, and I know that. You're right though. I want to come. I need to come with you."

Connor drew in a breath, intending to deny Noah's request.

"I was hoping I wouldn't have to say this," Noah continued, "but of everyone in this room, Lars has the most to answer for to me. I know the location, and I'm going to get there with or without you."

"It's going to be dangerous. Everything Lars has done points to a man you don't know anymore. What makes you think he won't take a shot at you while he's trying to escape?" Connor said.

Noah stared at Connor for a moment. They both knew it was dangerous to make assumptions, especially about people who'd once been close to them.

"He won't," Dash said. "As much as I hate him and blame him for what's happened, Lars stopped his men from engaging the CDF squad that was protecting me and Jory."

Connor shook his head. "That's the thing. The conflict has escalated, and that makes people reckless. Now he's backed himself into a corner, and I'm coming for him."

"He's still a colonial citizen," Noah said. "He's still subject to the law."

"They'll have a chance to surrender. If they don't take it, then one way or another, I will root them out of whatever hole they are hiding in. You can count on it," Connor said.

"Fine, and you can count on me going with you," Noah said.

Samson bellowed a hearty laugh. "Ain't it something when the kids grow up? I like this one," Samson said, gesturing toward Noah.

Noah smiled and looked back at Connor. "They made a mistake before. I don't believe what happened at the Ovarrow city was . . . had undergone much long-term planning. It would explain some of the communications channels I picked up."

"You picked up?" Connor said in disbelief. "How . . .? You were in a coma. What do you mean you picked up?"

"Before my coma, I was working on something to help track down certain network traffic patterns."

"We were already doing that, and we haven't found anything."

"This is something new. You see, what I created was something that can adapt in almost real time. It generates a lot of noise, but sometimes it can lead you right where you need to be," Noah said.

That was when Connor knew Noah had, in fact, found the rogue group.

"Let me show you what I found. They've limited themselves to three bases of operation, but the one we're most interested in . . ." Noah said and went on to tell Connor and the others exactly what he'd found.

"Ovarrow military bunkers, or at least supply caches. They'd be well hidden. I can understand why it was so difficult to find them. Their movements were covered because of all the Ovarrow bunker-hopping we've been doing," Samson said.

"They'd have more structural integrity and be better hidden than the civilian bunker sites we've found," Connor said.

"I can task some of our reconnaissance satellites to survey the area. Perhaps we can send some stealth recon drones," Natalia suggested.

Connor shook his head. "No, at least not right now. We can deploy the stealth recon drones once we get on site. I don't want to alert them that we know where they are. We need to take them by surprise."

Connor looked at Samson for a moment.

Samson drew up his chin proudly. "We lead the way."

Connor nodded. "You two," he said to Noah and Dash, "you'll need these if you're coming with us."

The two young men walked over.

"You've upgraded my MPS design," Noah said.

"I field-tested it, too," Connor said. "Come on, let's get started."

29

CDF TROOP CARRIERS, along with their Hellcat escorts, ripped across the pale gray sky. The engines shrieked in dopplered wails as they came in low and fast over deep canyons.

"Easy to get lost in here. This is a good spot to hide," Samson said.

Connor looked at Noah. "I hope this tracker of yours is right."

"That makes two of us," Noah said. This drew a few glances in his direction. "They're in this region. That's what I can confirm."

Connor looked at the holoscreen in front of him, which had a video feed of the landscape. Samson was right; Lars had picked a good spot to hide. Connor could've hidden several battalions here if he'd wanted.

"It's enough for us to go on," Connor said. "Once we locate them, I want one of the troop carriers held in reserve in case they try to escape."

"Understood," Samson said and then relayed the orders. He looked at Connor when he was finished. "How many people do you think are at this location?"

"Intelligence estimates anywhere from fifty to seventy-five

people. Other estimates are for several hundred. We take their base of operations here and it will lead to the others as well," Connor said.

He saw Noah give them a sidelong glance.

"Only if we take their base intact," Noah said.

"Yes, and if not, we can use your tracker to find the other installations." Connor turned away. He didn't want to watch Noah's reaction. If he did, he'd say things he'd later regret.

"We're approaching the marker," Samson said.

"Send the Hellcats on ahead and do a sweep of the area," Connor said.

The Hellcats flew ahead, deploying recon drones as needed.

Interspersed between the canyons they flew over was low, level, forested grassland. Near the marker on the HUD overlay of the video feed, a gargantuan opening appeared. A slope led to an elliptical mouth that at its widest point was over a hundred and thirty-five meters.

"Easy enough to fly ships in there," Samson said.

A Hellcat flew down into the cave shaft and deployed reconnaissance drones. Connor had the other troop carrier and Hellcat escorts make a grid search of the area, looking for escape routes.

Several live video feeds from the recon drones came to prominence on the main holoscreen. The cave bottom was over fourteen hundred feet down and then narrowed away from the opening. They could land the troop carrier at the bottom, but they'd have to go on foot from there.

"Power source detected, and it looks like someone's been here recently," Connor said.

The recon drones made slow but steady progress and showed a path that led to a network of caves. Several shafts of sunlight were coming in through openings above.

"That's Ovarrow-made," Dash said. "That path right there. And then it leads to the walkway, so you don't have to climb to the bottom to make it over there."

He was right. Connor had seen similar structures at other Ovarrow bunkers, but they didn't have a record of this one.

"How far do you think these tunnels go?" Samson asked.

"It's hard to say," Connor said as several of the recon drones went dark.

They brought up the last images from the recon drones and tried to see what had destroyed them. Some Ovarrow military bunkers had automated defenses that still worked, but if the rogue group was there, then it could have been automated defenses they'd set up.

"I can't tell what took out the recon drones," Samson said.

"We're going to have to go in there," Connor said.

The troop carrier took them down to the base of the shaft. As they were making preparations to leave, the other teams reported in that they'd found another cave entrance about two kilometers away.

"That's close enough to be with within the same cave network," Dash commented.

Connor nodded and looked at Noah. "Are you sure you're up for this? You can stay behind and monitor from here."

Noah shook his head. "I'm coming."

He gave Connor a determined look, and Connor nodded. When Noah turned to grab his backpack, Connor caught Dash's attention. He tilted his head toward Noah and Dash nodded.

There were three platoons that made up the 7th Ranger company under Samson's command. Lieutenant Keith Mason led the way with his platoon, Connor and the others were in the middle, and another twenty-five soldiers followed them.

They made their way slowly through the tunnels the Ovarrow had carved out hundreds of years ago. Enough time had passed for moisture and sediment buildup to begin impacting what had once been a smooth path. The air was damp, but at least it was fresh. There were several smaller cave openings along the path that lit up the area and provided fresh air.

They deployed another reconnaissance drone and sent it on ahead, looking for what had taken out the others. Suddenly, several CDF automated turrets burst from the ceiling and fired their weapons at them. The soldiers on point activated portable shielding to protect them as they retreated back down the tunnel. Connor tried to send a command override, but he was locked out. Noah tried to use a back door to access them and shook his head. "They're hardened. They'll only respond to someone else's command. You'll have to take them out."

They made quick work of the automated defense turrets. There wasn't any doubt as to who was here. They'd found the rogue group the, but they were going to have to take it slow, removing whatever defenses were in place. The closer they got, the more dangerous it would become.

"Alert the other platoons about the automated defenses we've encountered," Connor said.

Samson relayed the information and they continued onward.

30

LARS LEFT the Ovarrow holding cell. It had been a frustrating conversation where nothing new had been learned. Over the past year, Lars had tried a number of interrogation techniques to glean information from the Ovarrow. Some had yielded results while others hadn't at all. Actual physical torture rarely yielded any useful results, despite the preconceptions of some. They'd used psychological techniques, some of which had worked, but ultimately the Ovarrow were an alien species. However, showing them the world they'd left was an effective technique, as well as showing them an image of an active arch the Krake had used to come to this world. The Ovarrow prisoners didn't realize that it was the colonists who were using the arch, and it was enough to get them motivated to speak about what they knew. After a while, Lars had to admit that it had become more of a rinse-and-repeat-type effort. The fact was that their entire operation had been disrupted by what Evans had done—what Evans had been ordered to do, Lars amended in his mind—and it had set their entire operation back. In addition, the CDF was now looking for them in earnest.

It had been easy to avoid Field Ops and Security since they restricted their activity to colonial cities and the nearby surrounding areas. The CDF was something different altogether.

When Lars had been recruited, he'd thought he was working to protect the colony, but the Ovarrow were far from innocent victims. They'd left a minefield of horrors that colonists had stumbled into, and they couldn't be trusted. He still believed in his mission, but the rogue group's activities had become more ruthless. He'd been kept out of the loop for the mission in the Ovarrow city. His superiors had believed Lars wouldn't have carried out the operation, and they'd been right. He'd never have done it, but he did have to deal with the fallout of such activity. They'd circumvented his authority. They'd betrayed him. The whole thing had made him watch the people around him with a fresh perspective. How much influence did his superiors have over his subordinates? There were believers in the cause just like him, but there were others who were becoming more ruthless—more like Evans.

Lars walked down the corridor toward the command center. Evans walked out of one of the adjacent rooms and looked at him. His gaze was calculating, and Lars felt his own survival instincts take over as if he were no longer looking at a friend but weighing the threat of a potential enemy. He didn't like it.

"Learn anything new?" Evans asked him.

"Just more of the same."

"Want me to dispose of them for you?"

Lars shook his head. "No. These things take time."

They were silent for a moment while they regarded one another.

"I've seen you dispose of prisoners in half the time you've spent with these. What makes them so different?" Evans asked.

"Maybe they're not different," Lars countered. "It's getting increasingly difficult to get more subjects to interrogate, and we need to make the most of what we have here now."

Evans looked away and nodded. "Have you read the latest intelligence reports? It looks like they found out some things about your friend Sean, indicating that the battle group is still around."

"I hadn't heard about that," Lars admitted. Both he and Evans had kept close watch for news about the Trident Battle Group that had gone missing months ago.

"They found a remnant, or at least a partial remnant, of one of the ships but nothing of the rest of the battle group."

"That's good. That means your sister is probably safe as well," Lars said.

Evans could be a bastard at times, but he was loyal to his family. He loved his sister, and it was hard for him to deal with the fact that she was missing.

A klaxon alarm blared in the corridor, shocking them both to silence.

"Come on," Lars said and ran toward the command center.

Less than a minute later, they ran through the doors to the command center. Tonya Wagner looked over at them. "The CDF is here. They're heading right for us."

Lars looked at her holoscreen, which showed that the CDF had found the main cave entrance to their base. Lars shook his head. He had over eighty people there, and they'd only just gotten settled in. How had the CDF found them so quickly?

"We're going to have to begin evacuation then," Lars said.

"We can't," Wagner replied. "Another CDF troop carrier just entered the cave network on the other side."

Lars looked at the video feed they'd captured before it went out. No doubt the CDF had taken it out with jamming. "Those aren't the only two ways out of here."

"We haven't fully explored that third group of tunnels," Evans replied. "We'd have to leave a lot of equipment behind if we went that way."

"I don't see that we have much choice," Lars said and looked at Wagner. "Order the evacuation."

"No," Evans said sternly. "We don't need to run from them."

Lars glared at Evans for a moment and then looked at Wagner. She hadn't followed his orders. The other agents in the room stopped what they were doing.

"The CDF is here. There's no stopping them from getting to us," Lars said.

"That's where you're wrong. My team is prepared for this," Evans said and brought up a secondary holoscreen. "While we were exploring the tunnels, we left a few surprises of our own in case the CDF found us."

Lars looked at the schematic Evans had put on the holoscreen. Explosive charges were deployed throughout the tunnel system.

"They won't detect them until it's too late. Not even their combat suits will protect them from tons of rock."

Lars's eyes widened as he realized that the CDF was already well inside the danger zone. "You can't be serious. You're going to collapse the tunnel on top of them?"

"I didn't tell them to come here."

Lars shook his head. "You're done. Shut it down, now."

Evans glared at him. "I don't think so. You see, the higher-ups thought you wouldn't have the stomach to do what needed to be done. They were right. I'm taking command."

"Like hell you are," Lars said and stomped toward Evans.

Dean Morris and Wagner pulled out their weapons and pointed them at Lars.

There was no way Lars could pull out his sidearm in time, and he didn't need to. He used his neural implants and shut down access to their computing core using his own authentication. The holoscreens around them became locked out before turning off.

Evans laughed. "That's cute, but the detonation signal can only come from me," he said, smiling wolfishly.

Lars dove toward Evans, taking him by surprise. Morris tried to fire his weapon but growled in surprise when it wouldn't respond. Lars threw Evans into Morris, and both men went down to the ground.

Wagner glanced at her weapon, which had been locked out along with the rest of the system.

"I can't believe you sided with them, Tonya," Lars said.

"Not with them. The work we've done."

"Killing colonists and CDF soldiers is not our work," Lars said. He walked over and took her sidearm from her. "Get over there with them."

His weapons worked just fine. Lars brought up one of the holoscreens and activated a camera feed, seeing a group of CDF soldiers coming toward the base. He saw Connor and his eyes widened. Then Noah walked into view. He felt a shiver run down his spine, and his mouth fell open in surprise.

Evans pushed himself to his feet, and Lars began to point his weapon at him.

"Not so fast, Lars," Evans said and glanced at the holoscreen. "Look who it is. The great Connor Gates and your friend Noah Barker. They should've joined us. Hell, Connor should've *led* us."

Lars raised his weapon.

Evans glared at him. "Are you going to kill me?"

"Are you going to kill them?" Lars countered.

Evans growled and stepped closer to Lars. "Take the shot. Take it. Take it!"

Lars hesitated. If Evans was the only one who could detonate the explosive charges, he might have a dead man's trigger set up.

Evans sneered. "That's right," he said and tapped the side of his head. "I'm the only one who can detonate them, and I'm the only one who can disable them. Do you want to say goodbye?"

Lars clenched his teeth and used his implants to increase the power output of his sidearm to maximum.

Morris regained his feet and reset his weapon's system, then pointed it at Lars.

"I'm giving you a chance to say goodbye to your friends," Evans said.

Lars regarded Evans for a moment and then squeezed the trigger. Explosive-tipped darts shrieked from his weapon, and the remains of Evans's body dropped to the ground. Lars dove to the side as Morris fired his weapon. Deep slivers of pain ran all through Lars's side as the high-velocity darts gouged through his light armor, hitting flesh. Lars swung his weapon up and shot at Morris's chest and then shot him in the head. Morris stumbled backward and went down. Dead.

Evans's dead man's trigger activated, and a new holoscreen appeared in red. Lars pushed himself up to his knees and scrambled over to the holoscreen. A countdown timer had appeared.

"You killed them!" Wagner cried out.

Lars glared at her for a moment. "Help me stop this."

Wagner looked away from Evans and Morris with a pained expression. She swallowed hard and came over next to Lars. "I can't access it. It's running on a secure subsystem. It's completely separate from our main system."

Lars tried to bypass the subsystem and shut it down, but it wouldn't work. "Dammit," he said. "They're going to die if we don't stop this. There has to be a way." He glared at Tonya. "Did you know what Evans was doing?"

"No," Tonya answered quickly. "I had no idea he did this."

Lars didn't believe her. He should have kept a better eye on Evans. The sting of betrayal felt like acid in his mouth.

"We have to warn them," Tonya said.

"They'll never believe us," Lars said. He accessed the base's computer system. Evans' secure subsystem had to be using their comms channels to trigger the signal. It was the only way for a signal to reach where he'd hidden the charges.

"Lars, we're running out of time," Tonya said.

Lars opened up a holoscreen that showed all the comlinks currently attached to their network and severed all of them, then shut the entire system down.

The countdown reached zero and they both froze for a few moments. Lars tilted his head to the side, listening for explosions, but didn't hear anything.

"Did you stop it?" Tonya asked. "You stopped it. How did you stop it?"

"I didn't stop it. I couldn't access the dead man's trigger, so I shut down the entire comms network."

Tonya's eyes went wide. "If anyone brings it back online, it will trigger the explosives."

Lars nodded. "I locked out the system. I'm going to bring up the emergency broadcast network. It's a separate system."

"You need to check—" Tonya began.

"I know," Lars said.

He brought up the emergency broadcast system one component at a time, checking that there were no latent protocols set to run by first bringing them up in a virtualized environment before bringing up the actual system. Once the system was up, he sent out a broadcast to all the people in the base.

"Stand down. Fall back to the main area. We're surrendering to the CDF," Lars said. He set the broadcast to loop three more times and then shut it down.

"We can still escape," Tonya said.

Lars shook his head. "It's over. If we try to escape, the CDF will hunt us down. The only way for us to walk out of here is if we surrender."

He dropped his weapon. It was dead anyway. The emergency

broadcast he'd sent had locked out all firearms and automated defenses.

"We're just going to go out there and surrender?" Tonya asked. Then she said, "What about the Ovarrow?"

"Leave them where they are," Lars said.

"We can't just surrender."

Lars gave her a long look, and Tonya looked away. He used the emergency comms system to open a comlink to the CDF. "This is Lars Mallory. I'd like to speak to General Connor Gates."

He broadcast the channel so everyone in the base could listen.

"This is Gates," Connor said. "Lars, if this is really you, I'm giving you one chance to surrender."

Lars stood up, staggered over to a chair, and sat down. Tonya left him, saying she was going to get a medkit.

"It's me, Connor. I'm broadcasting this conversation to my people in the base," Lars said.

There were a few moments of silence. "Understood," Connor replied.

"One condition for our surrender is that I want your personal guarantee my people will be unharmed. We walk out of here in your custody. In exchange, we have fifteen Ovarrow prisoners we'll turn over to you."

Lars paused for a few moments, waiting for Connor to respond. He didn't, and Lars sighed. "I know what you want."

"You need to do better than that. We're coming for you whether you want us to or not. The moment your operations put colonial lives in jeopardy was the moment you lost all credibility for this cause you serve. I'm within my rights to blow this place sky high with all of you in it," Connor replied.

Lars winced, knowing Connor was right. "What happened at the Ovarrow city wasn't my operation. I didn't know about it until after the fact. I don't expect you to believe me."

"Your credibility isn't what it used to be."

"I can give you evidence of who was involved, including the leaders of our organization, in exchange for my people remaining unharmed. Otherwise, you'll get nothing," Lars said.

He glared at the comlink channel on the holoscreen. He'd just laid all his chips out on the table. He had nothing left to barter with. If they'd found their hideout here, then they'd no doubt be able to find the others. He glanced out the door to the command center. A crowd of people were gathered outside, waiting to hear. They looked angry and scared. They'd been backed into a corner, and they all knew it.

Lars waited for Connor to reply. "The ball is in your court. What do you say?"

"We'll talk about it. Since this is a broadcast and the rest of your people are listening in, you should all know that anyone who doesn't surrender or tries to escape will be shot on sight. You're all fugitives and enemies of the colony. If you walk out now, you'll live. This is your only offer," Connor said.

Lars stood up. Tonya had applied medi-paste and numbed his wounds, which had sealed and were no longer bleeding. He walked through the throng of people. He'd recruited most of them, and he had to be the first to walk out so they could see him surrender. Lars walked toward the main entrance, leading everyone to the CDF. What had started out as a rebellious effort to help defend the colony had morphed into something Lars hadn't anticipated. Even now at the end of it all, he couldn't pinpoint where everything had gone wrong. How had they lost their way?

He walked to the main bunker doors and entered his authorization. The large doors swung outward to grim-faced CDF soldiers. Lars held up his hands and walked toward them in defeat. Connor stood out in front, and Lars flinched from the fury he saw in Connor's gaze, but he also saw a small amount of remorse. It hit him like a punch in the gut. The only thing that would be worse was when he faced his father.

"There's someone who wants to talk to you," Connor said.

Behind Connor stood Noah.

His friend regarded him for a few moments as if he didn't know what to say. Lars thought he looked different. Noah had been in a coma, so how was he supposed to look? His throat became thick. "I'm sorry," Lars said.

Noah pressed his lips together, his mouth forming a grim line, and he shook his head. CDF soldiers surrounded Lars and bound his wrists together. Noah watched and didn't say anything. What *could* he say? Lars didn't know what was worse—the fact that after all Lars had done, Noah pitied him, or that he was starting to feel ashamed. Lars clenched his teeth and his lips trembled. He wanted to scream, revile against the shame he felt. He'd done the right thing, but the argument frayed on the edges of his thoughts.

"Take the Ovarrow to Camp Alpha," Connor said to one of the soldiers and then looked at Lars. "How deep does this go?"

Lars looked away for a moment. "It's pretty deep," he muttered and then began telling Connor everything he knew.

31

Lester Brody glanced at the time in the upper right-hand corner of his internal heads-up display. No matter what, they couldn't escape the running of the clock.

He headed down the corridor toward McKay's ready room off the bridge. Lester knocked on the door, and McKay let him in.

"Is the science team still here?" McKay asked.

Lester nodded. "They've done their final diagnostics of the Krake equipment and are preparing the report."

"I can delay their shuttle departure," McKay offered.

"If we need to. It's just about time to begin," Lester said.

He activated the holoscreen above the conference table, and three destroyer captains appeared. Three of the four destroyer captains he'd reached out to had shown up. Captain Ryan Ward gave a grim nod, as well as Olaf McGee. The presence of the *Diligent's* Captain, Ida Ingram surprised Lester. He hadn't expected Captain Martinez or Captain Welch to join them, so he'd kept them out of the loop, but he hadn't been sure about Captain Watkins. Three was enough.

"Thank you for coming," Lester said. "As of right now, none

of us has done anything we can't walk away from. You came to me and voiced your concerns, and I took those concerns to Colonel Quinn's attention. He didn't listen, and the way he dismissed those concerns left me with little choice. I must take action."

Captain Ida Ingram raised her hand. "Major Brody, what do you intend to do?"

"I intend to use the space gate to return home and report in to COMCENT. It's my belief that when I try to do this, Colonel Quinn will attempt to take control of the space gate," Lester answered and paused for a moment. "I'm going to lay it out on the table. I'm disobeying a direct order from my commanding officer. For the record, I do believe that Colonel Quinn is unfit to command this battle group, leaving me no choice but to take command."

"But that's just it, Major," Ingram said. "We don't have the power to take control of the battle group."

"You're right," Lester said, "but we don't need to take control of the battle group. We need to control the space gate and use it to get home. Then this becomes a matter for the CDF brass to sort out, and I think they'll judge us more favorably than they'll judge Colonel Quinn."

Lester watched the other captains, trying to gauge their commitment. "I invite anyone here who has objections to voice them right now. If you're not fully committed to this, then say so, and you'll be excused from this operation, but it won't change what we're doing."

"I have no objections," Captain Ward said.

"Neither do I," Captain McGee said.

Lester turned toward McKay, who simply shook his head. Then he looked at Captain Ingram.

"We're supposed to be better than this," she said with disgust in her voice. "It shouldn't have come to this, but I don't see another way. You have my support," Ingram said and then closed her comlink.

"We will begin in fifteen minutes," Lester said.

SEAN SAT in his office alone, going over some of the latest reports. His intelligence analysts were going over the Krake message and would be providing him with another report in just under an hour. They had a little over six hours before they were due to go to the predefined set of Krake coordinates.

A comlink alert appeared on his holoscreen with Oriana's identification.

"Dr. Evans, how goes the diagnostic of the Krake equipment?"

Oriana was alone and not on the bridge of the *Yorktown*. Sean frowned for a moment. "Where are you?"

"I commandeered somebody's office. The diagnostic came back fine. I was actually done a few hours ago," Oriana said.

"This is the first I've heard of it," Sean replied.

"Our shuttle hasn't been given clearance to leave. Something about an issue with the hangar bay doors."

"I'm sure they'll get it fixed in no time."

"I checked the logs, and there's nothing in them regarding a maintenance crew dispatched to fix anything," Oriana said.

"Have you spoken with Major McKay?" Sean asked.

"He's the one who told me about the issue with the hangar bay doors. There's something strange going on here," Oriana said.

She looked away from the camera as if she'd heard something.

"What do you mean?"

"I spent enough time on the *Vigilant's* bridge to know when there's an operation going on," Oriana said.

"In a few hours' time, we're going to try to find the Krake using their own message. It's probably just that," Sean said.

"This is different," Oriana said and leaned in closer to the camera. "I feel like I'm being watched by someone from Major Brody's team. I don't know who they are, but something's not right here."

She sounded a little upset but not outright scared. And that wasn't like her at all. "There's a lot of people talking about going home."

This got Sean's attention and roused his suspicion. "I'm going to head to the bridge and see if I can get some answers. Are you safe where you are?" he asked and then felt stupid for asking the question.

They had agreed to keep things casual, but his pulse raced at the thought of something happening to her. "Stay where you are. I'll be in touch."

Sean left his office. Major Shelton glanced at him as he entered the bridge and frowned.

"What's the *Yorktown*'s status?" Sean asked.

"They're holding position," Major Shelton answered.

"Comms, get me Major McKay—" Sean began. "Forget that. Give me Major Brody."

There was a long pause while Sean waited.

"It'll be a few minutes, Colonel. Neither one of them is on the bridge," Specialist Sansky replied.

Sean narrowed his gaze and frowned. "Tactical, initiate control of the space gate."

"Initiating control, Colonel." Lieutenant Jane Russo's fingers worked furiously as she accessed the remote systems. "Colonel, I'm locked out of space gate control."

Sean clenched his teeth. He attempted to access the same system. *Denied.* "Run a diagnostic," he said.

While Sean waited for Russo to run the diagnostic, he sent Oriana a text message via comlink.

Col. S. Quinn: *Can you access space gate control systems?*

There was no reply, not even a confirmation that his message had been received by Oriana.

"Diagnostic has finished. All systems are functioning normally, Colonel," Russo said.

Major Shelton walked over to his side. "They could be having comms issues," she said, and Sean could tell she didn't believe it any more than he did.

He shook his head. "I was just speaking with Oriana," Sean said and leaned over so only Vanessa could hear. "She thought McKay was purposefully delaying her shuttle departure and that she was being watched. She finished her diagnostic of the space gate hours ago."

His XO's gaze hardened. "Colonel, are you suggesting . . ." she said and didn't include what they were both thinking.

"I don't know," Sean admitted, and then looked at the plot on the main holoscreen. "Comms, confirm communication status of the battle group. I want all of them to check in."

32

"Colonel, the *Dutchman*, the *Albany*, and the *Burroughs* all report status green. Captains Martinez, Welch, and Watkins are currently on duty. I received an automated standard check-in response from the *Babylon*, the *Acheron*, and the *Diligent*," Specialist Sansky said.

"Inform the *Dutchman*, the *Albany*, and the *Burroughs* to stand by for further orders. I want a second request to the others for verbal confirmation of status," Sean said and looked at the main holoscreen, which showed the current ship positions.

"Split right down the middle," Major Shelton said.

The *Babylon* and the *Acheron* were positioned closest to the *Yorktown*. The next closest ship was the *Albany*. Captain Lori Welch had replied, so she wasn't caught up in whatever Brody was doing.

Sean looked at Vanessa. "I want you to get on a secure channel with Captains Martinez and Watkins. We have a situation, and I need them to maintain their positions near the *Diligent*."

Vanessa leaned in so only Sean could hear. "Is it a mutiny?"

"Not yet," Sean replied quietly.

Major Shelton went to the auxiliary workstation and began working.

"Colonel, I have a comlink request from the *Yorktown*. It's Major Brody," Specialist Sansky said.

Sean went to the command chair and sat down. "Put it on the main holoscreen and broadcast the feed to the bridges of the other ships."

A few moments later Major Brody's face appeared, and it looked like he was on the main bridge of the *Yorktown*. "Major Brody, we've attempted to initiate control of the space gate and appear to be locked out. Can you offer any explanation as to why that might be?"

"Colonel Quinn, you've left me no choice but to take control of the space gate. I'll utilize the gate to report in to COMCENT," Major Brody said.

Sean's tone deepened. "Doing so puts you in violation of my direct orders. You will relinquish control of the space gate at once. You are hereby relieved of duty and will surrender to Major McKay's custody," Sean said.

The video feed zoomed out, showing that Major McKay was standing next to Major Brody. Sean caught a glimpse of the back of Oriana's head on the bridge.

"I'm afraid Major McKay and I are in agreement. You are unfit to command the battle group," Major Brody said. "Major Shelton, relieve Colonel Quinn and take command of the *Vigilant*."

The bridge on the *Vigilant* went deadly quiet. "Have both of you lost your minds?" Sean said with a sneer.

"This isn't personal," Brody said. "I'm going to open the space gate now."

Sean stood up and clenched his fist. "If any part of that space gate powers up, I will use the *Vigilant's* weapons systems to take it out."

"And destroy our only means of getting home? I don't think so," Brody replied.

Sean looked at Lieutenant Russo and gave her a nod. A few moments later, there was a commotion on the bridge of the *Yorktown*. "You can't be serious—"

Sean muted communications with the *Yorktown* so they didn't have to listen to Brody.

A message appeared on Sean's internal heads-up display.

Dr. O. Evans: *I can delay him for an hour.*

Sean's gaze darted to Oriana in the background. Brody and McKay had moved over to her and pulled her away from the workstation. Sean clenched his teeth for a moment.

"I've cut off the *Yorktown*," Sean said and addressed the rest of the battle group. "For the rest of you, if you've been pulled into Brody and McKay's foolish effort, it's not too late. The chain of command exists for a reason, and you don't get to question it. My orders stand. As for Lester Brody and Christopher McKay, you have a window of opportunity to do the right thing and surrender yourselves. You have one hour to comply."

Sean cut the comlink to the rest of the battle group. "Major Shelton, you're with me. Lieutenant Russo, you have the con. I'll be in my ready room if you need me. I want to be alerted at the slightest change in the battle group."

Sean left the bridge with Major Shelton. Once they were inside with his office door closed, he looked up at the ceiling. "Gabriel, I'm enacting command protocol blackbird one-two-one-three-two-zero-nine. Ident is Colonel Sean Quinn. Please verify."

"Blackbird protocol is verified. Establishing secure communications network. Online in twenty seconds," Gabriel said.

Major Shelton frowned. "I'm not familiar with this."

"It's not official fleet standard operating procedure. I'll explain in a minute," Sean replied.

His personal holoscreen became active, and Captain Chad Boseman of Spec Ops appeared. "Blackbird status confirmed. What are your orders?"

"I need you to get to the *Yorktown*."

"Mission objective?" Boseman asked.

"There are friendlies mixed with mutineers. We need to take back control of the ship and the space gate," Sean said.

"I can get aboard that ship, no problem."

"Not so fast. They'll be on the lookout for combat shuttles leaving the *Vigilant*," Sean replied.

Boseman smiled. "Who said anything about using combat shuttles?"

Sean smiled and listened to Boseman's plan for storming the *Yorktown*.

"You have less than an hour. I want to minimize the loss of life; however, lethal use of force is authorized against any mutineers," Sean said.

"Understood, Colonel. I'll contact you directly once we're aboard the *Yorktown*," Boseman said.

The comlink went dark, and Major Shelton shot him a questioning look. "Just so I'm clear, Colonel, a secondary function of the Spec Ops platoons aboard CDF ships is to ensure command authority of the officer on board?"

"Not exactly," Sean replied. "It's for the battle group. It's one of those things you try to account for—the risk, I mean—and hope you never have to use," Sean said and shook his head.

"You didn't expect this to happen from Major Brody—Lester Brody that is," Major Shelton said, correcting herself. The moment Sean had declared Brody a mutineer, he'd lost his rank.

Sean shook his head. "I expected better from him."

"What do you need me to do?" Major Shelton asked.

They spent the next few minutes going over the strategy. Sean received check-ins from the other Spec Ops platoons on board the destroyers. The timing had to be succinct, and they needed to wait for Boseman to get aboard the *Yorktown* before they executed the operation. In spite of all their precautions, Sean had to admit that there was an extremely high risk of the situation getting out of control. The fact that Brody and McKay had delayed Oriana and her team meant that they weren't averse to taking hostages.

"What will you do if Brody decides to leverage his assets?" Major Shelton asked. She knew of his relationship with Oriana, despite the assertions that they were "just casual."

"Let's hope it doesn't come to it, but if it does . . ." Sean said and paused for a moment. "There's no negotiating with mutineers. Ever."

Casual, my ass, Sean thought and hated it.

33

"Dr. Evans," Brody said, "I need to know what you did. More importantly, I need you to undo it," he said, trying to sound calm.

"It can't be undone," Dr. Evans replied.

"That's bullshit," McKay said and turned toward Kent. "Bring up her workstation session. I want to know what commands she used."

Lester noticed that Dr. Evans didn't appear concerned about that, and he was beginning to suspect she was telling the truth. "I thought you wanted to go home."

Dr. Evans regarded him for a moment. "I did, but not like this. I'd never betray Colonel Quinn or the CDF."

Lester sneered. "Don't you mean Sean?"

Dr. Evans met his gaze coolly and didn't reply.

Lester looked at McKay, who shook his head. "She put the gate control systems into a full diagnostic reset. It takes an hour to do. If we interrupt, it simply restarts, picking up right where it left off."

Lester shook his head and sighed. "A flaw in the system. So, we have to wait an hour."

Brody returned to the command chair and activated the secure comlink he'd established to Captains Ward, McGee, and Ingram. "It appears the delay wasn't a bluff."

Captain Ward nodded. "For a few moments, I thought he was really going to take out the space gate."

Lester shook his head. "That was a bluff. All of us need that gate."

"Major Brody," Captain Ida Ingram said, "are you at all worried about what Colonel Quinn will do? He seemed pretty certain he was going to take command—"

The comlink to the *Diligent* went dark. Then, the comlink to the *Babylon* and the *Acheron* went offline as well.

"Lieutenant Harish, can you get them back online?" Lester asked.

"I'm trying, Major, but they're not responding. I'll keep at it," Harish replied.

Lester's gaze swooped toward Dr. Evans, and he stomped over to her. "There has to be a way to stop the diagnostic. It's been thirty minutes. It can be cut short."

"Then by all means, cut it short," Dr. Evans replied, secure in the knowledge that she knew more about the space gate systems than he did.

She was right.

Lester clenched his teeth and growled.

"Major Brody," Lieutenant Harish said, "I have a comlink from the *Vigilant*."

"I THOUGHT we were done with crazy operations for at least a few days," Sergeant Benton said.

Fifty Spec Ops soldiers in full combat suits were daisy-chained to ten communications drones under Boseman's command.

"You don't like hitching a ride on a comms drone?" Boseman asked. They needed to get to the *Yorktown* as quickly as possible, and Sean had authorized him to be creative with meeting that objective.

"Oh, don't get me wrong, I like a good thrill as much as the next guy, but this is downright dangerous," Sergeant Benton said with just a hint of mock exasperation in his voice.

Boseman heard several of the other soldiers chuckle and joke in return, saying the mission was too dangerous and they wanted to go home. There was no risk of their comms being detected since they were all using line-of-sight communications. They'd been leapfrogging from ship to ship, making their way as quickly as possible to the *Yorktown*. Luckily for them, Trident Battle Group was in a tight formation—as tight a formation as any fleet maintained in space. The *Yorktown* had all its main hangars locked up tight, which Chad had expected.

"All right. Look alive, boys. We're closing in on the target," Boseman said. He marked it, and an indicator appeared on the heads-up displays of each of the soldiers' helmets. They were aiming for a maintenance hatch amidships that would put them between the primary and secondary bridges of the *Yorktown*. The carrier vessel was actually a converted freighter, which made certain construction points less secure than they would have been on a CDF warship. The comms drones slowed their approach as they reached the maintenance hatch.

"Twenty seconds," Corporal Brentworth said and brought up his wrist computer. Even though he couldn't access the main computer systems of the *Yorktown*, he could override the door controls while making it appear that the door had remained shut. "We're clear, Captain."

"After you, Sergeant Benton," Boseman said.

Benton went to the hatch and opened it, and then he and five soldiers went inside. There was an empty maintenance corridor beyond. Boseman configured the comms drone they'd hitched a ride on with a quick message back to the *Vigilant*.

"All right, we're going to split up," Boseman said. "We're going to secure the ship, starting with . . ."

"I SEE you've moved on to taking hostages," Sean said.

The officers serving aboard the *Yorktown* were all armed. There was no doubt the bridge was locked down, but Sean knew it wouldn't be enough.

"Everyone here has volunteered," Brody replied.

"Is that a fact?" Sean replied. "They don't look like volunteers to me," he said and glanced pointedly at Oriana. "Some of them may have volunteered in the beginning, but much like you, they're in over their heads."

Earlier, Sean had had Gabriel attempt to gain control of the *Yorktown*'s systems, but that had been unsuccessful.

"We're about to bring the space gate online. Shall I convey anything to COMCENT on your behalf?" Brody asked.

Sean glared at the image on the holoscreen, wishing he could reach through it and choke Lester Brody.

"You're alone, Lester. Right now, my Spec Ops teams have taken control of the ringleaders of your little conspiracy. This farce of a mutiny is over. It would be better for you to surrender."

Brody glared back at him, his eyes full of contempt and hatred. "Like hell I will! You are so self-righteous, as if the great Sean Quinn couldn't be wrong. If you fire your weapons on the space gate, it'll alert the Krake, and then we'll have no choice but to go through it."

A message appeared on Sean's personal holoscreen, and he glanced at it. He typed a response but didn't send it yet, looking back at the main holoscreen on the *Vigilant*'s command bridge.

"History will judge whether I'm right or wrong, but what's important right now is that I'm in command"—he sent the message—"and you're finished."

"Colonel," Lieutenant Russo said, "I'm detecting power fluctuations from the space gate. They're bringing it online."

"Acknowledged," Sean replied.

There was shouting from the bridge of the *Yorktown*, followed by several loud concussive blasts as Captain Boseman and the Spec Ops team stormed the bridge. Sean felt acid creep up into his throat, and he kept his mouth clenched shut as he looked down at the message he'd sent Boseman.

Execute the mutineers.

The first mutiny in the brief history of the Colonial Defense Force had come to a bloody end.

34

SEAN POWERED off the holoscreen at his desk and leaned back in his chair. *A mutiny,* he thought and grimaced, feeling as if the bile in the back of his throat had taken up permanent residence. The whole thing made him sick. He stood up and looked at his hands, wanting to wash them again. All he needed right then was the Krake to attack them. Considering the state of the Trident Battle Group, they'd be hard-pressed to put up a fight, considering that half the senior officers from three destroyers were on their way to the *Vigilant.*

The Spec Ops teams aboard the destroyers had successfully taken control of the bridges without any loss of life. Former CDF captains Ryan Ward, Olaf McGee, and Ida Ingram, as well as several senior officers and security personnel on their respective ships, had surrendered in the face of heavily armed Spec Ops soldiers.

The armed mutineers on the primary bridge of the *Yorktown* had attempted to hold the bridge by use of force, hoping in vain for the space gate to activate. Lester Brody, Christopher McKay, and half a dozen other bridge officers had been killed, and Sean had just finished filing the report for his official log.

"Colonel Quinn," Gabriel said, "two combat shuttles have just arrived from the *Yorktown* with the mutineers."

"I'm on my way to the main hangar bay," Sean replied.

He walked toward the door and straightened his uniform. Major Shelton met him outside with a squad of CDF soldiers behind her. He'd gotten back control of Trident Battle Group, but the cost had been high. How could he have been so wrong about Brody? Lester had been his XO for the entire battle group.

"I want you to do a complete shakedown of the *Yorktown's* crew. We need to identify anyone else who was involved," Sean said.

"Understood, Colonel," Major Shelton said. "I just finished Captain Boseman's report. There were civilian mutineers as well who attempted to hold the bridge."

Sean couldn't keep the bitterness from his voice. "If we discover any other civilian mutineers, they'll be taken into custody and held for trial when we get back."

"Permission to speak freely, Colonel."

They walked down the quiet corridor. "Go ahead."

"For the record, I believe you did the right thing. The chain of command must be preserved; however, we now have a demoralized crew with junior officers who're going to have to function in senior posts," Major Shelton said.

"Thank you for that," Sean replied. "If I could clone you and have you command those destroyers, I would. The junior officers are simply going to have to grow up faster than we'd originally intended, but I see your point. We're going to have to do a full review and maybe shuffle some people around. If you have any recommendations, send them over to me and we can discuss it. You're now second-in-command of Trident Battle Group, and I'll be relying on you more than ever."

Major Shelton considered his words for a moment, her

intelligent brown eyes appearing a shade lighter than her dark skin. "I won't let you down. We'll get them past this."

"The mutiny is finished, but as the commanding officer in charge, I need to review my actions and see if there was a way all this could've been avoided. I want you to think about that when you write your own report. The CDF brass will review the reports to look for an honest accounting of events, and I encourage you to point out any faults you see with how things were handled."

Major Shelton frowned and then straightened her shoulders. "Understood, Colonel," she said and meant it. "Brody sowed dissension in the ranks, and that's unforgivable in an officer, but this is going to take some time to overcome. Soldiers need to obey without question; however, given our circumstances, I believe they must also have hope, or they'll fail to perform their duties. I'm not saying we should share our reasons for the decisions we make, but perhaps we can do a better job of keeping the crew informed."

Sean thought he'd already been keeping the crew informed. What more did they want? The attitude of the crew was a reflection of its leadership, and Sean needed to salvage Trident Battle Group's remaining senior officers—build them up so they could keep the crew in line.

They reached the door to the main hangar and Sean stopped. "Major Shelton, I'm lucky to have you serving under my command. I can't think of a higher compliment than that."

Major Shelton stood up straight and saluted him. "Colonel Quinn, the honor is all mine."

Sean stepped through the threshold onto the main hangar bay floor where two squads of CDF soldiers surrounded the combat shuttle. He gave a curt nod to the lieutenant, and the soldiers escorted the mutineers off the shuttle. They had their hands bound in front of them, and hardly any of them dared to meet Sean's gaze. The civilians who'd participated in the mutiny had been separated from the others and stood off to the side. They would bear witness to what was about to happen. Sean spared a brief glance at Oriana as she walked off the shuttle, and his mouth went dry. He could tell there was a lot she wanted to say, but they couldn't right then.

The rest of the mutineers were lined up just outside the airlock doors. Over fifty soldiers had been implicated in the attempted mutiny, from senior bridge officers to engineering crew. Armed CDF soldiers fanned out on either side of Sean, holding their weapons at the ready but not pointing them at the mutineers. Three destroyer captains, as well as their first lieutenants, stood with slumped shoulders. Some of them glanced at him, hoping for some kind of leniency.

Sean stepped closer to them, glaring. "Mutineers," he said, "each of you has dishonored the oath you swore when you put on the uniform. That oath represents a commitment to duty and honor to the Colonial Defense Force—a cause greater than yourselves."

"Colonel Quinn," Ida Ingram cried out, "we're sorry. Please, we were coerced by Major Brody. It was Ward and McGee who came to me. I just want to go home."

The rest of what she'd been about to say died on her lips. Sean looked at Ryan Ward and Olaf McGee. They'd been good men, but now they stared defiantly back at him.

Sean looked at Ingram. "You were in command of a CDF warship. You don't get coerced into anything. You follow the orders of your commanding officer, and you execute those orders to the best of your ability—neither of which you did," Sean said, sweeping his gaze across all of them. "Do you know the difference between a mutineer and a prisoner?"

Ingram looked away from him, and Sean glared at the others. The knowledge of what was about to happen was reflected in both Ward's and McGee's pallid faces. Some of their subordinates began to shift their feet.

"A prisoner has rights," Sean said and gestured toward the CDF soldiers. A klaxon alarm blared as the airlock doors opened to the inner chamber. "Mutineers do not."

The soldiers forced the mutineers into the inner chamber of the airlock, and the door shut. Sean saw panic ensue, along with muffled cries for mercy. He walked over to the door controls and looked through the airlock window. Several of the mutineers banged on the window, begging to be let back onto the ship. But not all of them. There was a defiant few who, whether through false bravado or sheer stupidity, refused to accept the inevitable. Sean slammed his palm on the exterior airlock door controls, and the mutineers were sucked into the vacuum of space.

He stood there for a few moments, watching until the last body disappeared from view. It had been over in seconds, but he'd keep seeing their deaths for a long time.

Sean closed the exterior airlock doors and turned around. The soldiers on the hangar bay floor saluted, and he returned it, forcing his queasy stomach into submission. It wasn't the first time he'd killed, but there was a big difference between killing an enemy and executing people who'd once been comrades. He hated the coldness he felt inside.

He came to stand before the civilian mutineers, and several of them flinched at his approach. "You are all prisoners and will be held until we return to New Earth. Remember what happened to the mutineers. If any of you ever feel the urge to complain about your treatment, I want you to think about the people who were just in that airlock," Sean said, gesturing behind him.

None of the prisoners would look at him as they were escorted out of the main hangar bay to the holding cells.

Sean headed back toward the bridge. Once off the main hangar deck, he leaned against the wall and swallowed several mouthfuls of air. He wanted to scream with rage that Brody hadn't been taken into custody so Sean could deliver the justice he deserved. But it wouldn't have been justice where Brody was concerned; it would have been vengeance. Sean hated that somehow this mutiny was a reflection of his own actions, that he'd contributed to this mess and didn't know what he should change to avoid it in the future. But perhaps there was nothing he could have done to avoid it. He would never apologize or regret the orders he'd given. He believed wholeheartedly in what had to be done, but he felt a knot weighing down his stomach at the thought that this dark business had only just begun.

"Colonel Quinn," Gabriel said, the ship's AI's voice coming through the speaker in the corridor. "There are three hours remaining until the first set of Krake coordinates is to be followed."

Sean walked down the long corridor. "Understood, Gabriel."

Sean went into his office near the main bridge, intending to splash some cold water on his face, but when he walked in, he saw that Oriana was there waiting for him. He stepped inside and the door shut.

Her shoulders were drawn up tight, and she looked at him. "You killed them," she said.

"I did," Sean answered, not offering anything more than that. He hated how she was looking at him, and he felt a small urge to justify what he'd done, but it didn't last longer than a few seconds. If Oriana was going to be with him, she had to know and accept him for everything he was.

"I'm sorry you were caught up in this," Sean said.

"He tried to use me as a bargaining piece to get to you," Oriana said.

"I know," he said quietly. He wanted to reach out to her, but he didn't know how she'd react.

Oriana looked away from him. Her eyes were red. "They took us prisoner. Me and my team. Is this how it's going to be?"

Sean swallowed hard. "No, this never should have happened.

Brody was desperate, but maybe it would be better if we didn't spend so much time together."

Oriana winced and looked away from him. "Our casual relationship," she said, and he abhorred how it sounded.

"It was never casual. I think we can admit that now," Sean said.

Oriana looked at him. She was angry, hurt, and scared, but she also cared about him. He could see it in her eyes, but something was holding her back. She must think he was a monster.

"I need to get to the bridge. You can stay here as long as you need to," Sean said and stepped back toward the door.

"No, don't go," Oriana said quickly and stepped closer to him. "I'm not that fragile," she said with a bit of steel in her voice. "I'm just not used to . . . this."

Sean stepped toward her. "No one should be used to this. It was a nightmare."

"It doesn't have to be," Oriana said, and reaching out, she took Sean's hand in her own. "No one should get in the way of us."

Sean pulled her into his arms, and they were quiet for a few moments. He wanted to stay there like that, but he couldn't.

He left his office, and Oriana followed him.

Sean stopped just before the bridge. "Are you sure you're all right?"

"I'm furious, but that doesn't mean I want to go somewhere and sulk," Oriana replied.

"That makes two of us," Sean said.

35

THE TROOP CARRIER left Camp Alpha. Connor leaned back in his chair and rubbed his hands over his face, taking a few deep breaths and sighing.

Dash cleared his throat. "I'm starting to feel a little outnumbered here. I think I'm the only civilian on this ship."

The prisoners were being taken to the CDF base at Sanctuary.

Connor shrugged and didn't say anything.

"I'm a little surprised you let me tag along," Dash said.

"You're an official witness, and Noah wanted to be alone with Lars," Connor said.

When Lars had offered a confession, Connor thought he'd had a good idea of who was involved. He'd been mostly right, but almost as surprising as who *was* involved were the people he'd suspected who *weren't* involved at all.

"So, what happens now?" Dash asked.

"That's a bit vague, don't you think?" Connor said and smiled a little. "What happens now?" he repeated. "We're going to upset the natural balance of the entire colony. Or at least its leadership."

"I understand that, but how do we do it?"

Connor chuckled. "You think I know? I wish I did. I really do," he said soberly.

Samson joined them. "We should reach Sierra soon."

Connor nodded. "I sent a message to Damon Mills. He'll be showing up with Field Ops security agents, but first I want to talk to them."

"They're too smart to confess, but I don't know so much about that stuff. I'll make sure they don't get away," Samson said and left them.

Connor had sent a message to Franklin Mallory that they had his son in custody. It was a simple and straight-to-the-point message. Mallory had sent a quick acknowledgment.

The troop carrier made a temporary stop over the colonial government building, and Connor and a squad of soldiers deplaned. Dash walked by his side.

Carl Flint, in civilian clothing, met him along the way to the offices of the Colonial Intelligence Bureau. "I'm sure glad to see you, General."

Connor arched an eyebrow at him. The entire corridor was filled with Spec Ops soldiers, but they were all dressed in civilian clothing. Officially, they weren't CDF soldiers at the moment; they were merely concerned citizens who had a right to make their voices heard to the colonial government. Connor had no doubt that Dana Wolf would see right through it, as would a lot of other people.

A few CIB agents attempted to forestall Connor's advance, but it was short-lived.

He strode to Meredith Cain's office and opened the door. Governor Wolf was inside, as well as Kurt Johnson.

"Just the people I wanted to see," Connor said and walked inside. Dash followed him in, and everyone else waited outside. "Damon Mills will be here shortly."

"Connor," Governor Wolf said, "there have been a number of alarming allegations regarding CDF special forces in Sierra."

"I don't doubt it, Governor. They're here on my orders," Connor said.

Governor Wolf glanced at the others for a few moments and then looked back at Connor. "Are you conducting a coup?"

Connor shook his head. "Never," he said. "I had to act quickly and positioned my people to prevent the escape of any of the conspirators," Connor said, glancing at Meredith Cain and Kurt Johnson.

Johnson harrumphed. "You can't be serious. There is no evidence to support this."

"Interesting you should say that because I have Lars Mallory and about seventy-five other people in custody right now. Most have given video testimony as to what they've been up to over the past year," Connor said and looked at Meredith Cain.

She smiled back at him. "Good work. You've finally found the terrorists. But all your so-called evidence is hearsay. You're not authorized by the colonial government to take anyone into custody."

Connor glanced at the governor for a moment and then looked back at Meredith Cain. "Does the governor know? Does she know you ordered the operation that put her daughter's life in jeopardy? The operations that endangered the lives of colonists, all so the alliance with the Ovarrow would fail?"

Meredith remained unperturbed by the accusation. "I'm still waiting to see evidence."

"You'll see a lot of evidence. If one thing can be said about Lars Mallory, it's that he was very well trained. He's very thorough when he puts his mind on a task. He believed in your initial cause, and he told me how you, in particular, recruited him. Protect the colony. Be able to do the things that no one else can. Does any of that sound familiar? But where you faltered was when you began seeing colonists as pawns. What was the plan? Expend a few lives here and there? Ignite fury against the Ovarrow?" Connor said.

"I believe *you* went to the Ovarrow city with a battalion of soldiers and took control of the disaster area. *You* entered into a military conflict with the very people you wanted to form an alliance with. I didn't do any of that," Meredith Cain said.

"He didn't say you did any of that," Dana said, "but you could've orchestrated events to move pieces around. Is this true?" she asked Connor.

"Lars Mallory surrendered. He told us everything. I've transferred all those files to your office so you can review them with Selena Brown and Rex Coleman for legal review," Connor said.

Meredith Cain laughed. "Now you want to use the legislative and judicial branches of our government, right after your reckless abuse of power. There've been reports in Sierra, New Haven, and Delphi of people being taken into custody."

"By Field Ops, not the CDF."

"At the behest of the CDF. They arrested Mayor Clinton Edwards in Delphi," Meredith said.

"I know, and now it's your turn."

"You can't arrest me," Meredith said. "When are you going to accept that the Ovarrow can't help us? The only thing they can tell us is how they were defeated by the Krake. Why don't you run along until I'm ready to use you and the rest of the CDF for your real purpose?"

"That's enough, Meredith," Governor Wolf said. "There's going to be an accounting here. And, in fact, I'm going to leverage the investigative arm of my office, the CDF, and Field Ops and Security to identify everyone involved in this monstrosity."

Damon Mills showed up with several Field Ops agents as Meredith Cain rose to her feet. "You can't undo what I've begun," she said, sneering at Connor. "Your precious alliance is going to fail. The Ovarrow will never trust us now, and the colony will never trust them."

Connor regarded her for a few moments. "We'll see," he said.

The security agents escorted Meredith Cain, and Kurt Johnson shouted in surprise when they took him into custody. He thought he hadn't been caught.

Connor was alone with Governor Wolf. She rubbed her eyes for a moment and then looked at Connor. "Since I'm not one of the people being arrested, I assume you found no evidence to implicate me. What about Bob Mullins?"

Bob Mullins was Dana's other advisor, and Connor didn't like the man at all. "He's clean, as far as I know. I would've let you in on the investigation, but everyone involved was part of the system, and there was no way I could communicate what needed to happen without alerting them. That's why I had Spec Ops soldiers here in plain clothes. Their orders were to provide observation and intelligence to Field Ops."

Dana regarded him for a few moments. "I know you really believe that. Your intentions were well placed, but Connor, this is a serious abuse of power. *Your* power, I might add. Regardless of your intentions, you conducted a military operation here in Sierra and the other cities. Good intentions aren't enough justification for breaking the law."

Connor had been expecting this. "I know. I knew it when I gave the orders, and I know it now."

"And you did it anyway," she said.

"It was necessary. It had to be done, regardless of what comes next."

Dana shook her head. "I don't know what's going to happen."

"Neither do I, and maybe that's a good thing," Connor replied.

Dana frowned for a moment. "Are you talking about what happened here or with the Ovarrow?"

"Both, but I'd recommend that we return the Ovarrow

prisoners to the warlord and high commissioner, as well as admit our role in what's been happening. It might kill any chance of an alliance, but they also might respect honesty," Connor said.

"Perhaps, but we still don't know which of the Ovarrow we can trust. They have their own rogue groups among them."

"We do have other options. There are other avenues we can pursue, but not until all this is sorted out," Connor said.

"They might call for both our resignations," Dana said. "Right now, I'll need a replacement to take over the Colonial Intelligence Bureau. There's been abuse of power all around."

Connor didn't know what to say. She was right. He'd acted in accordance with what he thought was the best way to protect the colony. Meredith Cain had been gathering power, but she'd had the same convictions.

"I'll comply with whatever the Colonial Defense Committee deems appropriate," Connor said.

"Haven't you learned? News of this will get out, as it should, but it's the ideas that are dangerous. They'll see what you've done and what I've allowed to happen, and then plan accordingly. I really don't know where we go from here," Dana said.

"We keep things running, and we keep doing what we can to protect our homes."

"Until the next crisis, you mean," Dana said dryly. "Don't answer that, but I do have to ask. Lars Mallory, the intel he provided..."

"He has evidence, too. I'm not going to lie to you—this is going to hurt us. There were a lot of people involved, and a lot is going to change as a result," Connor said.

"I was afraid that was the case," Dana said and gave Meredith Cain's office a cursory glance. "I trusted Meredith. I had no idea what she and Kurt were up to," she said and looked at Connor. "I allowed this to happen."

Connor returned her gaze. He knew what it took to lead, and

Dana needed time to confront the abuse of power that had occurred under her stewardship as governor. None of the evidence Lars had provided led to her, and Connor was grateful for that. Otherwise, the rift that divided the colony would be much worse.

"How would you fix this?" she asked.

"We need to figure out exactly what's broken, and we need to understand how and why their recruitment methods worked so well. I've known Lars for a long time, and I can tell you that he believed in what he was doing. The brutality of what he did to the Ovarrow is something that has changed him more than he realizes," Connor said, pausing for a moment. "I would advocate for going public with the whole thing and putting forward a strong, decisive stance. We either form an alliance with the Ovarrow or we don't, but we can't do our jobs at the whim of popular opinion."

Governor Wolf smiled a little. "Thank you for that. Sometimes I wonder what kind of governor you'd be."

Connor chuckled and shook his head. "My brief time as mayor of Sanctuary was enough."

"Who would you nominate to head the Colonial Intelligence Bureau?" she asked.

Connor frowned in thought. Dana was already looking ahead, thinking of the work that had to be done. "I'm not sure, to be honest. The people I've recruited for CDF Intel need to have an analytical mind and be capable of following the facts, but they also need to be capable of logical leaps. Whoever gets the job from here on out will require oversight from your office."

Dana nodded. "So, you're not interested in the job then."

"I have a job."

Dana gave a slight nod. "Technically, I'm your boss, and I'd just be giving you more work to do."

Connor couldn't argue with that. Instead, he said, "There

would be a lot of objections if you turned the CIB over to the CDF."

"I'm not turning it over to the CDF per se. You said before that oversight is needed, and I think you're right. What I have in mind is a partnership within the CIB."

"A partnership by whom?" Connor asked. He had enough to do. Why was the governor looking at him that way?

"The CIB needs representation from the CDF, and that's where you come in, but also from Field Ops, as well as from someone appointed by the defense committee."

"The defense committee," Connor said, thinking out loud. Then he understood. "You're giving them a stake in the future of the CIB while also doling out the responsibility. I hadn't thought of that."

Dana arched an eyebrow toward him. "Are you sure you wouldn't want to be the next governor? Don't answer that. Each group would have their support staffs, but in order for the CIB to be truly effective, we'd have to mix them up a bit."

Connor was impressed by the alacrity with which the governor threw herself at solving problems. It reminded him of Lenora. He'd known there were going to be a lot of changes in the way the colony was organized, but he hadn't expected the CDF to be affected all that much. Now, he was beginning to suspect he'd been wrong about that.

36

CAMP ALPHA WAS a buzz of activity. There were over fifty large storage crates full of Ovarrow equipment the CDF had brought back from the base of operations where Lars had surrendered. They'd nursed the Ovarrow prisoners back to health, and with their help, they'd identified equipment and even some vehicles the Ovarrow could restore to full operation.

Connor watched Dash and Lenora check the storage containers, along with the last Ovarrow at Camp Alpha. Trust was slow in coming, and he hoped relations with the Ovarrow would improve over time.

A C-cat landed nearby, and Franklin Mallory stepped off the loading ramp. He glanced around and walked over to Connor.

"This is quite an operation you've got going on here," Franklin said.

"It's an olive branch. We were always going to release the prisoners. Why not also deliver some of the equipment we found? It'll give the Ovarrow a little bit more independence, which I think they'll appreciate," Connor replied.

"After they accept the fact that they wouldn't have had the equipment without our help."

"Everyone needs help sometimes," Connor said.

Neither of them spoke while they watched the storage crates being loaded. Connor knew Franklin hadn't come there to discuss the Ovarrow, but what could he say to the father of the person he'd almost had to kill? Lars had saved CDF lives by stopping Colton Evans from triggering the explosives he'd hidden in the caves. There were lines that even Lars wouldn't cross. There would be some people who'd view Lars's actions as self-serving. He'd been caught, and every action he took from that point on would come under intense scrutiny. Connor wanted to believe Lars had done it because he genuinely didn't want the blood of colonists on his hands. But how Lars could brutalize the Ovarrow and yet be stalwart about protecting colonists was a sticking point. It had changed him, but it had changed people like Colton Evans even more. Objectives and beliefs had become more important than the means by which they achieved those goals. As a veteran, Connor had seen both the best and the worst in people. Some people embraced becoming a monster and the allure of power through violent means. Others glimpsed the monster in themselves and came to a breaking point where they decided who they were going to be.

"You're probably wondering why I'm here, so I'm going to cut to the chase," Franklin said. "The colony's first prison is being built in Delphi. Lars and most of the other conspirators are going to be held there until the trials start."

"I'm sorry, Franklin. I know this can't be easy."

Franklin shook his head in derision. "No, it's not, but at least I'll have access to my son. I'm going to try to help him."

Connor nodded, not knowing what to say. What could he say to someone whose child he'd almost killed? He could see it in

Franklin's eyes as well, the knowledge of what had almost happened. "Noah never gave up on him."

"I know," Franklin said. "Talk about a test of friendship. Noah is something else. I know what you almost—had to do."

Connor was quiet for a few moments. "I'm glad I didn't have to."

"I'm glad you didn't either, but if it had come down to it, you would've been right. As much as I hate to admit it, you would've been right."

Connor's throat thickened. "I would've hated myself afterwards."

Franklin nodded, a hardened glint in his eyes. "I would've hated you, too." He was quiet for a few moments and then shook his head. "I had an interesting conversation with Noah's wife. She's a remarkable woman. She's a little mad at you, but . . ."

"I can hardly blame her. I almost lost Lenora, but Kara had to contend with that reality while Noah was in a coma for almost a year."

"Yeah, that must've been tough. She'll never forgive Lars, and I honestly don't blame her. But she did tell me something Noah said to her, and it's been on my mind."

Connor's eyebrows raised. "She spoke to you?"

"Not exactly. She sent me a message. She tried to stop Noah from going with you, and Noah told her something I can't get out of my head. I keep mulling it over."

Noah was still recovering from his coma. Sometimes he was like his old self, but other times he struggled. He'd lose his train of thought midsentence, seemingly at random. Connor hated watching him struggle, but there was nothing he could do about it.

"What did he say?" Connor asked.

"They were arguing about Lars, and he said that it's the times when you're alone and you've crossed the line a little bit that you need your friends and family the most." Franklin's voice sounded hoarse and his eyes welled up. He blew out a breath and wiped away the tears. "I don't know if Lars realizes how lucky he is to have a friend like that."

Connor drew in a deep breath and exhaled. "He's one of the good ones."

Franklin nodded. "You've got that right. I figure that after all he's been through, the fact that he can still find it in his heart to try and help not just my son but another human being is remarkable. You can't teach that kind of integrity. I figured if he could do that, then who am I not to do the same?" he said and extended his hand toward Connor.

Connor's eyes tightened and he shook Franklin's hand firmly. They separated and Connor swallowed hard. The tension left his shoulders and he felt a sudden lightness, as if he'd been weighed down by guilt and hadn't realized it.

"I keep wondering if I did something wrong when I raised Lars."

"You've been a father a lot longer than I have. I don't think it's anything you did or didn't do. Lars made his own choices."

"And we get to try and help them when they stumble. I get it," Franklin said.

"If you wouldn't mind, I'd like to come to Delphi and check in on Lars from time to time," Connor said.

Franklin swallowed. "I think that would be good."

FRANKLIN LEFT and Connor walked over to Lenora.

"I saw you two were talking, so I thought I'd give you some space," Lenora said.

"Thanks. I appreciate it."

Dash and Darius Cohen joined them.

"It looks like we're ready to go," Connor said.

"I think they'll appreciate the gesture," Darius said.

"I hope it does more than that," Lenora replied. "At least this way we can set the record straight. How do you think the Ovarrow will react to the evidence that some of their own people were involved in sabotaging the support structure for the bridge?"

"They won't deny it, and I think they'll work very hard to find whoever was involved," Connor said.

Lenora frowned thoughtfully. "Do you think they'll find whoever it was?"

"I don't know," Connor replied.

"Regardless," Darius said, "we'll leave them with a way to contact us if they want to, but what do you think about an invitation to some of the Ovarrow to visit Sierra?"

"It won't be easy, but it's necessary," Connor said. "I told Governor Wolf it would be in everyone's best interest if she took a firm stance on the whole thing. She took that advice and then went above and beyond it."

Over the last week, Connor had come to appreciate just how shrewd of a leader Governor Wolf actually was. She worked with renewed vigor, and Connor could do no less. Connor shared a look with Lenora and smiled.

They headed toward their ship, and Connor saw Samson watching them. He was grim-faced and alert, a soldier standing the watch to his core. Connor nodded toward him and Samson did the same. Their work wasn't finished yet.

AUTHOR NOTE

Thank you for reading one of my books. I cannot express my appreciation enough. I hope you've enjoyed the latest book in the First Colony series and there will be more to come. I had such a warm response to my last author's note that I don't think I can top it. There are some people I would like to acknowledge who helped me get the book into its final form. A huge thank you to my editor, Myra, who has edited 15 of my books and has helped me grow as a writer. Tamara and Crystal, who gave my books that final read-through so I could publish the cleanest draft possible. Another huge thank you to my friend John, our monthly writer meetings have been a much-needed sanity check and respite from the day to day stuff. Last, but never least, Michelle, there really is too much to list here for everything you do.

Writing a book is a solitary undertaking, which I love and I get to continue to do thanks to you, but I wanted you to know that I do have a small team of very talented people who have helped me along the way.

Again, thank you for reading one of my books. If you wouldn't mind, please consider leaving a review for this book. Reviews really do help even if it's just a few words to say that you really like this book.

I do have a Facebook group called **Ken Lozito's SF readers.** If you're on Facebook and you'd like to stop by, please search for it on Facebook.

Not everyone is on Facebook. I get it, but I also have a blog if you'd like to stop by there. My blog is more of a monthly check-in as to the status of what I'm working on. Please stop by and say hello, I'd love to hear from you.

Visit www.kenlozito.com

THANK YOU FOR READING FRACTURE - FIRST COLONY - BOOK EIGHT.

If you loved this book, please consider leaving a review. Comments and reviews allow readers to discover authors, so if you want others to enjoy *Fracture* as you have, please leave a short note.

The series continues with the 9th book.

If you would like to be notified when my next book is released please visit kenlozito.com and sign up to get a heads up.

I've created a special **Facebook Group** specifically for readers to come together and share their interests, especially regarding my books. Check it out and join the discussion by searching for **Ken Lozito's SF Worlds**.

To join the group, login to Facebook and search for **Ken Lozito's SF Worlds**. Answer two easy questions and you're in.

ABOUT THE AUTHOR

Ken Lozito is the author of multiple science fiction and fantasy series. I've been reading both genres for a long time. Books were my way to escape everyday life of a teenager to my current ripe old(?) age. What started out as a love of stories has turned into a full-blown passion for writing them. My ultimate intent for writing stories is to provide fun escapism for readers. I write stories that I would like to read and I hope you enjoy them as well.

If you have questions or comments about any of my works I would love to hear from you, even if it's only to drop by to say hello at
KenLozito.com

Thanks again for reading *First Colony - Fracture*

Don't be shy about emails, I love getting them, and try to respond to everyone.

ALSO BY KEN LOZITO

FIRST COLONY SERIES

FIRST COLONY - GENESIS

FIRST COLONY - NEMESIS

FIRST COLONY - LEGACY

FIRST COLONY - SANCTUARY

FIRST COLONY - DISCOVERY

FIRST COLONY - EMERGENCE

FIRST COLONY - VIGILANCE

FIRST COLONY - FRACTURE

ASCENSION SERIES

STAR SHROUD

STAR DIVIDE

STAR ALLIANCE

INFINITY'S EDGE

RISING FORCE

ASCENSION

SAFANARION ORDER SERIES

ROAD TO SHANDARA

ECHOES OF A GLORIED PAST

AMIDST THE RISING SHADOWS

HEIR OF SHANDARA

BROKEN CROWN SERIES

Haven of Shadows

CPSIA information can be obtained
at www.ICGtesting.com
Printed in the USA
FSHW021950190819
61227FS